With Love

and

Peace

The Graduation

ISBN: 978-1-947573-10-9

Library of Congress Catalog number: 2017912047

The Carolee Collectables
Printed in the United States of America
www.crystalsforkids.org

Carolee O'Neill, pseudonym

Book has been handcrafted from cover to cover, including the watercolor illustrations by Carolee.

To The Sisters of Saint Francis

for the sacrifices they made

so that we,

their charges,

would be fully equipped

to meet our life challenges.

Acknowledgments

To all my friends and family who willingly gave of their time to edit the stories of my thirteen books; patiently taught me computer jargon; shared their computer skills with Indesign, Photoshop and GIMP; and guided me through the copyright, ISBN and barcode maze. I couldn't have done it without you.

The Graduation

by Carolee O'Neill

To: ______________________________

____

From: ____________________________

____

Class Ring 1952

Aim for the Stars

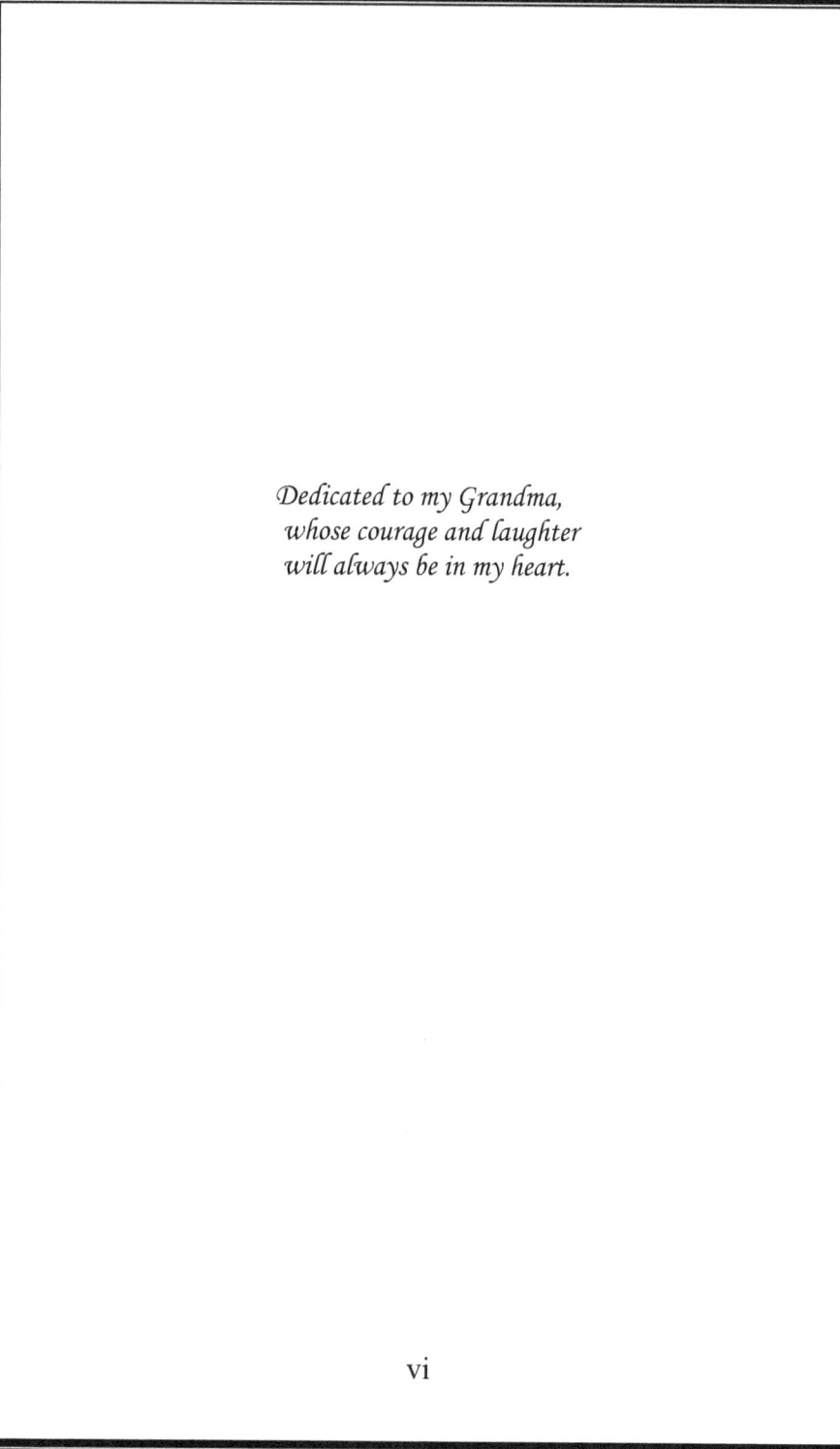

Dedicated to my Grandma,
whose courage and laughter
will always be in my heart.

The Graduation

Chapter One

Her ears rang from the sound of the iron gate slamming behind her. The noise echoed to her heart and reminded her of the goodness that had turned sour. The forthcoming nightmare was no longer just a possibility; it had given birth to the harshness of her fears. Her thoughts screamed her disapproval, only to be discarded. As her eyes filled with tears, she pleaded with her parents not to do this. But they didn't listen. They just kept saying it was for her own good.

As she looked down at her torso, her light-brown hair fell from her shoulders in soft waves and her skin shone a golden hue from swimming in the summer sun.

"Are we almost there, Dad?"

"It won't be long now, Annie—only a few more blocks."

Dad, with his lower jaw pushed forward from an under-bite, always wore a wide brim hat that dipped down over his soft, smiling eyes. His favorite past-time was teasing Annie more than her five older siblings, telling her wild stories she always seemed to believe. Today he was quiet, absorbed in thought. Annie had fallen into the same mood, thinking about all the guys she had crushes on, and the warm summer nights when she went swimming and played softball with her pals. That all ended now. She'd have to toe the mark, living in a convent school with a bunch of nuns.

Staring out of the car window as her father drove along Oklahoma Avenue in Milwaukee, Annie saw Lake Michigan become visible through the shadowy edges of the trees. Her petite fingers adjusted the brim of the wool hat her mother had chosen to complement her silk dress and the sea-green of her eyes. Noticing the light had cast her reflection on the car window, she put her face close to check to see if her teeth had anything stuck between them. Then she licked the tip of her finger and rubbed off what she thought might be a smudge on her cheek.

Annie hadn't noticed they had arrived in the school courtyard until she heard the iron gates slam behind them. Startled, she looked around to see how far the foreboding fence reached. A cold shiver ran through her when she saw that the six-foot wrought iron fence seemed to surround the grounds.

Gee whiz! What kind of a place is this anyway? They've got enough iron around here to keep an army under lock and key forever. Why *would anyone want to be in a place like this? Maybe they're like me. They don't have a choice. Maybe they were put here for something they did wrong or worse yet—maybe nobody wanted them anymore!*

A newer five story red brick building stood attached to an older four story gray one by a long tunnel-like structure that hid partially underground. The older building had a smoky appearance like a fire had raged out of control, finding only the large expressionless windows on which to lap its soot-filled vengeance. The sun painted patches of sunlight across the courtyard, attempting to lessen the effect of the morbid looking place. Yet the old building lurked in the shadows like a monster waiting to devour its prey.

Annie curled the material of her silk dress around her finger. Her thoughts flashed visions of giant rats lurking in dark passages. Fear of the unknown seized her imagination. What would happen if she opened the car door? Would bats swoop down followed by nun-witches? Would they seize her like a prize heifer to be sacrificed at the high altar of Count Dracula; or would they wait until her father's protection had left her more vulnerable? Indeed, they'd want to savor the moment, like a lioness, lying patiently, licking their chops in anticipation of what was to come.

With sweaty palms, she felt her heart skip a beat. She had to look for something to calm her nerves. Some beautiful flowers would do the trick. Seeing nothing, she rolled the window down, just a tad. If she could hear the flapping of bat wings, she could tell her dad. Then he'd never leave her at this place.

Annie noticed that the first floor windows of the old building were barred and the shades were all pulled down. *I'll never get out of here alive! I'd have to jump from a second story window. And if I tried that I'd be sure to break a leg or something. There I'd lie, waiting for hours or maybe even days for someone to have mercy on me. And what would they do to me for trying to escape?*

Oh my gosh! Why are all the shades pulled down? You couldn't see in or out if you wanted to.

That's it! They don't want anybody to know what they're doing to the poor souls they've captured. I bet they strap them to the walls just like they do in the Frankenstein movies. I can almost hear them as they cry out for food and water for their parched mouths and broken bodies.

Startled by the touch of her dad's hand on her arm, she looked into his face as he spoke. "We better go inside. We can't stay out here all day."

"But, Dad," Annie started to say.

Interrupting her, "I'll get your bags out of the back seat. Then I'll have to finish registering you."

"But, Dad," Annie pulled hard on his arm.

He turned to her, gently placing his hand over hers. "Don't worry, everything will be just fine. This is a good place for you, Stinker."

She cringed.

This was his favorite nickname for her, their special bond, even though she hated it. More than once, it had presented some embarrassing moments. On an afternoon that her friends had come to pick her up, he had inadvertently hollered upstairs, "Stinker! Your friends are here." Annie had stood in front of her mirror, watching her neck turn a patchy red that began to spread to her face. She would rather have died than go downstairs and face them. Somehow she managed to pull herself together, deciding that they wouldn't dare laugh unless they wanted a poke in the nose or their family secrets divulged.

"They have a fine conservatory here," he continued. "That'll give you an opportunity to advance with your music. Anyway, the education is supposed to be the best in the state. You know how important it is to your mother that you get a good education."

"Oh, Dad, I just want to go home."

He turned and got out of the car.

Hurt by his unwillingness to listen to her plea, she felt her tears begin to roll down her face. Annie batted her eyes and wiped the wetness from her cheeks. No matter what, she knew her mom would agree with whatever he decided.
They seemed to know what the other one was thinking. So going back and forth between them to get what she wanted never worked.

Thoughts of her mother reminded Annie how her grandpa used to laugh when he'd talk about how particular her mom was. He said she was just like her mother; you could eat off both of their basement floors. They even dusted the handmade doilies on the armchairs.

Every day her mom would brush her long, black hair one hundred strokes. Then she'd arrange it on top of her head in soft waves that bounced when she walked and did the housework. Annie thought it was such a waste of time to be so fussy, just to do housework. And she could never understand why anyone would want to suffer all day, wearing high heels.

Nevertheless, she'd beam when her friends complimented her mother, saying how nice she looked and how pretty she was. When Mom wasn't working, which seemed to be never, she'd spend time with Annie's older sister Jane, teaching her to knit, crochet and cook. Annie didn't want any part of that. She was too interested in riding horses, playing the piano and singing, especially when no one was home. Otherwise, as soon as Annie sat down to practice, everyone in the family would want to do the same thing. With four older brothers each playing a different horn and a different song, the chaos nearly drove her crazy.

Hearing the car door slam, she knew she would have to get out. *I've just spent the last eight years with nuns in grade school. Now I'm supposed to be thrilled about spending the next four years with more nuns?*

Annie opened the car door, listening for any unnatural sounds. She bent down to look under the car to be sure nothing would grab her by the ankles, pulling her into an endless black hole that led to tunnels of catacombs filled with dead and rotting skulls. Seeing nothing, she took a giant step outward, just in case.

Directly across the street was a beautiful park-like strip of land. Annie could see the tops of stair rails and assumed the steps led down to a beach with the lake visible on the horizon. Observing the scene she watched the sun skip across the waves, making them appear like pieces of dancing cut-glass crystal.

Her dad had removed the last piece of luggage from the car when Annie glanced at her watch, the one her grandparents gave her for her thirteenth birthday. The sterling silver band held the diamonds in place around its small, delicate face and fastened it to the silver band. Everything seemed to stop for a moment, even though the watch displayed almost two in the afternoon. Smiling, she placed her hand over it to capture the love with which it had been given.

After Annie's birth, her maternal grandparents raised her when her mother took ill. She remembered the little sled Grandpa O'Reilly built to take her for winter romps in the snow. He'd bundle her up so that the only things peeking out were her two little eyes. Sometimes the snowflakes were so big that Annie tried to grab one and throw it at him but they'd only disappear into her mitten. Then Grandpa would see her wiggling around and tuck her back under the warm woolen blankets. She knew her Grandpa would never put her in a place like this.

"Let's get going, Stinker."

Annie picked up one of the cases and watched him go up the stairs. As she remembered her grandma's advice, she struggled to regain her composure. "Sometimes you just have to pull yourself up by your bootstraps and do the best you can," her grandma had said. "And remember, honey, whatever happens—always keep smiling."

So Annie stood up as straight as she could and marched up the stairs right behind her dad.

The buzzer sounded harsh when he pushed the button. In silence they waited for someone to respond. Through the cloudy glass that was embedded in the two heavy metal doors, the silhouette of a tall, slender nun could be seen rushing down a flight of stairs. As she opened the door, a musty odor from old wood filled the air, and the sound of female voices seemed to come from everywhere.

"Good afternoon, you must be Mr. Charles O'Brien. I am Sister Mary Alicia," she said in a musical tone. "Please! Follow me." The nun ran up the stairs, ushering them into an office.

An old wooden structure divided the length of the room, separating them from the nuns. Sister Alicia turned and walked through the swinging half door at the end of the divider.

"There will be someone out momentarily to admit your daughter to the school." Then she vanished behind a closed door.

All that echoed through Annie's head were the words—admit your daughter to the school. Her heart banged so hard she thought it would explode. She wanted to scream at her dad and demand he tell her what she had done to be put in a place like this. But her strict Catholic upbringing silenced the words.

Education has nothing to do with it. It has more to do with my brother's fiancée, Melissa—the one who prized herself on proper etiquette. She just had to go and tell my parents I needed to go to a special school because I was a tomboy. So what if I played tennis and baseball with the guys? The girls never lasted long enough to finish a game. Patsy is the only one that even came close.

Annie walked into the barren corridor, mumbling under her breath and clenching her fists, "I guess I don't hold my little finger up just right? Oh! If I had that skinny straight legged prissy here now—I'd punch her lights out and leave her for the vultures."

The approaching sound of leather-cut heels silenced Annie. The nun passed in full stride with her arms folded into the sleeves of her habit and her head bowed, never acknowledging Annie's presence.

Annie began to walk back into the office. *Where did my brother find Prissity Melissa anyway? Whatever happened to that girl he used to date in Chicago? Betty was her name. She was so good to me when I cut myself going through Grandma's plate glass door. I could hardly do anything for myself. So she came over and entertained me. I remember playing Grandma's old player piano with her and we laughed and sang for hours. And when it was raining, and we couldn't do anything at all, we'd sit on the front porch and tell spook stories. Now she was a real person. I'll never forget her. Obviously my brother has. I wonder how long it will take him to learn to hold his pinkie up just right. By then Miss Prissity will have a ring in his stupid nose.*

Another nun passed Annie, saying her name was Sister Mary Edward. She had all smiles for Annie's dad but had a pat-on-the-head type attitude toward Annie. After Sister had completed her nicety-nice conversation, she left the room, and their attention was drawn to the blinking nun who had appeared behind the wooden divider.

"I'm Sister Mary Rejeta, the registrar. And you are Mr. O'Brien, I presume?"

Her expressionless face was lined with deeply carved folds of skin that moved with the twitching of her eyes.

"Yes, Sister."

She scanned the papers before her. "I see that the full tuition has not been paid. How do you plan to handle the fees for the room and board, Mr. O'Brien?" She stood motionless before them, communicating only what was necessary to perform her assigned duties. "You know that the bill has to be paid before school starts in three days, or we'll have to dismiss your daughter."

Annie thought for sure that her dad might listen to her now because she had overheard him saying that it cost more to send her to this school than it did to send her brother, Luke, to Saint Norbert's college.

Annie yanked at her dad's sleeve and whispered, "Save your money, Dad. Let's just go home. I don't have a good feeling about this place anyway."

Ignoring her, he searched through his coat pockets. Then his face flushed, "I'm sorry, Sister, I must have left my checkbook at home. I'll send you a check the first thing in the morning."

Feeling trapped and overwhelmed by the situation, Annie leaned against the wall, allowing her hands to slip into the pockets of her silk dress. Hard as she tried to understand family tradition, she didn't want to accept any reason for being put at St. Anthony's.

Her brothers went away to school, but they stayed with her grandpa and grandma, where they got home cooking. And Jane went to a girls' school, but Annie thought that was because she didn't like boys. Besides, she got to pick where she went—not Annie, though. She got to live with a bunch of nuns whose names she couldn't pronounce, much less remember. She got to stay in a prison.

Sister Rejeta directed her words at Mr. O'Brien when she called it a "finishing" school. "I am sure you will be pleased with the results."

"Well, Mrs. O'Brien and I have heard a lot about the school, Sister, that's why I'm here with Annie. Are there any more papers that need to be filled out? I'd like to get going as soon as possible. I do have a long drive ahead of me."

"We are almost finished." The blinking nun shuffled papers around on the divider, checking them as she did.

What about me? What will I be pleased about? Annie felt her Irish blood begin to boil. So far everybody's been acting as though I don't exist. In defiance, she stared straight into the nun's blinking eyes to get her attention, readying herself for the blast she wanted to deliver. Annie remembered staring into Jane's face, trying to irritate her, but no matter what she did her sister never changed her expression. She'd just go on with what she was doing, making Annie so angry, she wanted to pound on her forever. With that Annie conceded defeat. Screaming anything at this nun would only make matters worse. Besides, the deadpan blinking expression on the older nun's face told the story of having to deal with all sorts of obnoxious kids.

Annie swung around, turning her back to the nun and began rubbing the sole of her leather shoe back and forth on the warped wooden floor, creating a squeaking sound. We'll see who gets finished in your old finishing school. We'll just see.

After Annie's dad had completed all the paper work according to the blinking nun's satisfaction, he repeated that he would get the check in the mail right away.

He turned to Annie, "I've got to get going now, you know that."

Annie looked down so he wouldn't see the tears in her eyes. He put his arms around her and drew her close. Then he kissed her on the forehead. "I'm sorry I can't help you with your bags, but men aren't allowed on the premises except to pick up students or to bring them back to campus. I'll be seeing you soon anyway, Stinker."

He never looked back when he walked down the stairs to the car. Annie followed him to the entry doors and watched him wave goodbye as he drove out of the courtyard. As fast as the gates had opened to let them in, they closed behind him. He was gone.

As she lingered at the front door, her dad's final words struck home. "Men aren't allowed here?" Annie had never given it a thought that there would be nothing but women around. Guys were so much a part of her life that she didn't even think of them as guys, just friends. After staring at the empty space left by her father for several minutes, she turned and looked up the stairs at her suitcases on the top platform. In the background she could hear a voice saying, "Come on now, I'll take you to the dorm. I'm Sister Mary Joseph." Then Annie realized a nun stood next to her suitcases, stooped over and waved her sisterly hand at her. As she did, the sleeve on her habit flopped back and forth, and the rosary hanging at her side made a clacking sound.

Annie picked up her cases and proceeded to follow the nun down the first floor corridor. As she walked, she noticed that classrooms gradually replaced the offices that lined the corridor. Old pictures of popes, archbishops and cardinals hung side by side on either side of the wall with barely a breath between them.

Oh, I know that guy. That's Bishop Sheen. He's the one who has that funny show on television. What's he doing with this parade of straight-faced clergy?

"Hurry up. You mustn't loiter," the sister gestured again to her.

Annie annoyed by the nun's impatience, Annie dropped one of her cases and began to drag it on the marble floor. *For crying out loud! What's the hurry? Do you want to get me tucked away in your dungeon so you can get back to your beads? I'm only looking at a couple of your grumpy old pictures.*

When they arrived at the bottom of a staircase, sister positioned herself a step above Annie. "There are four flights of stairs up to the dorm. That's where you will be staying." Then she started to run up the stairs, leaving Annie to struggle with her bags.

Annie glanced around, looking for some sense of warmth, but everything was either marble, concrete or steel. Even the expressions on the old men in the pictures appeared to be chiseled out of stone. By the time she reached the second floor, the chattering of young women's voices had grown louder. With each flight of stairs the voices escalated more, ricocheting off the walls and through every fiber of her body. For four years she'd be listening to nothing but women. By the time she had reached the fourth floor, exhaustion claimed her spirit. Her grandma's stoic motto, "pull yourself up by your boot straps," had slid down around her ankles.

Never looking to see if Annie was still behind her, Sister Mary Joseph took a sharp left at the top of the stairs. At the end of the corridor, Annie could see a large room guarded by two doors with heavy locks on them. Except for the walkways, the room was filled with small square spaces that were separated by sheets.

Sister Mary Joseph entered one close to the entrance. Holding the sheet back she said, "You may come in. This is where you will be staying until you have passed the probationary period. It is called a cubicle or a cell."

Confused, Annie let her suitcases slide from her hands, hitting the floor with a thud, "What do you mean by probationary period?"

The nun smiled, realizing that Annie had not been told. "There is a period of six weeks where you will not be allowed to receive any phone calls, nor will you be allowed to call or see anyone. In other words, you are not to have any communication with the outside world."

"I can't have any calls from my family—my friends?"

"That's correct," the nun responded with her nose in the air.

I've been ambushed for six weeks. Weakness seeped into Annie's body until she thought her knees would buckle. *Why didn't Mom and Dad tell me about this? Didn't they know what these people were going to do to me? Didn't they find out anything before they threw me in this place?*

In the midst of her devastation, she could hear the nun rambling on about the probation period. "This time is necessary in order for the new boarding student to adjust to the routine here. And there will be other rules you will be expected to follow. However, you will be given those later. In the meantime you will find an abbreviated list in your nightstand. Also, a sister stays in every dorm so she can help the students and monitor their behavior as required. The nun for this dorm is back in the far corner. Her name is Sister Mary Leah. "Please," she said as she bent over Annie, "Do not ever enter her cell. If you have an occasion to need her services, you may go to the cell and ask for her by name. She will respond, if she is in."

Annie stared at the nun as she recited her rehearsed message. The ringing in her ears made every sound seem muffled, making it almost impossible for her to follow the nun's painful words.

Sister stopped for a second and took a breath. “Supper will be at five P.M. sharp. Be at the top of the stairs by four forty-five to go down with the rest of the ladies. Right now, you can get settled in your cell. When you have finished, you can familiarize yourself with this floor so you know where the bathrooms and other dorms are located. You’ll also find you won’t need so many things to wear here. I’m sure your parents told you that all the students wear uniforms.”

As the nun recited her gibberish with no sign of compassion, Annie flushed with anger. Only too well, she remembered the straight navy blue jumper that tied in the middle like a sack and the heavily starched short sleeved blouse with a tiny T-like red bow to complete the hideous outfit.

How could she ever forget the hours her mother spent sewing her last name on everything? “Now nothing will get mixed up,” she said. Even Annie’s handkerchiefs had her name on them. Heavens, Annie would never want to drop one in front of some gentleman unless her pinkie was being held out “just right.” Whatever would he think?

As Sister continued to speak, her fingers shook some when she absent mindedly stroked a piece of Annie’s leather luggage and eyed the silk dress Annie wore. For a brief moment, Annie noticed that Sister Joseph’s gaze seemed distant and her thoughts elsewhere. Often Annie had seen the apprehensive faces of young boys and girls as their parents bragged about how many of their children would be sent to become priests or nuns. They were so proud of it, as if it were a way to buy their way into heaven. Could it be that this nun was one of them? The possibility brought a twinge of sadness to Annie's heart. Perhaps the bitterness that Annie felt from Sister came because sister had no more control over her lost dreams than Annie did. Going to high school with her friends had been important to Annie, but her mom and dad didn't want to hear about "that" school. It wasn't a proper place to train a young woman for the future.

Annie heard a rustling sound when Sister Mary Joseph turned and left the cell. Attempting to steady her wobbly legs, she reached for the back of the chair and sat down. In front of her was the crisp, white sheet that hung around her cell. Thoughts of childhood crossed her mind and how her dad used to make animal shadows and show home movies on such sheets. After he had finished making Annie giggle, he'd play his favorite features, "Mickey Mouse" and the "Skeletons." Mickey Mouse's voice crackled as it came out of the old speakers, making it difficult to understand what he was saying. And her dad never seemed to thread the projector right, so it would jerk every frame, exaggerating the movement of the characters. Annie didn't mind the bad sound so much, but the distorted movements of the skeletons put the fear of God into her as they danced around like puppets on a string with their bones flopping loosely up and down. The ghoulish smiles on their faces, the empty spaces between their rotten protruding teeth, and the vacant eyeball sockets sparkled as the light from the projector flickered through them were horrid memories.

Over the years she had been plagued by recurring nightmares, until her mom forbid her to watch any more. In one such dream her body would be stuffed into her doll's double-decker bed. Then the skeletons would toy with her, jabbing her over and over again in her back with their knives. She'd wake up in a cold sweat, still feeling the pain from the torture they inflicted. Now she'd have to deal with a real nightmare.

A clock sounded. Her gaze centered on the steel-framed bed that held an old pinstriped cotton mattress that sagged in the middle. Next to the bed stood a nightstand and right across from the bed a small oak dresser and a chair. The dull finish on the furniture attested to their lack of care over the years.

"I guess I'm going to have to figure out where to put my things," Annie said. "At home Mom sure tried to surround me with a lot of girl stuff in hopes that I wouldn't swing from the trees and play 'Cowboys and Indians.' I guess it didn't work, because I still hung with the fellows. And why not, all the girls wanted to do was sit around and giggle about the boys. My parents must really be desperate to try to make a lady out of me if they have to send me to a place like this to do it."

Annie picked up one of her smaller suitcases and looked around to see where she could put it. As she placed it on the chair, her eyes began to well up. If she started to cry now she'd never stop. Determined to control her feelings as much as possible, she bit her lip so hard she thought it had to be bleeding. She didn't care! Nobody was going to see her cry like a baby.

Chapter Two

Annie sobbed, "Angel of God my guardian dear, to whom God's love commits me here. Ever this day be at my side, to light, to guard, to rule and guide."

With the back of her hand, she wiped the tears from her eyes as she attempted to regain her composure.

"I'll never get all of my things in this little dresser and nightstand. I guess I'm not going to. I'll just sort out a few things I know that I'll need and leave the rest in my cases."

Opening the drawer to the nightstand she saw an 8 X 13 inch card. The card the nun had mentioned with the rules on it. Picking it up she noticed it had a patchy yellow-gray appearance and the edges were unraveling.

I wonder how many young women have looked at this with the same feelings I have. The doors are locked, aren't they, kid? And the key is gone. There's nothing like knowing how little your family cares.

As she began to read, her hands trembled. She flipped the card over, only to see more rules.

Oh brother! And these are just some of the rules? I can't believe it. What are the rest in, a bound volume? We'll be like robots walking around bowing to their every command.

Cynically, Annie curtsied to the four corners of her cell. *Yes, Sister! No, Sister! Morning to night—rules, rules, rules. Why am I not surprised that every rule has the word silence in it? Ha! And just look at this caption, will you!*

THIS IS THE PROPERTY OF
ST. ANTHONY'S ACADEMY

Who'd want the stupid card anyway, unless you could get enough of them together to burn the place down? Appalled, she scanned the card for more information. *What?! We have to get up at quarter to six! Then proceed promptly to the sink room. Each sink has been assigned to three or four ladies for a ten minute period. If you are not there at your specified time, the next lady may take your turn. This is gross! I have to share a sink with three other women I don't even know?*

She tossed her head back and rolled her eyes. Not wanting to read another word, but knowing she had to, she grumbled and continued.

Mass will be at seven and breakfast will be served right after that. You will need to check the schedule to locate your assigned time for kitchen duty and respond accordingly. Well, what do you know! We have to do dishes and take the garbage out, too. I can't believe my parents are paying for this. They must be crazy. During school hours you shall hold silence from 8:00 A.M until 3:45 PM. During that time you shall walk on the right side in single file to and from classes.

Annie threw the card back into the drawer and slammed it shut. *That's it! Bring on the strait jacket, because that's what it'll take to keep me here!*

Feeling like she was riding an emotional roller coaster, she struggled with thoughts that didn't provide the right answers to absolve her parents of their guilt. They had abused her good nature and trusting attitude! Why didn't she question them more? She had always been on the naïve side. Glancing around the cell, she wanted to grab all of her belongings and run until she dropped. Then the vision of the wrought iron fence and barred windows surfaced in her mind. She knew there wasn't an escape. Embraced by the hopelessness of the moment, she collapsed on to her unmade bed.

Annie woke to the sound of young women's voices. She glanced at her watch, realizing it was almost time for supper and she hadn't finished unpacking. She sorted her things, unpacked what she could and made her bed. She looked around to make sure that everything was straightened, took a deep breath and stepped out of her cell. She stood there for a moment and listened to her stomach rumble and felt her heart pound.

Guided by the chatty female voices, Annie slowly began to walk toward the stairs. As she turned the corner into the corridor, she saw about fifty girls standing in line, with no nuns in sight. At the same time, they saw Annie and opened a space for her to join them.

A hazel eyed, fair complexioned young woman moved next to Annie. "My name is Jeannie, what's yours?"

Annie turned, looked down into Jeannie's smiling face with its crooked nose and square jaw, and responded, "Uh . . . Annie. Annie O'Brien."

Annie couldn't help wondering how Jeannie's nose got so crooked. Did someone land a lucky punch? Or was it something less exciting, like falling off her hobbyhorse? Jeannie's dark-brown, frizzy hair reminded Annie of the times when the beauty parlor had fried her hair and then her mom would make it worse by rubbing oil into it. Jeannie responded to Annie's inquisitive gaze with a broad smile and a sheepish look. Annie respond and felt like Jeannie could someday be her pal.

"If you're an upper classman," Jeannie said, "You should be at the front of the line."

Annie laughed, "Don't I wish! Then I'd almost be out of this place."

"I sure know what you mean. My parents didn't know what to do with me, so they sent me here. How did you get here?"

"My parents don't like the high school in West Bend. So when my sister-in-law mentioned this place, they were thrilled. That's how I got stuck here. And I didn't have any say about it either."

A silence began to spread throughout the group. Annie could hear the faint sound of someone coming from behind the closed door at the end of the hallway. The sound was getting louder and louder.

Jeannie whispered, "The upper classmen said that whoever comes through that door will be our monitor for the next year. That means she will be the nun we'll have to answer to for everything."

Now Annie could hear the rustling of a habit and rosary. The sound stopped, the doorknob turned and the door began to open. Out stepped a slender young nun with a spring to her gait and a bright smile on her face. Her bird-like features gave her almost a comical appearance and her upright stature made her appear very sure of herself.

"It's Sister Mary Margaret," someone at the front of the line, sighed. "Boy, did we luck out."

"Good afternoon, ladies," Sister said as she approached. "We will be going down to supper now. We must move right along so we won't be tardy." She picked up the pace and headed towards the stairs, lifting her habit as she began to descend, displaying her black nylons and heavy, black leather shoes. In silence the students paraded down five flights of stairs to the lowest level. As they approached the bottom floor, the aroma of prepared food filled the air. After walking the length of the corridor, they entered a room that was partly underground. The windows were barred and the walls were painted a stark white, which gave the room a sterile look against the long set tables covered with stiff white linen.

Annie whispered to Jeannie, "Gee, it looks like all the work is done. Maybe we'll get out of kitchen duty tonight."

Jeannie laughed, “Don’t count on it.”

The line slowed as Sister directed everyone to her proper seating arrangements according to class standing. “Please remain standing until every lady is at her place. When the seniors begin to sit down, then everyone may be seated.”

After the racket of moving chairs on the bare marble floors had ceased, Sister began introducing the students to dining room etiquette. “The food will be placed toward the east end of the table. The individual who is seated at that end will pick up one platter at a time, serve herself, and then pass it to the left. Remember, whatever you put on your plate you must eat, whether you like it or not. We do not waste food here. So I suggest you take smaller portions until you see if you like that dish.”

The seven girls seated at the table with Annie were silent as the meal began. Everyone heeded the warning and took small portions except the girl sitting across from Annie. Her coal black hair and large brown eyes were accented by her pure white complexion and the dimple in her chin. Her build was strong and she looked as though she wasn’t used to being pushed around. Annie wondered if taking the larger portions was how she usually ate, or if it was just an act of blatant defiance.

The last dish passed to Annie looked like a type of stew. Hints of potatoes were floating in a light tan sauce along with tiny flecks of carrots and onions. Annie lifted the dish to capture its aroma but backed off when an odor of hot dog food nipped at her nose.

Annie elbowed Jeannie, “Yuck! This smells more like something that should be coming out instead of going in.”

Jeannie giggled, placing her hand over her mouth to muffle the sound as she watched Sister

Margaret leave the room. Then she picked up a piece of bread from the platter in front of her. "What's wrong with this bread? It looks sort of blotchy. Why, it's hard and wet in spots. It's stale, isn't it? They didn't want to eat it so they gave it to us—breaking us in early, aren't they? Now we know what Sister meant when she said that they don't waste food. They give us their rejects."

Annie looked around the table at the shocked faces. Then she noticed that the girl sitting kitty-corner from her began to gag on her milk.

"It's sour! And in case you didn't know it—the butter is rancid too." Lois set her glass down so hard some of its contents spilled onto the table. In disbelief she sat staring at the milk on the table. Lois looked at everyone to see their reaction and then began patting the spilled milk with her napkin. Her cracked, dry lips still held remnants of the milk and her thin scraggly hair hung alongside of her gaunt face. From the distressed look on her face, Annie feared that the frail looking girl wouldn't be able to endure many more surprises.

Helen, a very tall slender gal with long straight hair and a doll-like face spoke up, "I don't think it's so bad. We sometimes get sour milk or buttermilk on the farm. In fact I kind of enjoy it."

"You drink sour milk?" Jeannie asked with her face looking as sour as the milk. "Sure, once in a while. Sometimes we don't get the milk used up fast enough because we have so many cows, and it gets sour. Then Mom uses it for pancakes and stuff, but there are leftovers so we have to drink it. We can't afford to waste it."

"I sure would appreciate it if you would sort of test the milk at mealtime. Then nobody would have to drink it if it's sour. I'll owe you." Jeannie waited patiently while Helen looked around the table at all the expectant faces.

"Sure, why not! No big deal for me. Besides I may need a favor someday in this place. And I could sure use a friend."

"You got one for life. That is, if we survive the next four years."

Delighted by Helen's response, the girls turned to one another, laughing nervously and then back to Helen, expressing their thanks. One by one, they began telling their stories about how they had been placed in the boarding school. By the time the third story had been told the atmosphere at the table had changed. Identical stories forced them to come face to face with their feelings of abandonment.

The eyes of the brown-eyed girl who first appeared to be so strong filled with tears.

"Hi! I'm Lucie. And I don't know how anyone could say they cared about you, and then put you in a place like this."

"They never could figure out what to do with me. Oh, I'm sorry, my name is Mary Alice," she said as she twisted her mousy brown hair and slouched in her chair, "I should have been a boy. They wouldn't have sent me away if I was a boy. They never sent any of my brothers away. Just me!"

A deafening stillness came over the group. Annie could feel a lump in her throat as she listened and tried to convince herself that her parents tried to do right by her, even though they didn't tell her very much.

"Wait a minute, we don't have to surrender so easily, you know," Annie whispered. "We can give them a run for their money. Which is it going to be, you guys?" Everyone at the table stared, with blank expressions, at Annie except Lucie. She just kept on eating. With no response, Annie continued. "Well, whatever we decide, we'll be stuck here for the next four years. I'm for giving them a run for their money. Can you imagine the reputation we could earn in four years? I can see it now; our names projected on this huge marquee standing in front of the school." With her eyes sparkling, Annie announced with a wide sweep of her hands from left to right.

"THE CREATIVE AND INNOVATIVE
CLASS OF 1952!"

"Let's go for it," Jeannie said.

Several of the girls chimed in, "Yeah. Why not?"

The excitement of the moment filled the air with an electrifying energy. Annie felt herself bonding with this group of young women, never dreaming it would have been possible.

"We'll have to play their game for a little while until we get used to the rules. Then we'll begin to see some loopholes," Annie said. "So let's keep our ears open and find out what we can. In the meantime maybe we can think up some neat things to do. Does anyone have any ideas?"

"Well," said Lucie, still chewing her food. "I could see if I can get in with a couple of the juniors or seniors to help us learn the ropes. Everybody thinks I'm older than I am so that shouldn't be a problem."

Susan, a tall, heavy-set girl with a round face closed her eyes and pursed her lips as she spoke, "That's a great idea, but how do we get together to talk and share stuff if they don't let us out of their sight?"

"They can't watch us all the time. We're talking now, aren't we?" Jeannie interrupted excitedly. "It'll work out. I know it will. At least it will give us something to do to keep our minds off this place."

Lucie chimed in, "If we just go about our business nobody will have the faintest idea what we are planning. This is going to be an interesting game. They might not figure out what's happening until we graduate."

Susan shifted her weight in her chair and hung her head like a puppy that wasn't sure whether to play the game or run away.

Annie glanced around the table and saw new life coming into everyone's face, except for one girl who hadn't said a word. She was a small girl with an oversized head for her body. Her face appeared flat with small, gray-green eyes peering out from her olive complexion. Her silence during the excitement made Annie suspicious. They didn't need a squealer in the group.

Looking straight into her eyes, Annie asked, "What's your name?"

The girl pointed at herself in surprise and pulled herself up in her chair saying, "Sarah."

"Well, how do you feel about the plan, Sarah?"

Sarah tried to work up a smile, "Fine. It's fine with me." Her lower lip and the corners of her mouth quivered as everyone's attention was drawn to her. Annie glanced at Lucie to see her reaction. Their eyes met, exchanging the message that Sarah could not be trusted.

"Let's toast the occasion," Jeannie grabbed her water glass and lifted it up.

The glasses chimed out their pact. Their laughter had shaped the moment into the possibility of survival.

Sister Margaret had appeared at the end of the table. "What's so funny?"

Jeannie froze in her chair. Lucie came to her rescue after seeing the look on Jeannie's face. "Nothing much, Sister. We're just getting to know each other."

"That's wonderful," Sister said.

Annie turned her head to keep Sister from seeing the smirk on her face.

Then Lucie delivered a sing-song, “Thank you, Sister,” as she walked away.

“I thought I saw her go out of the room after the food got served,” Jeannie choked out. “Where did she come from?”

Ignoring Jeannie, Lucie whispered. “This may be easier than we think—like taking candy from a baby.”

“I don’t know,” Annie said as she thought about Jeannie’s question. “I’m not so sure. Nuns have a way of appearing from out of nowhere.”

Sister Margaret walked up to the front by the barred windows. She clapped her hands, saying, “Ladies! Could I please have your attention? Thank you. I would like to explain our agenda for this evening. After dinner, please go back to the dorms as quietly as possible. You may finish unpacking or familiarize yourself with the fourth floor. I’m sure by now you have all found your sink room and the water closets.”

“What’s a water closet?” Annie whispered to Lucie.

“Shhh!” Lucie put her finger to her lips. “I’ll tell you later. You sure want to get in trouble, don’t you? Just listen to her, will you?”

“Remember, you must be in the study hall promptly at seven this evening for a briefing on some pertinent regulations so everything continues to run smoothly. Also our mother superior, Sister Mary Florentine, will be visiting us. After the session is over, you will go to your cell and get ready to retire. The lights will go out at nine forty-five sharp. Remember, eating is not allowed in the dorms at any time. If you have brought food from home, you will have to keep it in your locker on this floor. Please do your best to follow the rules as you will be held accountable for them. You will not be reminded. We consider you to be adults and expect you to act accordingly."

Hup two, three, four, went through Annie's head and she found herself humming, "You're in the Army Now."

Lucie kicked her under the table and whispered, "Are you nuts? Everybody can hear you humming that crazy song, you know. You're going to be dead meat, if she does."

"This will be your regular routine," Sister continued. "There will always be a sister monitoring your activities in case you have any questions, of course."

"Are you listening to what she's saying?" Annie muttered. "There'll be a prison guard at every corner to keep us in line. That's closer to the truth, right?"

"Yes! But it's your funeral if you get caught right now, so cool it."

The disturbance drew Sister Margaret's attention to their table. Looking directly at Annie she paused, turned and paced back and forth for several minutes with her hand cradled over her mouth. Her head was bent down and cocked to the one side, her brow furrowed. They all waited in silence for Sister to decide their fate.

"I do expect that you will have the courtesy to listen to me when I am speaking to the group. I know you ladies are new so I will excuse you this time. However, I warn you that these types of disturbances make it difficult on everyone and will not be tolerated."

Continuing to watch the freshman table, Sister began to speak again. "Tomorrow morning we will start attending Mass as a group. You'll need to be at the top of the stairs by six forty-five. I'm sure you'll all fall into the routine quite easily as there's nothing complicated about it." Sister looked around the room and smiled.

Then one of the seniors stood up, saying, "Sister, I know I speak for the rest of us when I say thank you for agreeing to be our monitor this year. With you helping us, it should be a good year."

"You're welcome, Mary. It will be a new experience for me. I'm sure a good one."

Half-empty platters of food lined the center of the table along with a pitcher of milk. Annie slouched down in her chair, examining the remains. She wondered if she would disintegrate into a pile of bones with nothing left for even the buzzards to snack on. How could she survive four years of this kind of food, much less keep her fears hidden? She had always been good at hiding her feelings. Now she would find out just how good she really was at it.

The racket of chairs scraping on the floor filled the room. Sister clapped her hands saying, "Just a minute, ladies, I haven't dismissed you and we haven't said our prayers yet." After the prayer, she clapped her hands again and said, "Dismissed! We'll see you promptly at seven in the study hall."

The upper classmen filed out first, leaving the freshmen in the room until last.

"I guess I have to find the sink rooms. Does anyone know where they are?" Annie inquired.

Everyone shouted, "Sure I do."

"It's no big deal," Lucie butted in. "I'll give you a guided tour. Come on I'll race you to the fourth floor."

The twinkle in Lucie's eye excited Annie. *Wow! A little competition, this is fantastic.*

Glancing both ways down the corridor, they saw that the coast was clear. They dashed out of the doorway with everyone but a couple of girls right behind them. The marble floor blurred under their giant strides, leaving only their laughter echoing in the hallway. When they reached the bottom of the stairs, Lucie started taking the stairs two at a time. Seeing this, Annie picked up her pace to take three steps at a time. It didn't take long before Lucie changed her stride to match Annie's. Helen, with her long legs, was able to keep up with them, but then began to drop back. All were oblivious to the risk they were taking and enjoying the boldness of their game.

Laughing and gasping for air, Lucie and Annie reached the fourth floor about the same time, neither conceding a victory to the other. Jeannie lead the rest of the group while Helen kept pace right behind them. Almost at the same time, Lucie and Annie extended their hands outward to give them a quick boost to the top.

"Now that's the way to get some fresh blood flowing in your veins," Annie shouted.

"You'd better cool it," Lucie turned to look down the hallway. "There's got to be nuns all over the place up here. I'm surprised we got this far with all the racket we made."

"You're right! No sense ruining our good behavior record already." Annie laughed as she turned and waved to the rest of the girls. "I'll see you in the drill hall--I mean the study hall." Then she raised her arm as though she were charging into battle. "On to the water closets!"

Lucie laughed, "Boy, you're really full of it, aren't you? Come on, I'll give you the treat of your life—a good look at a water closet."

Light streamed into the dim shadowy hallway as if a spotlight was shining through the open doorways on the right. In the darkness, a long room could be seen on the left side with pulled shades on the closed doors. Wondering what it was, Annie walked into the shadows to see if any of the doors had been left unlocked. When she touched the doorknob, she felt like an unknown had been revealed to her, but she didn't know what it was. Fear struck like a bolt of lightning, causing her to step back. *Geez, this is a spooky place. I feel like I'm standing next to a tomb. Why do they have this room locked? I've had enough of their wicked witch games. That's right. You can just stir your pot of dried skeleton skins and spider web moss, trying to inflict your potion, but I won't be the one that will fall under your spell. The worms crawl in, the worms crawl out, the worms play pinochle on your snout.*

"Here we are at the first wonder," Lucie announced in a dramatic voice. "This is the sink room."

Annie walked into the room. At least fifteen small gray-pitted sinks stood in a row on either side of the room with no more than an inch between them. Just above them was a long partially unglazed mirror that covered the entire length of the wall. The three windows opposite the doorway were stopped by a dark lusterless, wooded sill. The lifeless wood continued up the sides of the windows, ending when it capped them at the ceiling.

"That's interesting," Annie spun around toward Lucie. "There aren't any bars or shades on these windows."

"And no privacy either, right?" Lucie stood looking down, facing the antiquated mirror that distorted her features. "God help the person who gets her hair on my toothbrush."

Annie put her hand to her mouth and gagged. "How disgusting! I can't imagine someone else's hair on my toothbrush."

"What do you expect? Look how close these sinks are. Everybody will be standing on top of each other. You can't help but bump into somebody or get an elbow in the eyeball. God help them because I'm not the friendliest person in the morning as it is." Lucie's eyes narrowed and her face flushed as she turned to Annie, "And what about having to look at the half asleep, bent out of shape, crabby faces with their hair every which way in the morning? Looks like you'll be living with a bear most of the time."

It doesn't seem like a good way to start the day to me either," Annie said. "There's not much we can do about it, I guess."

"Guess not," Lucie added. "By the way, the freshmen and sophomores are in this room, and the juniors and seniors are in the next one. We wouldn't want to mix the common freshmen with the upper classmen. It's getting late, so we'd better look for our names on these sinks and move on with the tour. Here's mine. Hey! Guess what—there's yours. You're right next to me. Just remember what I said about hair on my toothbrush," she laughed.

"You're kidding." Annie walked toward Lucie. "Wow, this is too good to be true. They didn't know what they were doing when they did this, did they? Will this make it easy to exchange ideas or what? Hey, does your bathrobe have pockets in it?"

"Yeah, it's on the right side, I think," Lucie said.

"Mine does too, one on each side. We can pass notes that way. I hate clothes that don't have pockets. I don't know what we're supposed to do with our handkerchief with those ugly uniforms. Stuff the slimy thing in our bras, I guess."

Lucie sat down on the wooden sill, "You know the uniforms are bad enough, but why no makeup, not even lipstick? And look at these clumsy shoes! I always thought the nuns' shoes were bad, but what we're expected to wear is even worse. I waited all this time to be fourteen, just to get into high school. Then I could dress up with the latest fad clothes and wear makeup like my older sister. And here I'm stuck. Here! In this dreary old building with bars everywhere, sagging army cots for a first-class backache and not a guy in sight. You'd think we were criminals or something. Tonight they'll probably tell us we have to have permission to pee! As far as I'm concerned, they deserve everything we can think of. Hey, we may even get so good at our little schemes that we get expelled."

"Maybe." Annie felt as if the last speck of energy had seeped out of her body as she sat down next to Lucie. "They sure haven't been very fair, have they?" she asked as her eyes began to fill with tears. "Here we are, trying our best to ignore what's happening to us when down deep inside, our guts are coming apart. You're right! Why should we worry about how much trouble we get into?"

Both girls choked out a laugh as tears escaped from the corners of their eyes. Then they put their arms around each other's shoulders and proceeded to walk out into the hallway.

"It's on to the water closets," Lucie laughed, trying to sound happy. Skipping down the hallway, they passed a nun standing in the shadows. In unison they responded sweetly, "Good evening, Sister."

"You ladies should walk down the corridor, not jump around like some kind of animals," the withered looking nun grumbled.

They kept on skipping, ignoring her comment and giggling, assuring each other of their mutual support.

Arriving at the end of the corridor, Lucie opened a door announcing, "Are you ready for this? Ta-dum! Here we are."

Inside the room were eight wooden stalls, four on either side. Annie opened one of the doors, "This is a water closet? Why, it's just an old toilet, a funny looking one, but a john nonetheless." As she turned to the opposite side of the room, she saw that the other four enclosures housed tubs and chairs. Then she noticed that the partitions around the tubs didn't go all the way to the ceiling, and the room appeared to be attached to another room.

Puzzled, Annie looked at Lucie. "Do you know what's on the other side of this wall?"

Lucie shook her head no, "I didn't notice it before."

Annie walked back into the hallway ahead of Lucie. They saw a door next to the one they just came out of. Annie reached to open it.

"Ladies! That room is not for your use. It is to be used by the sisters only."

Startled by the nun's harshness both girls spun around to see a short, fat nun with a scowl on her face. Annie looked at Lucie who stood motionless.

Give us a break! You're acting like we committed the crime of the century by touching this sacred doorknob. What's so holy about what's behind this door anyway? And who the blazes are you? I guess it doesn't matter. I have to play their game right now. We aren't the ones with any advantages.

Annie attempted a smile, thinking the nun would warm up. "Excuse us, Sister, we were only trying to get acquainted with the floor. We didn't mean any harm."

The nun did not respond. Without a word, the girls began to withdraw. They turned and walked toward the dorms, looking back to see if she was still watching them. The nun held her sentry, her facial expression and stance, frozen.

Annie whispered to Lucie, "I think the secret room is another room attached to the tub room so they can listen to what we are doing. I sure don't like this at all. It's getting pretty bad when you can't even go to the bathroom without somebody listening."

"At least we know what they're up to, total captivity," Lucie said. "I wonder how many more hiding places they have around here that we don't know about? Do we even stand a chance?"

"Right now I don't want to think about it. My guts are so upset that if there are any more surprises, I'm going to lose everything that's down there."

"No kidding! We'd better make a beeline for the dorm because time is running out, Lucie said. "We only have a couple of minutes to find each other's cells."

"What a delightful ring that has to it, don't you think? Cells. It sort of fits right in with everything else around here," Annie said as they walked towards the dorms. Then she remembered the room on the one side of the hallway that gave her such a fright. "Do you know what's in here?"

Lucie laughed, "Oh that—that's the study hall. Oh, I mean the drill hall."

"Funny! Very funny, Lucie."

Water Closet - 1948

Chapter Three

It was six forty-five in the evening when Jeannie poked her head into Annie's cell. "It's time to go; we don't want to get in trouble for being late or anything."

"Sure! Sure!" Annie snapped. "To tell the truth, Jeannie, I don't give a damn."

Annie cringed, remembering how upset her parents would get with her off-colored language. One of these days she'd have to quit that, especially since she was living with the nuns. The punishment could be quite severe if it's a mortal sin to touch a doorknob.

"Come on," Jeannie pleaded, "If for no other reason than not to get me in trouble. Besides you don't have to take it out on me. I'm no better off than you are."

"OK. You're right, let's go." Stepping out of the cell, Annie saw Lucie coming from her cell in the back of the room. Annie waved at her in an attempt to make her hurry up. "We don't want to be late," she yelled. "If you were a better kid they wouldn't have put you so close to the monitor's cell. See I'm way up here in the front of the room." Annie cupped her hands around her mouth and whispered, "They looked at this sweet innocent face and knew they could trust me."

"What a bunch of baloney! Am I going to have to listen to that for the next four years?"

"Maybe my shining personality will rub off on you, and you'll become just as sweet as I am."

"That's a crock! They probably didn't know what to do with you so to be on the safe side, they put you where the nuns stand guard."

"Come on, you guys!" Jeanne threatened. "If you don't stop horsing around, I'm going without you. I don't want to be causing any trouble right now."

"Don't get your girdle in a bind, we're coming," Lucie said as she reached Annie's cell.

"Thanks loads!" Jeannie pouted as she glared at Lucie. Then she turned to Annie with her hands planted on her hips. "What more do you think they'll throw at us tonight?"

Before Annie could answer, Lucie interrupted. "Who knows? For sure, we're going to get to meet the bigwig," Lucie paused, emphasizing every word as she announced, "Sister—Mary—Florentine. She'll probably be the one to lay it on us."

Most of the girls had gathered into small groups in the back of the study hall. Giggles and excited conversation filled the room as Jeannie, Lucie and Annie made their way through the group.

"See! You guys made me late," Jeannie moaned. "Now I'll have to sit up front."

Lucie laughed, "We did you a favor. Now you can stare at the nuns at close range and make them nervous."

"That's enough cornball stuff." Jeannie sat down on the first chair that was available in the third row while Lucie and Annie sat in front of her.

Sighting them, Helen made her way forward and sat down next to Annie. "I've been waiting for you guys. I thought you were going to be late."

Within seconds, Sister Mary Margaret came into the study hall, interrupting Helen's conversation. She clapped her hands. "Thank you for being prompt, ladies. I'm sure you will find this evening very informative."

Lucie turned to Annie, pointed her finger down her throat and proceeded to make a gagging sound.

"What was that?" Sister asked as she turned and looked around the room.

Lucie slid down in her chair as if she thought she would vanish. A moment of silence melted into years.

Sister continued, "We need to go through some rules before Sister Mary Florentine stops by to greet you. First of all, have the new ladies had a chance to read the card that was in your nightstand?"

"Yes, Sister." They all responded,

"Good! Are there any questions?"

Heads turned to see if anyone was brave enough to ask one.

"All right then, I'll get right to the business at hand. First thing tomorrow morning, right after breakfast, we will tour the grounds and school buildings. Please, do not ask questions while we are touring. We will get too far behind and that would interfere with the other sisters' schedules. If you have questions you may approach me later. In the afternoon you will have time to pick up your class schedule and locker assignments at the registrar's office."

"That's the blinking nun again I bet," Annie whispered to Helen.

"Then you may proceed to the bookstore to pick up the books that are required for your classes. The individual who is responsible for your finances will be billed for the books you select."

Annie looked at Lucie and then back at Sister. *The individual responsible! Doesn't everybody here have parents?*

"There are some used books, but they go fast. Please do not get into any unruly discussions over these books. Tomorrow evening you will have some free time. You can spend it in the lounge, the conservatory, or just visiting and getting to know one another. The sisters asked that you be considerate of others by keeping the noise in the dorms to a minimum."

Annie tried to concentrate on what Sister was saying, but in spite of her efforts her thoughts drifted. Daydreaming, she imagined herself playing the music she wanted to play and not something she was told to play. Melodies floated through her mind, "Il Trovatore," Chopin's "Minute Valse" and then the love songs, "Someday My Prince Will Come," "They Tried to Tell Us We're Too Young," songs that sometimes made her feel happy and sometimes made her feel sad.

Annie envisioned her new piano teacher, a middle-aged nun with a happy smile and a sparkle in her eyes. She spoke in a gentle tone and kept telling Annie how much she loved to hear her play. Beautiful compositions were spread out on top of Sister's grand piano and not a razor sharp ruler, waiting to be used as a weapon. A metronome stood silent on the left side where Sister sat next to Annie but sister would rarely use it. She would allow Annie to set the tempo and fill the room with glorious sounds.

It seemed like forever since there weren't so many rigid rules. The last time that she remembered she had just turned three. Her dance instructor had put her on a Chicago stage with her brother, Luke, they tap danced to the tune of "School Days." Right in the middle of the song, Annie dropped her books. Laughter rang out from the audience when she stopped dancing, looked at the books with her hands on her hips and then picked them up before she continued dancing. Things were different when she was little. If she made a mistake singing or dancing, everybody thought it was cute. Teenagers have to follow rules and nobody thinks they're cute.

This sobering reality snapped Annie's thoughts back to Sister Margaret's briefing.

"I want to take a minute and explain demerits to you so there are no misunderstandings. You will be given five pink cards tomorrow that will have the word demerit on them. Be sure to carry them with you wherever you go because they are used to monitor your behavior. You can lose them by breaking the rules, such as talking in the hallways or classrooms, being late for class, or being disrespectful to the sisters, to mention a few. Every week you will show your demerit cards to your homeroom teacher. She will record how many you have lost that week, and she will also note if you lose them on a regular basis. If you lose more than two cards a week, you will be sent to the principal's office. The principal will then decide how you are to be disciplined. However, I'm sure you ladies will not have that sort of a problem."

Annie noticed that Lucie was beginning to slouch in her seat with her head bobbing up and down.

Sister Margaret stopped and turned toward the front doorway. "I see Sister Mary Florentine is ready to greet us now."

Annie jabbed Lucie to wake her up. Lucie immediately brought herself to an upright position. As Sister entered the room, the students stood to greet her.

Annie glanced at Helen and heard her whisper, "Wow!"

A smile crowned Sister Mary Florentine's eyes, making them sparkle, and her soft aged skin glowed under the overhead lights. Annie felt a thrill pass through her body as she delighted in Sister's saintly appearance. Sister stood tall in spite of her robust figure, like someone who had always walked with a book on her head.

There had been a lot of nuns in Annie's life during her parochial school training. Most of them were not much fun to be around. And then there were the stories her older brothers and sister brought home, like the nun who had hung Michael Castle on the hook in the clothes closet because he hadn't finished his homework. Somehow this one seemed different. She reminded Annie of her favorite teacher, Sister Mary Mark, an energetic nun, made learning a delight instead of a chore. Sister would spend as much time as necessary going over problems. She made her students feel like she really wanted them to understand. Sister Mark's olive-gray complexion, black bushy eyebrows and little mustache made her look old for her years. Annie never gave her appearance a thought because her smile and gentle manner were foremost. It seemed like Sister Mary Florentine might have some of those same qualities. She sure didn't seem like the old bat type, but for that matter, neither did Sister Mary Margaret. They may have some good stuff inside them after all.

"Please be seated, ladies, and welcome to St. Anthony's Academy," Sister Mary Florentine said in a soft flowing voice. "We have many wonderful things to share with you. First I want to tell you about the chapel that is connected to the convent because it's my favorite place. Oh no," she said. "It's not because I spend all my time there, though I wish I could. It's because I want you to know there is a place to go if you ever have a special need. Or if things seem to have no answers or are too overwhelming. It's a small chapel with a gold tabernacle and tapestries of wine and ivory. The Sisters keep fresh flowers on the altar, making it such a special place that it warms your heart. I go there when I have some difficult decisions to make, and I always leave with answers. I guess you'd say it's my place to connect with God. We will be visiting it soon so you will know where it is. Always remember to ask Sister Mary Margaret's permission before going over so she will know where you are. There is also a church connected to the convent. That is where the sisters have daily Mass and say their vespers. Sometime you'll have an opportunity to hear the sisters sing. And at Christmas time the seminarians come over and sing for us. It's a delightful time. The grounds include the seminary and the convent, but they are separated by a fence. Fresh breezes off the lake, great sweeping lawns, tall pines contrasted by the oak trees and red maples, make this a wonderful place to study or meditate, especially on these warm fall days. So be sure to enjoy this wonderful gift we have and celebrate every moment you are here. If you decide that you would like to go over to the lake for a special occasion, you'll have to ask permission to go outside the grounds from Sister Mary Margaret. You are fortunate that Sister has accepted the position of monitor for this year. She is a very congenial and fair sister, and I know you will all grow to care about her. Lastly, I want you to know my door will always be open to you. I must go now. I've taken up quite a bit of your time. God bless you."

As Sister Mary Florentine walked toward the door, Sister Margaret began addressing more rules, and Annie did not want to listen to her. It all happened too fast. Annie had questions that needed to be answered, like where could she find Sister Mary Florentine. She felt Sister's gracious ways had to be genuine. And if she could just talk to her, even for a moment, perhaps it would relieve the sick feeling she had in her stomach.

After that Annie found it impossible to pay attention to what Sister Margaret was saying. Thoughts of home, thoughts of her music, thoughts of Sister Florentine took preference. Annie had no conception as to how long Sister Margaret had been talking when she realized everyone was beginning to leave the room. In a raspy whisper Lucie spoke her disapproval to the girls as Annie sat in silence. "She's really something, isn't she? She didn't fool me though. I bet she isn't so sweet when you end up in her office. Just like all of them; they put on this goody-two-shoes facade and, as long as you don't breathe out of turn, you're safe. When it comes right down to it, all they hit us with were rules, rules and more rules. Then we'll get the ax when we can't remember them. I guess there's not much to the whole thing anyway. Is there? Just shut your mouth and stay in line, that's it."

Helen looked at Annie and then at Lucie. "I guess you're right. But Sister Florentine sure looks good to me right now."

"I don't know what to think," Annie said. With the vision of Sister Florentine fresh in her mind, Annie wanted to believe her instincts, that Sister was what she appeared to be. "She might end up being our only saving grace."

The next thing Annie knew she was standing in her cell, looking down at the bed. She recalled how she had been taught never to sit on the edge of a bed. If she did, the springs would break and then the bed would sag. It didn't seem to matter much with this bed because it sagged all over anyway. No matter what she did, it wouldn't make a difference. She was going to be stuck there for a long time.

Confused and yet resentful, Annie threw herself down on the bed. She lay there, unable to cry and forced to listen to the students in the surrounding cells who were readying themselves for bed, without a word. Suitcases snapped open, the sound of dry wood against dry wood scraped as drawers opened and closed, the noise of shuffling slippers going in and out of the room as the students went to their assigned sink rooms—under it all was the soft chatter of rosary beads as the guard nuns paced up and down, keeping a close watch.

It's funny. I had everything, my own room with all the trimmings, I could come and go as I pleased, silk dresses, wool ensembles and fur wraps filled my closet. Now I have nothing. Not even this cell is mine. They could take it away anytime and put me somewhere else. They are in complete control of everything I do, my comings and goings—everything that I am.

Annie glanced at the chair beside her bed where she had placed her favorite teddy bear, Chocolate. She reached out and picked him up, caressing his soft body against her chest.

"Please, dear God, don't let them take Chocolate too," she prayed.

Chapter Four

DING - - -DONG- - - DING - - DONG- - -
DING - - DONG!

Most of the night Annie tossed and turned on her sway-back cot, trying to get comfortable. After several hours, she fell asleep, only to be awakened by the clanging sound of a bell ringing. Struggling to sit up, she threw back the covers, managed to scramble to the edge of her cell and pulled back the curtain. A nun was going through the dorm with a cowbell, swinging it as hard as she could. Annie clasped her hands over her ears in an attempt to soften the overwhelming decibels. Nothing seemed to help until the nun headed out of the dorm with the weapon in her hand.

Shivering from the icy cold floor, Annie grabbed her slippers and bathrobe. "Don't they ever heat this place?" she grumbled. "What a rotten thing to do to a bunch of new boarders. This is more than a little sadistic."

Continuing to complain, she gathered her toiletries and made her way to the sink room. Annie wasn't surprised to see the girl, who was next in line after Annie, was already there. Annie had arrived a minute before Mary Ann had finished. *I bet Francis would have loved it if I hadn't showed up. Not that I'd blame her. You can't get dressed or do your hair before you get washed up. Anyway I can't.*

Lucie was standing in line, looking like she had slept on her face. "How did you like the treat we got this morning with the cowbell?"

Before Annie could answer, a nun poked her head into the room. "Ladies! Keep moving along with your tasks and do keep the silence."

Annie turned and whispered to Lucie, "What a heartless thing to do to someone when she's sound asleep. You can bet your booties they won't get me again because I'll just set my clock and wake up before that crazy nun makes her rounds."

Lucie looked over her shoulder and then turned back to Annie. She put her finger to her lips and nodded toward the mirror. Following Lucie's direction, Annie realized the nuns could see everything they were doing.

"Opportunities will present themselves," Lucie whispered. "We'll just have to watch for them."

Annie left the sink room as soon as she finished rinsing out the sink. Frances smiled and nodded a thank you. Annie wondered about this pleasant looking girl who seemed old for her years with her reddish and ruddy, freckled complexion. Annie knew Frances must be at least a sophomore, but she looked more like a senior. Maybe after class some afternoon Annie would have an opportunity to get to know her.

Back at her cell, Annie hurried to get dressed and put her things in order. She had just finished when a nun poked her head in her cell and said, "Good, you've made your bed." She left, leaving Annie standing in amazement at her lack of manners. *Whatever happened to the courtesy of announcing yourself before you enter? There sure isn't any consideration for us, but they expect us to have big time consideration for them. Well, I'll keep my list and we'll see what Sister Mary Florentine has to say about this. First I'll have to find out who that was. Put this in your memory bank, kid—a pudgy little nun whose red face pops out from behind her head-piece because there isn't enough room for it. The rest of her looks like a typical nun, glasses, white and black habit, rosary, cord around her waist and plump. Too bad the cord isn't around her neck.*

The little clock from home that stood on Annie's nightstand reminded her that she'd better stop thinking about that nun and finish what she was doing. As she approached the top of the stairs, the tired eyes of the students turned slowly to exchange a morning greeting. As Annie stepped into line, she could hear the footsteps of Sister Mary Margaret coming from behind the door at the end of the hallway.

Lucie poked Annie and whispered, "Just think, we have four years to stand here every morning waiting for a nun to come through that door."

"Sister Margaret doesn't seem like such a bad egg," Jeannie interrupted. "It'll be fun to see how much we can pull over on her, anyway."

Sister led the group down the stairs to the first floor, walking past the same group of pictures Annie had seen the day before.

"What's that smell?" Lucie grimaced in a half whisper. "Is someone smoking pot?"

"What's pot?" Annie asked.

"You know," Lucie said. "You smoke it and it makes you high."

"Yeah," said Susan. "I've heard of it, but I've never had any. My parents would kill me if they ever caught me with that stuff."

"I don't have a clue about what you guys are talking about. I've never heard of pot," Annie said. "Pots you sit on, but that's it. The only thing I smell is incense. Maybe that's what you smell, incense. You can't be Catholic, if you've never smelled that before."

"Naw! You're kidding? Just because I'm here doesn't make me Catholic. I've got enough problems without that too."

"I never had gotten used to the smell of that stuff. It gives me an instant headache."

"So what is this incense?"

"It's the stuff the priest puts in this capsule-like thing that's on a chain. Then he walks around whatever he wants to bless and swings it back and forth at it. The incense is what's supposed to bless stuff. You'll know what I'm talking about when you see it."

Sister Margaret had stopped the group. Walking back to them with her finger to her lips, she said in a low tone, "Ladies, you need to be still. We are going to be entering the chapel now and we will be in the presence of Our Lord."

Annie took a deep breath and let it out as Sister walked away. "I thought we were dead meat that time," she whispered.

"For those of you who are new here, there are veils on the table outside of the chapel," Sister said. "Please take one and cover your head with it. It will be your responsibility to keep it clean and to have it available for all of our chapel services until you graduate. So be sure to keep it in a safe place."

Sister Margaret continued to lead the students down the corridor toward the chapel. Just before the entrance to the school, Annie caught sight of an embossed door that read 'Sister Mary Florentine.' With her discovery, she hadn't noticed that the group had stopped, and she walked right into Susan.

"Ouch!" Susan hollered.

Sister Margaret turned quickly, picking up her pace on her way back to the freshmen. "What's the matter?"

"Oh it's nothing, Sister, I just tripped a little. I'm sorry for the disturbance."

"Very well," Sister said. "All right, ladies, please make your way into the chapel with the seniors and juniors on the left side, and the sophomores and freshmen on the right side."

"Gee, thanks for covering for me, Susan. I guess I got distracted when I saw Sister Mary Florentine's name on the door back there."

"That's OK. We need to stick up for each other."

The young women shuffled their way into chapel like a herd of cattle that knew their own stalls. The sophomores filled the back pews first, causing the freshmen to have to go into the front pews. All remained standing as they waited for the chaplain. He entered by way of a door at the side of the chapel altar. He was a tall erect man with an elongated face and slightly graying hair. Looking around the group, he broke out in laughter, making his Santa Claus tummy wobble under his long white vestments.

The freshmen stood in amazement, never expecting to hear a priest ready to say Mass, laughing out loud in the chapel. The upper classmen responded with, "Hi Father!"

"Welcome, welcome, welcome, I see that I have startled a few of our newer ladies. Don't worry, I haven't committed any mortal sin by talking in church. This is the house of God. He has a sense of humor too, you know. My name is Father McBride, and I'd like to have a couple of our new students tell us something about themselves. This is a kind of 'get acquainted' day, so we have a little more time than usual. What about you? What's your name?"

He was looking at Susan. She looked around to those next to her in an effort to avoid his question. Annie could see her bottom lip start to quiver and little beads of perspiration begin to pop out on her forehead. "Yes you—come on now. Don't be bashful. We'd like to get to know you."

"Susan, uh, Susanne Blatts is my name," she managed to stammer out. "I'm from a small town just outside of Milwaukee called Germantown."

"Now that wasn't so bad, was it?" Father asked.

Annie looked at Susan who was very pale and perspiring profusely. Susan forced a smile and again looked back and forth, trying to draw the attention away from herself.

"OK now, who is next?" Father asked.

"Me, I'll go next. My name is Lucie Young. I came here from Lake Geneva, Wisconsin. You know, the place where they have the Bunny Club! A lot of big money people go there. It's a beautiful area with the lake and all. There're plenty of places to spend your cash between the casinos and the bars with strippers that are really stacked. And…"

Father McBride interrupted Lucie, "Mary Ann, it's good to see you again."

"Thank you, Father."

Annie looked at Lucie and saw that she was standing tall and grinning. *I wonder what else was on its way out of her mouth. This should be a very interesting year.*

"I understand you won some awards this past summer in music. Would you like to tell us about it?"

"It seemed like I spent my whole summer practicing, but it turned out to be worth it. I found out about the contest just before I left school last spring. I knew my competition would be stiff when I learned that it was in Chicago."

"How did you do? I bet very well. Come on now, don't be shy," Father coaxed.

"Somehow I managed to squeak out a first place."

"You're too modest, Mary Ann. Anyone who has heard you play knows what an accomplished violinist you are."

"Thank you, Father."

This is getting to be too much. I'm starving and we have to sit through at least a half hour of Mass yet. Annie looked around to see if anyone else was getting restless. Lucie was still looking pleased with herself. The rest of the lower classmen were either shrinking or had their heads hanging down so they wouldn't be the next ones to be called on.

"I guess it's time we get started. You'll find your hymnals in the pews so you can follow along with the Mass. Sister Mary Loretta will lead the singing with the organ."

Annie turned. She stiffened in surprise. It was the same nun who had poked her head into Annie's cell. *Oh no! This is not good. What if she is the head of the music department?!*

It was Thursday afternoon, almost three weeks after school had started. Annie had gone to see Sister Mary Florentine with her list of complaints, but she couldn't bring herself to talk to Sister about them. Her instincts told her it was alright, but her past experiences with a nun when she was in fifth grade changed her mind. Annie had turned sideways in her desk because the girl sitting behind her started cutting her hair off. When Sister Mary Ann saw Annie's position, she attacked Annie, telling her to sit properly in her seat. Annie tried to explain, but Sister interrupted her, saying the only reason Annie went to Communion was to show off her face. No tears came, only speechlessness, followed by a pain that burned Annie's body to her very depths. That night she tossed and turned, wondering whether she should ever go to Communion again. By the next morning, Annie decided to receive Communion because what Sister Mary Ann did was very wrong. Right then and there, Annie vowed that nobody would ever get away with saying such terrible things to her again. Sister Mary Florentine had been pleasant enough, but Annie decided it would be wise to leave her list tucked in her sweater pocket until Sister Florentine got to know her better. Annie's grandma used to say that first impressions were lasting ones, and Annie did want to make a good impression.

The monotonous routine and the bad food, complicated by having to climb five flights of stairs to her homeroom and four flights to the dorm, made it difficult for Annie to be happy about anything. The only solace she had was when she escaped into the raptures of her music when no one else was around. That didn't happen very often because her new teacher's practice room was right across from Annie's. Sister Mary Elizabeth would practice endless amounts of exercise scales on her cello with her door open. Then she could keep a watchful eye on her students.

Sister Elizabeth was a huge woman who hobbled when she walked from sitting for long hours practicing the same exercises that she assigned Annie, with her cello propped between her legs. The repetitious sounds vibrated through Annie's body like a buzz-saw out of control. Her only protection was to play something that would be loud enough to drown out Sister's noise.

Today Annie had gotten out of class early, hoping to go to the conservatory to play some of her favorite melodies from home before her teacher showed up. She wanted to make the most of the few precious moments she had. Paging through her music, she searched for melodies that sparked her inner feelings of expression. "Somewhere Over the Rainbow" was the first one she picked, then "The Blue Danube," the "Merry Widow Waltz" and finally "Claire de Lune." As she played, feelings of sadness turned into feelings of joy. She slipped into the world of melodies and memories as she lost all sense of time.

All of a sudden, there was a knock on her door. Annie froze in place, thinking a punishment lurked behind it for not practicing her scales. She opened the door to find a nun whose eyes had a sparkle when she smiled. Her face seemed too pretty to be surrounded by a habit.

"Good afternoon! My name is Sister Mary Louise, and I'm the head of the music department for the college that is affiliated with the high school. I hope I didn't startle you, but I couldn't help listening to you play. You seem to be enjoying your music very much. You play with such passion."

Grinning, Annie said, "Thank you Sister."

"I came over because I have room for one more student in my teaching schedule. So I thought I'd see if I could select a high school student. After hearing you play, I would like to invite you to be my student."

Annie wanted to scream with delight but restrained herself instead. "Yes, Sister, I would be honored." Then she saw Sister Mary Elizabeth walk into the conservatory. Annie's heart sank.

"But what do I do about my present teacher?"

"Don't be concerned about that. I'll talk to Sister Elizabeth. Your lesson will be at four o'clock on Monday afternoon. I hope that's convenient for you?"

"Oh yes—sure Sister! That'll be fine," Annie stammered.

"You'll find me on the fourth floor in the college building." She smiled and left.

Annie stood in the doorway, so excited she hardly noticed that Sister Elizabeth had begun practicing her scales again. Closing the door behind her, Annie leaned against it to catch her breath, looked up, rolled her eyes and said in an airy tone, "She's just like I imagined." Then she went to her school bag and dug out "Malaguena," the most demanding piece she could find to express her elation.

*   *   *

Golden colors had begun to streak the leaves of the stately oaks and maple trees as the days grew shorter. It was the end of the first week of October. The probationary period was almost over, and the first year boarding students had just been put in a dorm together. Their beds were lined up against the wall in barracks style, with one row down the middle. Whatever the reason for the change, all were grateful to have people around them, instead of sheets.

Surviving the monotony of the routine had been especially difficult because the girls rarely had an opportunity to meet. However, that didn't stop them from planning a prank or two when they did. Notes were passed in the hallway as they'd drop things or run into each other deliberately. They shared their ideas when the guard nun was out of hearing range. A week after they had gotten settled into the new dorm, Annie, Susan and Lucie initiated a plan to "get" Jeannie.

"You'll have to get to Jeannie's bed before the lights go on in the dorm, and make sure Sister Eunice isn't in her cell," Annie said to Susan. "I'd do it myself, but Jeannie will suspect something if I leave study hall early. I've been watching Sister Eunice; she usually goes to her cell about the same time that we begin to get ready for bed, around 9:00 o'clock. So if you retire early, you'll have plenty of time to get in there and get the job done."

Lucie laughed like the rascal she was, "It's about time we have some fun around here."

"Remember, Susan, don't tell anybody about this, and you don't know anything either, OK?" Annie said.

"Gotcha! I've never done anything like this before. I hope I don't screw up. What do I tell Sister Margaret so she'll let me retire early?"

"Tell her you're sick," Annie suggested. "She'll believe you with that innocent look you can fake so well. And don't worry about screwing up. You won't. You'll do just fine." The three girls burst out laughing, excited for their adventure to begin.

Early the next morning Jeannie crawled out of her powdery den. As she walked around her bed, little white footprints marked her journey. Her hair was matted and stark white, and her face looked as if someone had smacked her with a giant powder puff.

After the wake-up bell had sounded, Sister Eunice came out of her cell to greet the girls, stopping abruptly at Jeannie's bedside. "Whatever happened to you?" she asked, shocked by Jeannie's appearance.

Barely able to open her eyes to look at Sister, Jeannie said, "Oh, I just spilled my talcum powder during the night, Sister, that's all."

Sister paced around Jeannie with her hands propped on her hips, shaking her head in disbelief. She was an older nun. Her short, slender frame allowed her habit to hang straight to the floor, not billowing out like the chubby nun's did. Sister's disposition sparkled through the devilish light in her eyes. It seemed likely that it would be hard to pull anything over on her. A blend of smile marks and crow's feet around her eyes, complemented her face. More than likely put there from laughing at all the pranks young women thought they were getting away with.

"Well, I guess you'd better get busy and clean this mess up."

All in the dorm busied themselves getting ready for Mass, trying to hide the smirks on their faces. Annie was on her way out of the dorm to go to the sink room when she passed Susan's bed and whispered, "How much stuff did you put in her bed? Are you crazy?"

"It was your idea! I just thought that as long as I was doing it, I'd get her good," Susan chuckled with a mischievous grin. "Besides, I couldn't see what I was doing. It was dark, you know."

Annie glanced over at Jeannie. The frown on Jeannie's face had cracked the powder around her eyes, mouth and forehead. Annie struggled with a sympathetic look towards her, but the scene tickled her insides so much she had a hard time not laughing.

Jeannie did not share Annie's delight, from the harsh glare in her eyes. She probably had a good inkling who was behind the prank. Lucie and Susan wouldn't have said anything, but then there was Sarah. Annie just didn't trust her. Sarah could've overheard the three of them planning things and then gone and snitched to Jeannie to win her over as a friend. But then Jeannie wouldn't have gotten into bed. The possibility that Annie held the most guilty position for Jeannie to suspect, couldn't be ignored. One thing for sure, sooner or later, Jeannie would get back at her. Whatever Jeannie tried, Annie planned to be ready for it. That would be another challenge to liven up their dull routine. In spite of the nasty looks from Jeannie, Annie felt proud of her. She took it like a real trouper and didn't rat on any of them. And that said something. The most amazing thing seemed to be that Sister Eunice might have actually bought Jeannie's story.

Not sure of how Jeannie's revenge would play out, Annie examined her space every night—under her bed, in her bed, behind her bed. She wanted to make sure that if the revenge was something that crawled, that she got to it before it got to her. The other girls watched the game proceed between the two friends, enjoying every moment.

This suspense is killing me. It's been a week already. If she's going to do something, I wish she'd get on with it. I bet that's part of her strategy, making me sweat it out. Maybe I'm making too much of a thing out of this. Jeannie might just be glad Sister Eunice didn't make more of a stink. I suppose the only way to find out is to ask her. Now that would be stupid. She has to be fuming.

By bedtime Annie had convinced herself that Jeannie was too chicken to do anything. She opened her bed, and took a quick look and jumped in. That's when she realized her bed had been short sheeted.

Disappointed by what she thought to be a feeble attempt, she walked over to Jeannie and said, "Couldn't you come up with something more original than that? Short sheeting beds went out with Girl Scouts—two years ago!"

"I don't know what you are talking about," Jeannie insisted.

"Oh, come on now. You don't think I'm as gullible as Sister is, do you?"

"Why don't you tell me how gullible I am, Annie?" Sister said when she stepped out of her cell.

"Oh my gosh!" Annie whispered. Afraid to turn around, Annie stared into Jeannie's face, watching her suck in her cheeks to keep from laughing.

Annie stammered, "Oh, Sister, I didn't mean that—I . . ."

"Yes, Annie, what did you mean then?"

Annie knew that horror had to be written in the blush of her entire torso. Her heart banged so hard she could feel the pulsating throb in her head and neck. She had buried herself deeper than any powder bath and decided not to dig a bigger hole.

"I'm sorry, Sister. Even if I was just horsing around, I had no right to make a comment like that."

"Clever, Annie. Very clever. I'll accept that as an apology." Sister paced back and forth for a moment. "You know, Annie, the Home Economics floor has been looking a little dingy lately and could use a good scrubbing. Would you like to do that for me?"

"Uh . . . sure, Sister. "When would you like that done?"

Annie tried to appear matter of fact, but inside she felt like her stomach had eaten her internal organs.

"Why don't you meet me at my classroom tomorrow after school? That way you'll have plenty of time to finish the job before bedtime."

Jeannie grinned as she turned and began to open her bed. *She got me and with my own big mouth. And Sister—I could swear she had a smile on her face as she walked back to her cell.*

Chapter Five

The following Monday evening, Sister Margaret announced that the probationary period was over for the freshmen. Sighs of relief echoed through the study hall, with hopes of freedom on the horizon. The next day, Annie received a message that her dad was going to pick her up on Friday afternoon to go home for the weekend. She was so excited she ran to the dorm to tell everybody her news.

On her way, home cooking popped into Annie's head. She imagined such glorious dishes on the table that her mouth began to water. Along with that, she decided to take her long list of atrocities committed by the nuns she had prepared with the help of Lucie and Helen.

Annie hoped that she might not have to go back to St. Anthony's once her parents realized what had occurred at the school. However, that idea lost its glow once she remembered all the things her parents hadn't told her.

She'd have to be prepared for the worst case scenario, or the chance that her plan might run aground. That meant bringing food back that wouldn't spoil so they'd have plenty to eat. The possibility that her other friends could bring something back surfaced. Then they'd have lots of variety.

The first person she ran into when she got to the dorm was Susan. "Guess what! My dad is picking me up on Friday for the weekend. Is your dad coming?"

"No, I'll have to take the bus home. That's OK, I'm just glad that I'm lucky enough to get out of here. Helen is the only other one who'll be leaving this weekend. I guess Lucie and Jeannie are pretty bummed out over this, not to mention some of the others. So don't be surprised if they don't share your enthusiasm. Believe me, I found out the hard way."

Annie didn't know what to say to her friends. She tried to reassure them that there were a few more days left before the weekend so they could still get a call.

"I don't think so," Jeannie responded. "I'll be lucky if I get out of here for Thanksgiving. Unless they have some work that needs doing, then they'll come and get me."

"Yeah, same for me," Lucie chimed in. "There's too much going on in Lake Geneva. That means they'd have to keep an eye on me, and that would be too much trouble."

"Can I bring you something back? Or do something for you?"

"If you can get your hands on some food, like a treat or something, that would be great. Wish we had a refrigerator to keep our own stuff in," Jeannie said.

The three girls sat together for several minutes, not saying a word. Annie got up, using the excuse she had to practice. Nothing she could say would relieve their pain and she couldn't imagine what she'd feel like if she had to stay while everybody else went home. If it were only possible, she'd take them with her.

Sitting on the front steps with her luggage, Annie tapped her foot as she waited for her dad to arrive that Friday afternoon. The air felt fresh with the soft autumn breeze. The fall had always been her favorite time of the year, especially Indian summer. She'd sit in the warm sun, drinking in the energy from the brilliant colors that were displayed everywhere; then she'd imagine the new crop of apples hanging heavily on the trees, waiting to be picked and baked into a fresh apple pie.

As the iron gates began to swing open, she saw her dad's black sedan drive into the courtyard. Annie jumped to her feet. She grabbed her suitcase and ran to the car before it stopped, opened the car door, jumped in and said, "Let's go!"

"Wait a minute, not so fast. Don't I even get a hello?"

"Ah. Yeah. Sure. Hello!" She leaned over and kissed him on the cheek.

"First I have to go in and sign you out and find out when you have to be back."

Annie didn't move. "I'm not going back in that place one second before I have to."

"OK, OK," he said, disappointment written on his face. "I'll be back in a minute." As he turned to get out of the car, he added, "I think you have to be back by five on Sunday afternoon or you'll be campused."

"Campused! What's that? Oh, never mind. I've heard something about that, but there was so much I had to pay attention to every second that I didn't bother about something that may happen whenever. I bet it's a real joy though, just like everything else around here. And why would I suspect there might be other surprises hanging around that nobody told me about?"

"I didn't come all this way to argue with you, Annie. I thought you'd be glad to go home for the weekend, but if you're going to be sassy, perhaps you'd rather stay here."

Annie folded her arms and proceeded to pout, feeling she had every right to say what she did with the way she had been treated. Neither one of them said anything for a couple of moments. Then he cleared his throat, trying to regain his composure.

"Being campused means if you don't come back on time, you'll lose your weekend privileges. Then you'll have to work at the convent the following weekend."

"What?" Annie shouted. "What if I get sick and can't get back? Or you have a flat tire? Or my train is late? What then? I'm stuck here forever?"

"Don't make such a big thing out of this, Stinker. I'm sure there must be exceptions to the rule."

"You'd be upset, too, if you had to stay in this place. Besides, I doubt if there are any exceptions to anything here. I haven't seen any in the last six weeks."

Annie kept silent on the way home. She felt unsettled about the realization that her parents knew more than they had told her. The ugly truth had shown itself and she had to deal with it. The possibility of trying to convince them of anything about the school seemed useless.

They were about half an hour from home before Annie spoke. "Did anyone call?"

"Yes, Michael did. He said he would meet you at the bleachers around seven-thirty for the football game and the dance. I guess West Bend is playing Port Washington. Your mother and I have decided that I'll pick you up at eleven. That's late enough for you to be out."

"The dance lasts until eleven-thirty. Can't you reconsider? It's bad enough that I'll be the only kid being picked up by a parent, but leaving early, too?"

"Sorry, but if you want to go, you'll have to follow the rules. We both feel you are too young to be going to a dance."

You can't do this. You can't do that—more rules only from a different place. I'll probably be ninety before they let me live a little. Sounds like just another type of prison to me. Maybe that's all life is, going from one prison to another.

It was almost six in the evening by the time they arrived home. Annie had "ants in her pants" from thinking about the excitement of going to her first dance. She wanted everything to be perfect—her hair, her clothes and her shoes. As soon as she got home, she ran upstairs and rolled her hair into tiny curls, fastening them with bobby pins. When she had finished, she headed straight for the kitchen.

Having a marvelous bounty set before her after six weeks of bad food, she stuffed herself with homemade mashed potatoes oozing with butter and rump roast browned to perfection and topped with sautéed onions that were submerged in a savory, dark-brown gravy. Although Annie didn't care much for peas and carrots, she relished every morsel. She waited for her mother to tell her to stop chasing the peas around on her plate, but she never did. The final course was a rich homemade yellow cake loaded with whipped divinity frosting and fresh grated coconut. The rest of her siblings were away for the weekend so all this food would be Annie's.

Due to the lateness of the hour, Annie asked if she could be excused from doing the dishes. She still had to get ready and she didn't want to be late. Her parents agreed, but her mother added, "Just this once, and don't expect this to happen every time you come home for the weekend."

Annie said her after meal prayers. Then she pushed herself away from the table, wondering if she would be able to get up, much less dance. She thanked them, excused herself and ran up to her room. On the way, she envisioned the outfit she planned to wear. As she sorted through her clothes closet, looking for her dark-wine skirt, she pulled hard past some wool skirts her mother had made, causing one of them to slide from its hanger.

"I'm not wearing these box-pleated skirts," she grumbled. "They flare out at all the wrong places and make me look fat. I don't know why Mother keeps making them when she knows I hate them. Oh! Here it is! My favorite skirt or shall I say my only skirt." Annie held up the straight-cut gabardine to make sure it was clean and pressed. The fad for the area specified that skirts should be down to the ankle and the saddle shoes scuffed. Only a hint of the bobby socks should be visible.

Her skirt would do just fine, but getting the shoes scuffed would be a challenge. Her parents' rules were unconditional. Your shoes were always polished, and you didn't go anywhere until they were. The makeup rule about choked Annie when she heard it. *You do not wear any makeup until you have started high school. If you do, you will pay for all of it for the rest of your life.* Being very frugal or probably a miser, Annie would rather give up the makeup than take a chance on getting caught with it and lose money. Ever since she could remember, she exploited every opportunity to collect coins for her piggy bank. With the most innocent smile, she'd present her piggy bank for donations. Everybody thought it was so cute. Then she'd sit in her room and shake it, listening as the coins clanged together.

Being a freshman she could wear all the makeup she wanted, without hiding it.

Knowing she'd have to take care of the shoes after being dropped off, donned her matching set of cashmere sweaters and skirt. Then she selected a wine colored scarf with hints of almond to complete the ensemble. After dressing, she dashed into the bathroom, pulled the pin curls out of her hair and brushed it. Applying a little rouge to her already flushed cheeks, she ran down the stairs with her shoes in hand, hollering at her dad to start the car.

"I'm ready. Let's go!"

Her dad lifted himself with effort as he got up from his favorite wingback chair, annoyed by her impatient demand. "What's your hurry? You have all night, and the dance doesn't start for a couple of hours. And I know you're not interested in football."

"Come on, Dad," she pleaded.

"OK. I'll be right out. Wait for me in the car."

Annie could feel her heart skip beats as her dad neared the school. Cars were scattered on the grass as well as at the curb. Young people were gathered together over the great lawn, while others were beginning to hurry toward the football field, mounting the bleachers in hopes of getting the best seats.

"I don't know how you'll ever find Michael in all this confusion," he said, watching so he didn't hit a darting teenager.

"Stop. There's Patsy. It's OK, I'll get out here," Annie said as she began to open the car door.

"Hold on! Not so fast. Where am I suppose to pick you up?"

Annie had hoped that if she got out of the car fast enough, her dad wouldn't have time to make plans. That would've opened a world of possibilities for her, like going home with one of the fellows.

Ignoring the disgusted expression on Annie's face, he said, "See that platform over there at the back of the school building? I'll pick you up there at eleven sharp. You stay right there until I come to get you. I don't want you walking around in the dark late at night. If I can't find a place to park, I'll walk up and get you. Alright?"

"OK," Annie said with head hanging down.

"Have a good time now."

Annie jumped out of the car and screamed Patsy's name as she ran across the lawn. Several heads turned to see where the racket came from. Hearing Annie's voice, Patsy turned, waved and started walking toward her.

"How are you? You look great!" Patsy said. "That place couldn't have been that bad. Now was it?"

"Bad isn't a bad enough word for it," Annie said.

Looking around to see if anyone had noticed, Patsy said, "The shoes, Annie, the shoes. Here, I have a brillo pad we can rub them with, and then a little dirt and everything will be fine." She bent down and began rubbing Annie's shoes.

"It's worse than awful. You'll never believe what they make us do." Annie was rattling off sentences in rapid succession with her hands moving in expressive gyrations. "We are like prisoners of war, marching up and down the hallways in uniforms. They might as well have stripes on them. You know how strict the nuns can be around here? Like when they used to hang the boys on hooks in the cloakroom and whack us with rulers? Well, believe me, they are nothing compared to how they are in that place. They even watch to see what you are doing in the bathroom. And the food! How does moldy bread, rancid butter and sour milk grab you? I didn't know food could be so terrible. Why, even my cooking is better than theirs. You know how bad that is."

Patsy listened while scuffing Annie's shoes as Annie went on and on about the academy. Patsy and Annie had met the previous summer while taking a Life Saving class at the city park. While comparing notes on the techniques, they discovered they both lived off Highway 33. From then on they enjoyed each other's company, walking home together.

Patsy never seemed to worry about fancy hairdos, the makeup scene or silly talk about guys. Her dishwater blonde hair was cut short to keep it out of her face while swimming. Annie marveled at the way Patsy manipulated her body to get under and behind a drowning victim, and she could hold her breath for what seemed like an eternity. But no matter what, Annie felt that Patsy's best quality was that she could keep a secret.

"Well, at least you're here now. Try not to think about that place. Otherwise you won't have a good time tonight. I saw Michael just a little while ago over by the bleachers." Patsy laughed, "Now that your shoes look like they belong, we can see if we can find him. I'm sure he'll be watching for you because he has the biggest crush on you."

"Come on! Michael? Why, he is so serious about his studies. I didn't think it was possible for him to have a crush on anything except his books."

"Afraid you're wrong. Hey! There he is, over there, see him?"

Moonstruck, Annie said, "Yeah."

"Will you look at that grin on his face? He looks like he could swallow you whole. We'd better hush before he gets within hearing range."

The girls exchanged mischievous glances and then waved and hollered at Michael.

Annie had met Michael in seventh grade. He had to be at least six feet two now, making his lanky body appear more slender. Having an ill mother, Michael cared for his younger siblings and still became the family scholar. During this period his dad worked two jobs, allowing Michael few freedoms; even events like the free movies that were put on by the fire department were off limits.

One evening when his dad didn't have to work, Michael begged his father to let him go to a movie with his friends. His mother interceded and managed to convince her husband to let Michael go. As it turned out, the gang decided to go to the junkyard after the movie to get some extra parts for the car they were building. Michael didn't want to go, but he didn't want to look like a chicken either. Fifteen minutes after the gang arrived at the dump, the police showed up, sirens blaring and lights flashing. The gang scattered in different directions with officers right on everyone's heels. Michael panicked and headed for the river. He thought he could outsmart the police if he worked his way downstream.

The water had been drained for cleanup so he had to make his way through the muck. With each lunge, Michael sank up to his knees, doing his best to stay upright. The vision of what his father might do, kept him motivated. After an hour of struggling, he emerged saturated in mud, only to be greeted by two police officers who had a good laugh at his expense. Off to jail he went!

Everybody talked for months about how red in the face Michael's dad got when he screamed that Michael had disgraced the family. That put an end to Michael's social life for the next year.

As the rhythm of the marching band announced the start of the game, Michael ran towards them effortlessly "I didn't think you were going to make it," he said, still smiling. "I've got some seats saved right on the fifty yard line. Can you believe it?" He grabbed Annie by the hand as he walked, leading her toward the bleachers. "Come on, Patsy, I saved room for you, too."

Annie glanced at Patsy, shrugged her shoulders and allowed Michael to guide her. The bleachers were full of students cheering for their team as they began to climb to the seats that Michael had saved. As they made their way through the crowd, Annie could hear some derogatory comments amongst the girls, asking who she was and why she was sitting on their school bleachers.

Hearing this, Michael squeezed Annie's hand as he looked into her eyes and told her to ignore them. They were just jealous, he whispered. Regardless, the comments made Annie very uncomfortable, so she sat safely between Michael and Patsy. It wasn't her school and she didn't belong there, no matter how much she wished that she did.

It was a glorious night for Annie. Sensual feelings she had previously ignored were running wildly through her veins as Michael sat holding her hand, never letting go, even when there was a touchdown. His considerate nature blossomed in Annie's heart when he wrapped his blanket around all three of them to make sure they were warm as the cold night air set in. Annie never had a guy hold her hand before or stir the rush of warmth that ran through her body. They were feelings Annie didn't understand, wonderful yet scary.

After they were beginning to get warm, Michael bought hot dogs and hot chocolate loaded with marshmallows for all of them. So intent on cheering for the team and smiling at Michael, Annie noticed her hot dogs had already begun to cool before she took her first bite. Seeing Annie's glow, Patsy took an occasional peek to see their embracing hands and then winked at Annie.

As the end of the game neared, it became obvious that their team would win. Everyone, especially the girls, screamed and jumped up and down on the bleachers so much Annie thought they would collapse. Through hand gestures and attempting to shout over the crowd, Michael indicated to Annie and Patsy that they should try to get off the bleachers before the other students. The cheering began to die down as they made their way through a group of young girls who were having a giddy conversation about how sexy the quarterback was, especially when he ran away from them down the field. Hearing the conversation, Annie noticed that Michael's neck flushed under his chin and around his neck. He had turned away from Annie, she assumed, so she wouldn't notice his embarrassment from the raw innuendoes. When he sneaked a glance at her, she smiled to reassure him which only seemed to make him blush more. Attempting to overcome the suggestive conversation of the students, Michael talked about how great the band would be at the dance. All three of them continued to hold hands as they made their way toward the school gym. Annie didn't care one bit about those silly girls. It was the promises the evening held that ran through her veins. Feeling the warmth of Michael's hand as they walked along, she wondered what it would be like to dance so close to him that she could sense his body against hers. Annie felt sure she must be falling in love and she never wanted it to end.

The weekend ended much too soon. It seemed like she could still feel the warmth of Michael's hand in hers as she sat next to her father in the black sedan on her way back to St. Anthony's. Radiance flowed through her as her thoughts recaptured dance after dance with Michael. She wanted him to kiss her. At times she was sure he was going to, but he never tried. He just kept looking down into her eyes, melting her insides with his soft deep-blue eyes. They glided across the floor, intoxicated by the romantic evening and the sweetness of the music.

All too soon, it was eleven o'clock. Feeling like Cinderella, Annie dashed out of the gym toward the back of the school, knowing her dad would be there on time. She excused herself, explaining to Michael on her way that her dad would be waiting. Michael pleaded with her to stay as he escorted her towards the door. Realizing she would have to leave regardless of how he felt, he asked if she would write to him. When would she be back home again? Could he call her? And what about the Homecoming dance next month? He would be honored if she would go with him. Annie blurted that she would love to go with him. Then she promptly added that she would have to check with her parents and let him know.

Trees flashed in front of Annie's eyes as she stared out of the car window. The bag of fresh fruit in the back seat filled the air with its sweet aroma. Her parents didn't buy the stories about the school and the bad food. Yet they didn't stop her from taking bags of food back with her either. She figured they allowed her to take the food so she'd stop complaining about the school. They probably thought she'd soon tire of hauling things back and adjust to her new way of life. Annie knew she would never give up her mission as long as she could get the food out of her parents and her friends still needed her. She knew that with all the hungry souls she had to feed, they'd be lucky to get through the week with what she had, even if she rationed the supplies.

The iron gates slammed behind them when they drove into the courtyard, a sound that Annie swore she'd never get used to. Lucie and Jeannie were sitting on the front steps. Both of them jumped to their feet, waving with wide smiles on their faces.

Annie opened the car door before her dad had stopped and shouted, "Wait until you see all the stuff I brought with me."

"Annie!" her Dad scolded. "Don't ever do that again. You keep the door closed until I have the car stopped. That's the second time you've done that in the last couple of days and I won't have it again. Do you hear me?"

"Yeah—yeah!" came her sassy response.

His face reddened as he glared at her.

"You're not too big to be spanked, you know. You better remember that. And I don't have to be making this trip to pick up a sassy young woman all the time either. I think you owe me an apology."

Realizing she had just bitten the hand that had the power to get her off campus, if only for weekends, her toned softened, "I'm sorry, Dad. It's this place. It brings out the worst in me."

Still perturbed, he turned and started getting her things out of the car. "There. As your friends are so anxious to see you, maybe they'll take your things in for you, too."

"Sure, no problem," Lucie responded. "Hey, does this stuff smell good."

"When do I get to go home again?" Annie shouted at her dad as he got back in the car.

"I'll have to let you know. I'll call on Wednesday if I can make it next weekend. Don't forget to sign in or you'll be campused," he responded, then drove way.

"He was really upset," Jeannie said.

"I think I'm in pretty deep doo doo this time. How can they expect anything else from me? If they want to put me in a place like this, then they'll have to put up with a brat once in awhile."

Jeannie stood with her mouth open in disbelief.

Lucie rummaged through the bags of food, taking out an apple and sinking her teeth deep inside its juicy pulp.

"What? Why are you looking at me like that, Jeannie? Am I supposed to be happy about coming back here? Sure! That'll be the day. What am I supposed to do, just swallow it all?"

"That's the best apple I've ever had," Lucie said as she chewed.

"Well, no," Jeannie said. "But if I talked to my dad like that I'd be rapped on the head and then knocked across the room, for sure."

"You're kidding me, right?" Annie said in disbelief.

"No way. I'd never get away with that," Jeannie emphasized.

"Forget the chit-chat, you two," Lucie interrupted. "It won't change anything. Look at the great stuff Annie brought back. We'd better get it into our lockers before anybody sees it, or else there won't be nothing left for us."

Lucie and Jeannie grabbed the food, leaving the suitcases for Annie to handle.

"Gee, thanks, guys! I get the fun stuff to carry. Right?"

"Sorry," Jeannie said. "Guess I wasn't thinking. Let's split up the bags and suitcases."

Lucie was already holding the front door open, while reaching over the bag in her arm to take another bite out of the apple.

"I think I'll leave my suitcases in the foyer while we take the food downstairs to the lockers."

"Good idea. Hurry up before somebody sees us," Lucie whispered. "The coast is clear right now, so come on."

Annie and Jeannie slid the suitcases into a corner of the foyer so they would be out of sight. "Wait here until I sign in. I'll be right back."

One by one they departed toward the staircase as the sun began to set. Meeting on the sly in the downstairs locker room, they closed the doors and began sorting the food. They ended up with three different groups of food: fruits, chips and pretzels, and sweets. Lucie put the sweets in her locker, Annie took the fruit and Jeannie got the chips and pretzels. Then they made a pact not to touch the food without the others knowing about it. Lunchtime was never a problem as the day students were served more edible food. It was after school and in the evenings when their stomachs howled and growled for nourishment. So they decided to meet every day right after school, except for Monday when Annie had her piano lesson, to take what they needed to get through the rest of the night. The next thing to do was to find out if anybody else was able to bring some food back. They could add that to what they had and maybe share with more girls.

They had just finished putting the food in their lockers when they heard the sound of the boarding students, parading down for dinner. Lucie turned off the light and opened the doors to the locker room before Sister Margaret saw her. Then they hid in the shadows, waiting to sneak into line as the brigade passed by.

"What are you guys doing down here?" Susan whispered and looked around to make sure Sister Margaret didn't see them sneak in line. "I thought for sure Sister would start looking for you. Did you just get back, Annie?"

"Yeah, my dad dropped me off just a little while ago. How about you? Did you have a good weekend?"

"Sure did, and I was able to bring some food back with me, too."

"Great!" Annie whispered. "We'll talk later. Until then, mum's the word."

After Annie had retrieved her luggage, the three girls met with Susan in the locker room and saw that she had brought back a healthy donation. So they shared their secret about the food and put Susan's food with the rest. Then they repeated their original vow. After settled, both Annie and Susan rambled on about their weekends. Susan's weekend fizzled out with seeing a few old friends and helping her mom around the house. Annie mesmerized them with the thrill of watching the team win, how Michael held her hand during the whole game, and how he melted her insides as he gazed into her eyes on the dance floor. The girls all listened and sighed.

"Now that's the way it's supposed to be," Lucie said. "Every day we should be having these thrilling experiences, not a prison walk to the guillotine."

Chapter Six

Just as Sister Mary Margaret had predicted the night of orientation, everybody fell into a routine. The silent march was on, to the sink rooms, to the bathrooms, to the chapel, down for meals, through the tunnel that separated the school building from the dormitories and cafeteria, up the stairways, and through the hallways to classrooms. As Annie made her way through the school corridors, she watched the students in the same sacks of uniforms march by her with dullness in their eyes. Once in awhile someone would smile at her, but it was obvious that the joy of being taught new things had been overshadowed by the drudgery of the routine. Days melted into one another with nothing to look forward to except more routine. Silence haunted Annie's life. She only found solace in the melodies she carried in her subconscious.

The students were only allowed to break silence after school and after they entered the lunchroom. Then they were expected to keep the level of noise to a minimum. The lunch period had been spread out over three class periods to accommodate the five hundred students who ate in the cafeteria. Annie's boarding school friends all ate during other periods, leaving her with no one to eat with. Out of necessity, Annie decided she'd have to make friends with some of the day students. It would also be a way to keep in touch with the outside world and not feel so isolated.

"Do you mind if I sit with you?" Annie stood in front of a circular booth in a corner of the cafeteria where three of the friendliest looking students were eating.

"Course not," was the quick, congenial reply from the young blond. Her warm, brown eyes twinkled as she smiled and pulled out a chair for Annie.

"My name is Betsy, and this is Lois and Joanie. We all ride the bus from Wauwatosa and Elm Grove. We don't know anybody else here so we decided we might as well eat together, too."

"You're lucky they didn't separate you," Annie said when she sat down with her tray. "All my friends are eating during the earlier class periods, and I don't know anybody else either."

"I guess it's nice to get to know someone new once in awhile," Betsy said. "Out where I live, in little old Elm Grove, everybody knows everybody else. It gets rather boring at times. Besides, it takes an hour and a half on that bus to get here. So it's nice to have someone to talk to. You know, to pass the time. Where do you hail from? Are you a day student?"

"Don't I wish," replied Annie. "I'm a boarding student. I came from West Bend, which is like Elm Grove. Everybody either knows everybody, or else they're related. Sometimes I think half of them have nothing better to do than gossip and keep up on everybody else's business. So I know what you mean. I must admit I didn't think there was anything good about being a boarding student. But at least I don't have to ride a bus every morning in all kinds of weather."

"You're not kidding," Lois emphasized. "I get so tired of being shook all over the place. The drivers are crazy. They zigzag in and out of traffic and never look to see if anything is coming. I guess they think that just because the bus is big they can drive any way they want. It makes me nervous. And to think I have to go through four years of this." Lois was a tiny fragile-looking person with dried out brownish-black hair. Annie didn't care what she looked like as long as she had a brain in her head, and only time and conversation would determine that. Annie felt very comfortable around Betsy, almost like she had known her all her life. Annie sensed that Betsy felt the same way after only a couple of lunches together. Now Joanie, a chubby girl with heavy eyebrows and black peach-fuzz under her nose, never said much. She did manage to get everyone's attention when she reached for the pepper shaker, blacking her food.

"I'm sorry, but I have to do something to give this food some flavor. It is so bland," Joanie said with a snap in her voice.

"If you think this is bad, you should see what they give us," Annie said. "At least at lunchtime we can pick what we want from the buffet. Otherwise we're looking at sour milk, watered down stale bread, rancid butter…"

"You're not serious, are you?" Betsy interrupted.

"Sure I am," Annie said.

"How do you survive?" Lois asked. "That would kill me. If that's the case, I'm not going to complain about riding the bus."

"Me neither," Betsy and Joanie said together.

"That's OK. What are friends for anyway? Besides, if you don't complain about the bus ride, then I don't get to complain about boarding here. Just look at all the interesting conversations we'd miss."

They all chuckled. The more Annie listened to Betsy as she expressed herself within the group, the more Annie knew that someday Betsy would be one of her best friends.

In the middle of November, Annie would be going to the Homecoming dance with Michael. Annie's dad had called on Tuesday and said he would pick her up on Friday afternoon about four o'clock. Both Jeannie and Lucie were going home for the first time since school started. Of course this stirred some pretty energetic and romantic notions between the girls that they found difficult to contain. Every night they'd talk about their adventuresome plans, the anticipated dates with their dreamboats and then the needed supplies. On Thursday, the night before the big day, Lucie and Annie decided to retire early so they could get some extra packing done and perhaps talk some more about the coming weekend. All went well until after the lights were turned off and they headed for their beds.

Not able to contain herself, Lucie decided to express her vim and vigor with some unusual calisthenics. One minute Annie lay on her stomach beginning to count sheep and the next she was being catapulted four to five feet into the air on her floppy, cotton mattress.

Giggling, Lucie had crawled under Annie's bed and heaved her upward with all the power of a kangaroo's kick. Annie tried to muffle her giddy laughter with her face in a pillow that wanted to fly higher than she did. Then she glanced in horror toward the lighted hallway. Silhouetted in the doorway against the darkened dormitory, Annie could see the outline of a tall nun. Without a word the nun leaned against the doorjamb and watched the antics of the two girls. Annie tried desperately to warn Lucie about their impending doom with hand signals over the edge of the mattress and by whispering, "Trouble at the door." She even tried to hold on to the springs to keep herself down when the mattress hit bottom, but that only resulted in having her shoulders almost yanked out of their sockets. High in the air she saw Sister's hand moved for the light switch. Light flooded the room at the same time that Annie's mattress hit bottom. Playing her role to the hilt, Annie sat up, rubbing her eyes as though she had been awakened from a deep sleep. Turning and fluffing her pillow in a nonchalant manner, she tried to see where Lucie was. Amazed, she saw that Lucie was back in her bed, all covered up, and acting like she was sound asleep. Annie casually fluffed her pillow and straightened her covers and pulled them up around her neck. She lay there with her heart pounding, waiting for Sister Margaret to lower the boom on each of them and then campus them for life. But nothing happened, just silence. Then Annie watched Sister reach for the light switch, and darkness flooded the room again. Annie wasn't sure, but she thought she heard a chuckle over the clacking of Sister Margaret's rosary as she turned out the light and walked away. Or it might have been wishful thinking. Regardless, Annie lay too scared to move a muscle or to ask Lucie how she managed to get back to her bed so fast. All she could think about was what would happen tomorrow. Would she be going home for the weekend or would she be spending it at school, scrubbing floors?

Sister Margaret's pleasant mannerism hadn't changed when she came to get the ladies before chapel the next morning. Sister didn't look at or mention Lucie and Annie's behavior the night before, but the two girls weren't surprised by that. They anticipated that Sister would approach them after breakfast, or worse yet, just before they were supposed to leave for the weekend. Of course, there was always the likelihood that they would be called out of class to Sister Mary Florentine's office. Annie dreaded that more than anything because she didn't want to fall out of Sister Mary Florentine's good graces.

As Sister Margaret taught English on the second floor of the school building, Annie avoided walking down that corridor or any others where she thought she might encounter Sister. By lunchtime Annie's stomach had flopped upside down from thinking about a possible confrontation. She wondered how she could even enjoy the dance without some relief. Spotting Betsy back in their usual corner, Annie made her way toward the table. At least she could talk to Betsy about the situation and maybe calm down a little.

"What's the matter with you, Annie?" Betsy asked. "You're as white as a sheet. Are you sick?"

"Lucie and I were goofing off in the dorm and we got caught by Sister Margaret. She didn't holler at us or anything. She just stood there, turned off the lights, and walked away. All day I've been waiting for her to pounce on me and tell me I couldn't go home for the weekend." Annie's eyes welled up with tears as she added, "I've got the Homecoming dance tonight with Michael. Can you imagine how that would goof things up?"

"Wait a minute. Just calm down and start at the beginning. What were you doing that was so terrible?" Betsy asked.

Annie related the events of the previous night, acting out the whole scenario.

"So you are still concerned Sister Margaret will come after you, right?"

"You better believe I am," Annie said, her hands shaking as she picked up her sandwich.

"Oh, I don't think you have anything to worry about. Sister would have done something last night if she planned to scold you or campus you. She believes in punishment right away, not hours later. Anyway, that's what she told us in her English class. And I believe her. Besides, you're punishing yourself more than she ever could. Sister Margaret is fair, and, may I add, one smart cookie. She knows you're sweating it out because you don't know what she's going to do. Not knowing is the biggest punishment there is. It's a real killer. I don't think what you did was all that bad. Sister probably got a kick out of it. You know, just because she's a nun doesn't mean she wasn't a kid once. Don't give it another thought and start planning for the big dance. How exciting! What are you going to wear? Have you decided yet?"

"You really think so? That she won't do anything to us?"

"I'm sure of it. Now stop worrying. Otherwise you'll be a pill tonight from making yourself sick all day," Betsy emphasized.

"I guess you're right. Worrying about it won't stop it from happening. I might as well think of the good things that are about to happen." Annie let out a squeal, "Oh, I have to tell you this. My mother took me to the French Room at Ema-Langes to pick out this gorgeous soft-pink dress." Gesturing, Annie indicated how the neckline swooped down to her bosom, embracing her body and showing off her slender figure. "The neckline is open and sort of off the shoulder. And the whole top of the dress fits. I mean really fits—if you know what I mean," she said and grinned as she moved her eyebrows up and down. "The skirt goes out with just the right amount of flare to accent the tiny rows of lace going all the way down to the hem. It is luscious."

"Wow! The French Room at Ema-Langes, no less. That's pretty impressive!"

"I know!" Annie flushed with embarrassment. "Mom always takes me there for all my clothes. It's the neatest place and they spoil you rotten. That I don't mind a bit. All I have to do is stand in their dressing room and wait for them to bring the clothing to me. Of course, Mom spoils it some because she wants things on me she thinks are stylish. You know me, I always manage to get my two cents worth in."

Betsy pulled on Annie's uniform skirt and said, "Did she get this lovely there also?"

Barely able to keep a straight face, Annie responded in a raspy voice. “Why, of course, my darling.”

Four o’clock finally came. Annie hadn’t run into Sister Margaret, and she wasn’t about to take chances now. She didn’t waste any time putting her hair in pin curls and getting a couple of last-minute things together. Hurrying down the stairs, she arrived in the foyer at exactly four, slid her suitcases over to the stair landing, perched herself on top of one of them, and then sat tapping her foot while she waited for her dad to arrive. Of all nights, Annie prayed her dad wouldn’t be late or, worse yet, forget her. Michael would be picking her up around six-thirty to go to dinner before the dance, and she didn’t want to be late. Her mother saw to it that Annie had well-groomed in etiquette, you should be polite and not keep a gentleman waiting.

Sometimes it was difficult to be on time with a dad who had a tendency toward forgetfulness. He’d always apologized, in a sheepish sort of way, and then made an excuse like he got preoccupied with business. As a rule it was the Cubs’ baseball game. A couple of weeks before, Annie had waited for hours for him at the Plankinton Hotel in downtown Milwaukee. When he hadn’t shown up by seven in the evening, Annie began to worry about being abandoned in the city by herself. Betsy told her she had to be careful whom she talked to downtown. It wasn’t uncommon for a young woman to be approached by drug dealers or street bums asking for handouts. To get her mind off of her dilemma, she decided to check the prices on the hotel restaurant’s menu. She had no intention of spending a lot of her money on food. That was her parents’ job. As it was getting late, she knew she’d have to eat something. She had enough money in her pocketbook for a bowl of soup, so she ordered the French onion.

The restaurant was in the front of the hotel, with windows that looked out onto the street. A long brass bar ran horizontally across the bottom half of the window, holding up velvet café drapes that were attached with brass rings. The restaurant window continued on past the entrance and into the hotel lobby, allowing Annie to watch the revolving door for her dad. The waitress smiled as she set the soup in front of Annie.

"Are you alone?" she asked.

Concerned as to why the waitress asked her the question, Annie told her she'd been waiting for her dad, and he would be there any moment. The soup came covered with tons of melted cheese and half slices of toasted garlic bread that night. Even this didn't appeal to Annie. She still couldn't get her mind off being stranded. She didn't want to call home and upset her mother, but when it got to be eight, Annie decided that she had better. She dialed the operator and placed a collect call. Her mother must have been next to the phone because she answered it on the first ring, inquiring if Annie was all right. Hearing that her daughter was safe, her mother told Annie that her father, in his absentmindedness, had come home without her. Annie was told to stay right at the hotel because he'd be there in a little while.

Annie hoped this would be the last case of forgetfulness that her dad ever had. Deep down inside though, she knew this behavior was already a well-established habit.

Annie's dad swung the black sedan into the academy courtyard at four fifteen that afternoon. With the excitement, she kept dropping things. Grabbing at the items that had fallen, she spewed out a couple of curse words under her breath but recaptured her poise before her dad heard them. Seeing her struggle, he went to Annie's rescue and helped her pick up a couple of the things she had dropped and put them in the back seat of the car.

Annie talked non-stop all the way home, shooting questions at her dad in rapid succession. "Did Mom get my dress picked up OK? I hope it's as pretty as I remember. Did anybody call? What time do I have to be home? And don't tell me eleven because I don't want to hear that. I hope nobody is planning to use the bathroom for an hour or so. Who else is home this weekend?"

"Hold your horses," her dad said. "Do you want an answer to all of those questions or are you just talking to yourself?"

Annie giggled and said, "All of them, of course, and all at once please."

"I'm glad to see you're in such a good mood. You must've had a good week at school."

"Not really! Nobody could ever have a good week in that place. The only thing that's good about it is getting out of there. That's it!"

The still night and clear night accented the full moon that had cast its light across the O'Briens' front yard. Mary O'Brien peeked through the living room lace curtains and could easily see Michael walking toward their porch.

"It's six twenty-six. I respect a young man who has the courtesy to be prompt."

Walking to the bottom of the stairs, she called to Annie that Michael had arrived.

"I'm ready—I'm ready," Annie said shortly, feeling the pressure of being ready on time.

"Don't take that tone with me, young lady," her mother said. "Unless you'd like to stay home this evening?"

"Yes, ma'am."

"That's better. I'll be right up to see how you are doing. In the meantime your father can let Michael in and entertain him for a minute."

As Mr. O'Brien opened the front door, he greeted Michael with a firm handshake and a smile. "Come on in. Annie will be down in a moment. I see you brought some flowers for Annie."

"Ah. Yes, sir, I did," Michael stammered. He stood as stiff as a board with a grin pasted on his face. His black wool topcoat hung open over his dark gray suit, accented by a crisp white shirt, and a black bow tie.

Aware of Michael's strict upbringing, Mr. O'Brien responded to Michael's formality in a jovial manner. Patting Michael on the shoulder he said, "Come on, Michael, relax. I'm not going to bite your head off. Unless, of course, you bring Annie home too late," he laughed. "We can sit down over here for a moment until Annie comes down. How are your studies coming? Annie tells me you are quite a scholar."

Michael flushed with embarrassment at the comment and sat down on the edge of the sofa, "Oh, I guess I'm doing quite well, actually. Trig is a bear at times, but I have an excellent teacher who is willing to explain things until I understand them."

"Trig, huh? Are you planning to go on to college?"

"Yes, sir. I'd like to be an engineer like yourself, sir."

"Well that's refreshing. So many young folks today seem to be more interested in having fun than taking their studies seriously."

Just then Annie walked into the living room. Her hair had been swept on top of her head with deep waves that accented its beauty, dramatizing the milky-white of her exposed shoulders.

Michael jumped to his feet.

They stood staring at each other for a moment as though they had never seen one another before. Mr. O'Brien shook Michael's arm to bring him out of his trance.

"Michael, don't you have some flowers for Annie?"

"Oh, yes, sir. I mean—Annie, you look great," Michael sighed. "Here I got you a pompom. They're the in things this year. I hope you like it. I got white because I wanted to make sure it would be perfect for your pink dress, which is . . . wow!"

"You look fantastic yourself, Michael, all dressed up in your suit and tie." Annie blushed and her eyes sparkled with excitement as she gazed at Michael.

"OK, you two, it's time to get going so you're not late for dinner," Mr. O'Brien said. "Now, Michael, I want you to keep your eyes on the road and not on Annie. You really look sweet, honey," he said as he kissed her on the check. "Be careful now. I don't want to get a call saying you've been in an accident."

"Yes, sir, I will be careful. I wouldn't want anything to happen to Annie, ever," Michael said as he helped Annie on with her mouton fur coat. "What time do you want me to bring Annie home, sir?"

"What time does the dance end, Michael?" he asked.

"One o'clock, sir."

"Right about that time would be fine. Now go and have a good time. Just be careful. There're a lot of crazy drivers out there."

"Yes, sir. One o'clock it is. And I'll be very careful, sir."

Annie's mother came into the living room as Michael opened the front door for Annie. Delighted with the scene, she hugged Annie and shook Michael's hand earnestly.

"You both look so grown up, and, Annie, you are beautiful," she said as her eyes welled up with tears. "I can't believe you are growing up so fast. Whatever will I do when my baby leaves our home?"

"Now, Mary. It's only a dance, not a wedding," Charles said as he put his arm around her shoulder.

"I know, I know, they all grew up too fast," she said as she wiped a tear from the corner of her eye. "Go now and have a good time. Just forget about my silliness."

"Don't worry, Mrs. O'Brien," Michael said as they walked out the door. "I'll take good care of Annie."

Charles stood next to his wife inside the front door, watching Michael help Annie into the car. The word s*ir* was still ringing in his ears, making him feel nostalgic about his high school days when he attended St. Mel's Military Academy. The top ranking position for a member of the student body was major. He had worked hard to achieve that respected position. Often he had been addressed as s*ir* as a matter of protocol, just as Michael had addressed him tonight. How clearly he remembered marching in front of the brass of the school in full dress, leading his classmates across the parade field.

Engrossed in the memory, he found himself standing at attention. "I like that boy," he said. "Annie chose wisely for her first big date. He's a fine young man with some good manners."

The soft overhead lighting at Nino's Supper Club added to the romance of the evening. During the meal, Michael spent more time looking at her than he did eating. Annie was flattered, but the prolonged silences made her uncomfortable. She had never eaten dinner at a supper club before with anyone other than her family. She wondered if Michael had. To ease the tension, Annie began talking about the trouble she managed to get into at school, and how her music saved her from the regimented lifestyle. However, neither of them relaxed until Michael brought up the story about how he ran down the river through the muck. Telling his rendition of the story, he could barely contain his laughter.

"Remember the night we were stealing parts from the dump for the junk car the gang built?"

"How could I forget?" Annie said, leaning forward to listen to his story.

Seeing that he had captured Annie's interest, he began his tale. "I felt like I had been sucked into the depths of that rotting, old riverbed as I plowed my way through slimy brown muck. It's a good thing I had worn my laced shoes! Even at that, I don't know how they stayed on," he chuckled. "By the time I got out of there they weren't worth much, and neither were my clothes, for that matter."

Annie scrunched her face into a grimace. "I never could've run down that river, Michael, especially in the dark.

Last summer, before the water had been drained, I got dumped into it. I guess I deserved it because I went with Leo and Marty in their small boat instead of going to Girl Scouts. We were just floating around out there, having a good time, when all of a sudden Leo hollered, "One—two—three," and over we went. Then I heard Leo screaming, 'Swim for your life. Swim for your life.' There I was with my heavy wool jacket on, trying to swim. Can you imagine?"

"Oh my gosh!"

"I could hardly lift my arms out of the water because of the wet wool. I continued to struggle like a crazy person to stay afloat. My head swished back and forth in the stench. I hit the panic button when I realized I might be swallowed up by the silt and muck. Then I said began sinking like a battle ship. One last swish of my head and I saw that those guys weren't swimming. The creeps had played a prank on me, so I tried to stand up. Of course I could."

"Oh brother."

"Believe me, they were lucky they weren't any closer to me than they were, or I would've beaten them to a pulp. I had waded through at least a hundred yards of weeds and who knows what else to get to shore. I could feel these slimy lumpy things under me as my feet slid over them. Of course, my imagination was working overtime and that didn't help. It all happened right by Joanne's house, about where you came out. Leo and Marty stayed in the water until they knew I couldn't get them. They needed a good soaking anyway. Don't you think?"

"That's awful! I can't believe they did that to you. They should've been tarred and feathered."

Laughing, Annie said, "Joanne's mom did her best to help me rinse out my clothes. Then she told me to stand in front of their wood stove in my wet underwear so I'd dry out. In the meantime she hung my stuff by their kerosene stove. I could hear her grumbling under her breath until she couldn't contain herself any longer. Then she gave me a good scolding. She said I should have gone to Girl Scouts like I was supposed to and this never would've happened. Parents! Can you believe it! As though I didn't know that."

"No kidding."

"Now my clothes not only picked up the color and stench of the river, but also the odor from their kerosene stove. I can't tell you which was worse. A horrible situation. By the time my brother John came to pick me up my clothes were still pretty damp, and I smelled less than desirable, I assure you. I remember shivering from their clamminess as I got dressed. I didn't have many options so I decided to act like everything was hunky-dory," she laughed. "After all that, my brother never said a word about it. Thank heavens he was more interested in listening to himself talk than in how I smelled."

"What a horrible experience," Michael said as he stared spellbound at Annie.

"I think you have it much worse than I did. Marty and Leo steered clear of me for a long time. You know, when you're one of the gang, you expect the guys to pull stuff like that. You're not always prepared, but you expect it nonetheless. I really wasn't that angry. They sure could've picked a time when I didn't have all my good clothes on though," she laughed. "The worst part was walking that river. That got to me, but I never let them know it, or they would've called me a sissy. Growing up with guys, I've been in a lot of scrapes since I've been a kid, but that's all behind me now that I'm in high school. What about you? You haven't finished telling me about what happened that night."

"Oh sure. Well, when I realized the cops were all over the dump, and that my chances of getting caught were astronomical, I headed for the river. Believe me, I had plenty of incentive to find the quickest way out of there, knowing what my dad would do to me. I ran all that way, smelling like I had fallen into an outhouse. You know what I mean. And so tired that I thought I'd die. And who greeted me? Two officers. I couldn't believe it. Talk about being frustrated. If you would've seen me Annie, you never would've wanted to be around me again."

"I doubt that, Michael. I heard all about it because the story spread through town like wildfire. I can't imagine how you got as far as you did. That took guts."

"I don't know if I'd call it guts or running on raw fear. Boy, my dad was mad. I can still see his face as he screamed at me. I thought he was going to have a heart attack. I had to walk on egg shells for the whole next year to keep him happy. He's not like your dad. I bet you are able to talk to him when you get into trouble, like with what happened in the junkyard, and when you got thrown into the river."

"I'll never know the answer to that because I didn't get caught either time. I don't think the cops were looking for a girl at the dump. I think they thought only guys would be there. I had ducked inside of a pile of old tires and just sat tight. I'm not sure what my dad would've done, but I don't think it would've been as drastic as what your dad did. I know because Mark, my older brother, a real chemistry nut, used to make these stink bombs and let them roll down under the seats during the movie at the Merrimac Theater. He'd brag about watching the effects of the bomb when it rolled under the people's seats. He said they'd begin to leave as soon as it hit their row. Then he'd escape with the group leaving. Believe it or not, he never get caught.

I can't say as much for my other brother, Luke. He tried the same trick when he was in high school, only he ended up behind bars down at the West Bend police station. Guess he didn't have as much finesse as Mark. Luke told me later that Dad did not appreciate being called by the chief of police to come and get his kid out of jail."

"I sure know what that's like," Michael said.

"But later though, when Dad told the story, he acted like he thought it was pretty funny. Maybe dads have to act a certain way when their kids get into trouble because they're dads. In reality they probably did the same stuff when they were kids. No doubt they think they have to keep a short rope on us so we don't get into as much trouble as they did. I remember my dad talking about getting it good with the razor strap behind the woodshed. We were lucky he didn't have one. So they couldn't have been such saints, or there wouldn't have been a need for the woodshed or the razor strap," she giggled.

"That's true. I should've followed my gut feeling and not gone with the gang in the first place. A year is a long time to be punished. Heck, I didn't want to miss the fun either. Guess I didn't miss much, not even my dad's swing when I got home. It looks like we have similar situations. Both of us are locked up in a way. At least I'm still at home, while you are stuck away in that dungeon."

"I never thought about it like that. I mean, you are pretty much stuck just like I am. Stuck is stuck. Really doesn't matter where, does it?"

Michael and Annie walked into the high school gym a little after eight o'clock. Hundreds of balloons covered the ceiling and the stage. They were joined with what seemed like miles of crepe paper. A large ball with small mirrored tiles hung from the center of the darkened room. As it revolved, the ball cast flickers of light on the ceiling, walls, and the floor as the spotlights on either side of the room struck it.

Looking around for Patsy, Annie said to Michael, "I didn't have time to write or call Patsy to find out if she would be coming, not that I'd write to anyone if I could help it. Did I tell you the nuns read all of our mail? Before it goes out and when it comes in."

"Are you serious?"

"I sure am. So you have to be very careful with what you write. They call it censoring. I call it invasion of my privacy. It's supposed to protect the reputation of the school from the likes of us, I guess. It's just another one of those little tidbits my parents forgot to tell me about."

"I never heard of such a thing. They really got you coming and going, don't they? I could write something real juicy and make their hair stand up," he laughed.

"Michael! You wouldn't."

"No, I wouldn't. Just kidding. Annie, I'd never do anything that might get you in trouble. Besides, I'd give them a heart attack if I did."

"I don't see Patsy anywhere."

"Come to think of it, I haven't seen her for awhile at school either. I'm sorry, Annie. If I had known you were hoping she'd be here, I would've called her. We'll just keep watching for her."

"It doesn't matter. It's just that she is the only real girlfriend I have around here."

"What about the girls you went to eighth grade with?"

"We moved when I was in sixth grade, and then again just before I started eighth. So I never got to know anybody very well. I got to know Patsy because we were in Life Saving class together. I'm sorry, Michael. I just don't trust very many girls. All too often I've overheard girls gossiping or dishing out catty remarks about their best friends, as though they hated them. I don't need those kinds of knives sticking out of my back."

"I don't understand why it has to be that way. I've noticed it a lot, especially with the younger girls. They seem to get better with age."

"I don't know about that. Remember the first football game we went to? Do you recall the snide remarks about who I was and why was I sitting on their school bleachers? It's been like that at every game, somebody is always saying something. In a way I don't blame them. This isn't my school, and maybe I wouldn't want girls from somewhere else invading my territory either. I suppose you think I'm crazy?"

"No, not at all. You'll be OK. Just stick close to me," Michael said as he walked her to the dance floor. "Your mom was right. You are so beautiful, Annie. I'm sure lucky to have you with me tonight."

She looked up into his eyes and smiled.

He sighed.

Annie made it a point to be a perfect lady at the dance. She allowed herself to be led by the hand to and from the dance floor, smiling politely and sweetly saying "you're welcome" after Michael had thanked her for the dance. Thoughts of Patsy melted into nothingness as they waltzed across the floor, turning and swaying to the music of the band. It all felt rather majestic, like a princess at a ball. Annie thought this had to be the way Cinderella felt when she danced with her prince as she captured hundreds of smiles, felt wonderful sensations, and time seemed endless. Glancing at the clock as Michael spun her around, she noticed there was only an hour left before her fairytale evening would end.

After finishing a set of dances, they walked to the punch bowl to refresh themselves. Michael had just dipped the ladle in the bowl when he heard a young woman shouting at Annie.

"Who are you anyway? And what are you doing here? We don't need your kind, so why don't you just get out!"

The girl stood almost a head taller and more heavy-set than Annie, with scraggly brown hair and a ruddy complexion.

"What's your problem, Michael?" she snarled. "You just have to bring Miss Prissity to our school dances, don't you? We've been watching you for the last couple of months and thought maybe you'd wise up. But no, you just kept bringing her. So I guess we'll have to straighten you out once and for all."

Michael grabbed Annie's hand.

Annie stood with her mouth open in disbelief.

"Come on, Annie, we don't have to put up with this. Shirley is nothing but a troublemaker and everybody knows it."

Shirley brought her fists out in front of her as she made her advance and shouted profanities at Annie. A crowd began to gather behind Shirley, cheering her on.

Snapping out of her stupor, Annie said, "What's your problem, Shirley? We haven't been doing anything but dancing and minding our own business. That's more than I can say for you."

"No, Annie," Michael pleaded. "Don't play into her hand. Let Mr. Kelley handle this. He's the dance chaperone."

"Why you little piece of crap!" she screamed at Annie and began swinging her fists in a circular motion, attempting to land a blow.

Upon seeing the disturbance from the other side of the gym, Mr. Kelley ran toward them. Not knowing what to do, Michael tried to step between the two girls, taking the blows that were meant for Annie. Before Annie could do anything, Shirley sidestepped him, landing a couple of blows on Annie's upper arms, scratching and bruising her. Anger invigorated Annie's Irish blood as she dodged Shirley's attempt to hit her again. Shirley's fists continued to whirl in a circular motion, out of control. Annie positioned herself and waited for an opening to throw a good solid punch. It came and Annie's fist went straight, landing right in the middle of Shirley's face. Shirley staggered backwards. The crowd moaned as she hit the floor. There she lay crying until Mr. Kelley arrived.

"That'll be enough," Mr. Kelley shouted. "This is a dance not a barroom, for heaven's sake. Can't you even get along at a dance? This is ridiculous. I can't believe it. Who started this anyway?"

"She did," Shirley sobbed. "She has no business being here. We don't want her here."

"Annie didn't start anything, Mr. Kelley," Michael said, trying to stop the bleeding on Annie's arms with his handkerchief. "She was just defending herself."

"Right now I don't care who started it. I just want it stopped. Do you hear me? You've ruined a perfectly good evening with your brawling," Mr. Kelley said, looking around at the students. "I hope you're satisfied."

"I'm sorry, Mr. Kelley," Annie said. "Michael, maybe it would be better if we just left."

"That's a good idea, young lady, and I use that term loosely. I saw that punch you threw. I don't think a lady would've done such a thing."

Aggravated with Mr. Kelley's attitude, Michael shouted, "What did you expect her to do? Let Shirley pound on her until she dropped? This isn't fair. Why should we be the ones who have to leave when we didn't do anything in the first place?"

"You seem to forget whom you are shouting at," Mr. Kelley said. "Maybe a trip to my office on Monday morning will teach you some better manners. Be there—nine o'clock sharp!"

Michael continued to apologize for the way Annie was treated by Mr. Kelley and his classmates while he drove toward the downtown area. The clear, cool evening had filled the sky with brilliant stars. The full moon stood high in the sky, lighting the roadway as if it were day. Then a cloud crossed it and blackened their way. Annie sat still while Michael continued to talk. She stared into the headlights of the oncoming cars. How would she sell her parents on the idea that this wasn't her fault? She had the opportunity to walk away but decided to stay and fight, jeopardizing Michael's welfare as well as her own. Her parents wouldn't be as upset over her punching Shirley as they would over where she did it and when she was dressed up. They'd see it as hoodlum behavior. Now they had the excuse they needed to say that Annie wasn't much of a lady, poking another girl in the nose at a Homecoming dance.

It didn't matter what the girl did. Knowing the consequences, terror ran through Annie's veins. She glanced over at Michael who had stopped talking. He seemed so far away on the other side of the car. He had the window open just a crack so she could feel the cool air brushing across the side of her face. Without thinking she slid over next to him. He turned and put his arm around her, pulling her close. She put her head down on his shoulder, trying to recapture the same warmth she felt when they were dancing. She lolled in the protection of his arm around her shoulder, watching the car lights change the interior of the car from dark to light.

It was like a reflection of her life, most of it seeming dark, especially with what she knew her parents were about to say. They never understood that she had had to learn to fight for everything, being the youngest in the family. She had to fight for her rights at school as well or get squashed. Often enough, she saw how miserable the gang would make a sissy's life with piercing remarks. Then they'd send Annie to beat the sissy up to prove her loyalty. She had taken some nasty blows, getting toughened up to run with the gang. The worst ones were when she'd get hit in the stomach. The pain often made her throw up afterwards. She never told anybody though. Now she had to worry about Mr. Kelley and what might happen to Michael. His dad could very well snitch to her parents, then what? The possibilities were real, especially with Michael having to go to Mr. Kelley's office.

"I don't know what gets into people to do this kind of thing," Michael said as though he was talking to himself. "What harm were we doing? I bet it all boils down to jealousy." Smiling at Annie he said, "I say that because there wasn't a girl there that could hold a candle to you, not in looks or brains. I'm really sorry, Annie. I never would've asked you to go, if I thought this might have happened."

"Please don't blame yourself, Michael. After all I should be apologizing to you for getting you in this mess. I could have left and I didn't. Besides, I wouldn't have traded the evening for anything. Up until Shirley making her appearance, I had the time of my life. So what are a few scratches and a punch in the nose in exchange for such a wonderful evening? The only problem is if our parents find out. I'll keep my arms covered so they won't see the scratches. Of course, if Mr. Kelley
calls . . . We better come up with a good story just in case. Do you think Mr. Kelley will call?"

"There's a good chance that he will, as mad as he was. Maybe we'd better go get a soda or something and figure out our plan of attack."

"That's a good idea. I'm sort of hungry after all that commotion. How about getting one of those great hamburgers at George's restaurant? He makes the best hamburgers in the world."

"You're amazing. You bounce right back, don't you? I'm not sure if I can eat anything. My stomach is pretty upset, thinking about what my dad is going to do when he finds out, not to mention your dad."

As Michael parked the car in front of George's, Annie said, "Let me worry about my dad. He's not going to blame you for this. I'm the one who threw the punch. I should've walked away when you took my hand, but no. I had to get my two cents worth in. Everyone in my family is going to have a good laugh over this one. At my expense I might add. I can just hear them saying, it's a good thing you've locked her up in that dungeon so she doesn't have a chance to embarrass the family more than she already has."

"I'm really sorry, Annie, that things went the way they did. Maybe Mr. Kelley will have time to reconsider by Monday and things won't be so bad. Now let's go get you that great hamburger."

As Michael swung his dad's car into the O'Briens' driveway, they could see the figure of a man talking to Annie's parents through the lace curtains in the living room. A cold chill burned through Annie's body, making her cringe.

"Who do you think it is?" she whispered.

"I hate to tell you this, but it looks like Mr. Kelley." Glancing at his watch, he added, "Well, it's not quite one o'clock. At least I got you home on time."

Annie's initial reaction of fear was quick to turn to sarcasm, "I can't believe this. I wonder if he went running to Shirley's parents, or are we the only bad apples here? I'm going to give him a piece of my mind."

Annie jumped out of the car, not waiting for Michael to open the door for her. Michael rushed to the other side of the car, "No, Annie, if you start a fight with Mr. Kelley, we may never be able to see each other again. Please! Stop and think about it for a minute. We don't have anything to gain and everything to lose."

Annie stomped her foot in frustration, "You're probably right, Michael, but I think we're going to lose no matter what we do. Why else would he have come all the way out here unless he wanted to get us? It makes me so angry that we're being treated like this." She looked down so Michael couldn't see her eyes swell with tears.

"Oh…what are we going to do? Nobody is going to believe us over Mr. Kelley." She began to weep and found herself in Michael's arms. She felt so safe for a brief moment.

Holding her close Michael whispered, "We'll get through this somehow. Now let's wipe those pretty eyes and try and compose ourselves. Let me do the talking. I'll try to stay calm. With any luck, I'll be able to get a word in edgewise. Mr. Kelley has been rather obnoxious so far so anything could happen." He patted Annie gently on her back and then moved her away to look into her eyes. "We might as well go in and get this over with. You know what they say. Things are never as bad as you think they are."

"Whoever said that wasn't standing in our shoes."

"Well, let's give it our best shot anyway."

As Michael began escorting her to the front door, Annie paused. "You know what? I just thought of something that my dad told us all the time. He says that no matter what we've done, we should always tell the truth. Then he'd back us one hundred percent. But God help us if he finds out later that we lied. So we have to start by convincing my dad we are telling the truth. If we can do that, maybe this whole thing will backfire on Mr. Kelley. Wouldn't that be something?"

Hearing loud conversation as they approached the front door, Michael squeezed Annie's hand in reassurance. When Annie entered the living room, her mother rushed to her side, asking if she was all right.

"She's fine," Mr. Kelley sneered. "It's Shirley who isn't, and her parents are very upset over this mess."

"Well, you two—what do you have to say for yourselves?" Mr. O'Brien asked. He stood with his feet slightly apart and his arms folded across his chest.

Michael pushed Annie a little behind him, "First of all, sir, I want to say we're not guilty. And that's the truth, sir. We were dancing and having a wonderful evening when Shirley started screaming at us and calling Annie some nasty names. The next thing I knew, Shirley was swinging her fists at Annie. I tried to protect Annie from the blows, but Shirley sidestepped me and hit Annie several times. Look at the bruises and scratches on her arms and see for yourselves. Right after that Annie hit Shirley in the face. I swear, sir, Annie was only protecting herself, and that's the honest truth. With all due respect, sir, Mr. Kelley wasn't even there when it began so he couldn't have seen what happened."

"Is this what happened, Annie? Don't lie to me. You know what will happen if I find out you lied to me," her dad said.

"This is ridiculous," Mr. Kelley grunted, and screamed, "Of course, they would try to blame someone else for this. Anything to get themselves off the hook."

Mr. O'Brien turned toward Mr. Kelley, "One thing I learned a long time ago is that there are always two sides to every story. Regardless of whether or not you agree with that is not my concern. I intend to hear my daughter's side of the story. She may have hit this girl, but she may have had good reason. And one thing I know for sure, when I tell Annie I want the truth—I get it—because she isn't a liar. So, if you please, I want to hear what she has to say."

"I'm not going to stand around here listening to this. I've said my piece. So I believe I'll leave you to listen to their cock and bull story. You can call me in the morning and let me know what you intend to do about the medical bill to fix Shirley's broken nose."

At that point Annie knew Mr. Kelley had overstepped his boundaries with her dad because his lower jaw jutted outward like it always did when he was upset.

"I suggest you do leave, Mr. Kelley. I will call you in the morning if I have something to say to you."

Grumbling under his breath, Mr. Kelley slammed the front door and left.

Turning to Annie, her dad said, "Back to my question. Is Michael's rendition of the story correct? Keep in mind what I said earlier about lying."

"Dad, I didn't know what else to do. She was swinging like a mad woman."

Annoyed because of the lateness of the hour, Mr. Kelley's attitude, and Annie's avoidance of his question, he interrupted, "You didn't answer my question. Do I have to repeat myself? You know your mother and I do not appreciate being awakened in the middle of the night to listen to stories about how you couldn't contain yourself as a lady."

Seeing the agitation in his eyes, Mary O'Brien interrupted, "Now Dad, it's late. Perhaps we should settle this in the morning."

"No, Mary. I'm sorry, but we need to settle this now. We have Michael's welfare to consider. The sooner we have the complete story, the better it will be for both of them."

"Yes, Dad!" Annie said. "Michael's story is right except for one small detail."

"And what small detail is that?" Her dad shifted his weight, trying to maintain his composure.

"We were having a wonderful time, and everything was going great when Shirley started to yell at me. I went into shock. I just stood there for a minute, not believing something like that could actually happen. I vaguely remember Michael pulling on my hand and saying something, but it didn't register. The next thing I knew Shirley came at me with her fists up. Something popped inside of me when I looked at her angry face. I began to feel my blood boil because too many times I've had trouble with stupid girls. Like the time when . . ."

"Stick to the story, Annie. We don't need you going off on a tangent in the middle of the night."

"I'm sorry. I know I should've walked away, but I didn't. Instead I told her we weren't doing anything except minding our own business, and that was more than I could say for her. Then she called me a piece of crap! That made me want to smack her. So I waited for the right opening and let her have it. The rest you know."

Charles looked at his wife and shook his head, "And you didn't think for a moment that such a comment would add fuel to the fire?"

"I guess I wasn't thinking about that. Besides, the fire was already blazing. And then her calling me "a piece of crap" in front of everyone--that did it. I'm not a piece of crap, and I wasn't about to let her get away with saying that."

"Obviously! That's enough for one night, I'd say. Annie—go to bed. I'll talk to you both in the morning. Goodnight, Michael."

"Goodnight, sir."

Chapter Seven

The days were long and dreary for Annie, having been grounded at school until the Christmas holidays. As she walked toward the office after her last class, she gazed out of the windows. The trees had already turned their usual dusky black with the winter winds, and the first snow hadn't amounted to much more than a damp chill. Patience was not one of her virtues, so having to wait another half an hour for a nun to sort the mail seemed like an eternity. She yearned for a letter from Michael, telling her about all the wonderful things he had planned and how much she meant to him. A letter that would bring a spark back into her shattered spirit.

Like a broken record, her mind replayed the scene with her parents. They said she needed to learn to control herself and staying six weeks at school might give her enough time to think about it. As far as Annie was concerned, Shirley got exactly what she deserved, and Annie was just the one to give it to her. Lucie and Jeannie didn't have any trouble understanding that. Didn't they both cheer when they heard? So why weren't her parents able to see that justice had to be done? No such luck! Annie would have to "do her time" no matter what she thought, and that meant six weeks without seeing Michael.

Entering the office, Annie slouched against the wood divider, openly showing her resentment. After all, look what she had gotten dragged through over this Shirley thing. And now she was supposed to tolerate having someone read her personal mail. Annie watched Sister Rejeta's staunch emotionless frame as her eyes twitched faster than the letters she sorted. Waves of apprehension flashed through Annie with each passing letter. Would the next one be for her, and would it be censored?

No one ever knew what prompted a nun to open a particular letter. The odds were pretty good that the letter wouldn't be censored if the student stood where the nun could see her. The exception to this rule was Sister Mary Edward. She relished making the students squirm. Many times Annie had seen Sister Edward hold a letter up to the light to check for any hidden messages written on the inside of the envelope. Or she would tap the letter again and again on her desktop while staring into the student's eyes. If found, an unacceptable letter would never be seen again. Annie dreaded the day that might happen. That would feel like someone had violated her privacy big time and had stolen another piece of her life.

After a couple minutes, Sister Rejeta turned and said, "Here, Annie, this one's for you. I'm sure that with losing your privileges, a letter is most welcome."

Annie grabbed the letter from Sister and then apologized for her haste, turning Sister's frown into a smile. When Annie saw it was from Michael, she stuffed it into her sweater pocket and ran as fast as she could to the dorm. Jumping onto her bed, she almost ripped the letter to bits in anticipation of the latest news and the thrill of feeling close to him again.

"My Dearest Annie,

I can't imagine how difficult the trip back to school was for you with your dad. I do know that the punishment of having to stay at school until Christmas has to be the worst thing possible for you. It certainly will be hard for me not to see you. You are such a free spirit that the thought of being cooped up for so long has to be very painful. I wish I could do something to change everything that happened so we could keep the wonderful memories we shared.

> My trip to Mr. Kelley's office turned out to be pretty painless. Mr. Kelley must have cooled off by the next morning so he never called my dad. I don't know why he had a change of heart and I don't care.
>
> Annie, there is something I've been meaning to tell you. I wanted to tell you over the weekend, but there never seemed to be a good time. Unfortunately, we ran into that snag with Shirley, and then we were out of time. I didn't want to tell you this in a letter. Please forgive me!
>
> A couple of weeks before you came home, I began to have some bad headaches. My parents thought maybe it was eyestrain, so they took me to Dr. Brent, an ophthalmologist. He checked me out, but he didn't think my eyes caused the problem. He sent me to a neurologist who ordered all kinds of tests, some of which were not much fun. Yesterday I had to go in with my parents for my follow-up appointment. That's when I got the news."

Annie dropped the letter. It lay on her lap as she sat in silence. She couldn't bear having anything happen to Michael, especially on top of all that had happened to her. She sat for a couple of minutes, fiddling with the corners of the paper. She wanted to know what was wrong, and yet she didn't. Hands shaking, she picked up the letter and began reading again.

> "It seems that I have a brain tumor, but they don't know what kind it is. The doctor said he wouldn't know until he got in there. So I'm scheduled for surgery next Wednesday. I don't want you to start worrying about me now. I'll be

fine. I'll just look a little funny for awhile because they have to shave my head. The doctor tried to tell me my hair would come back curly, but I think he was just kidding. Anyway, I hope so.

By the time you get home this will all be over, and we'll be together again. Maybe we can drive down to Milwaukee for dinner and a play.

You take care of yourself. I don't want anything to happen to you.

Fondly,
Michael"

Stunned by the news, Annie whispered, "Wednesday. He said Wednesday. That's today! What am I going to do? I can't even call home to find out if he is OK." Her body went limp and she began to tremble. She knew she didn't dare try to stand. She turned to see if one of her friends was in the dorm, but no one was there.

Annie dropped to her knees on to the cold floor. "Please, dear God," she cried out. "Don't let anything happen to him. Please…no. Please…nothing." Tears poured down her checks as she buried her face in her hands, weeping hysterically.

Sister Eunice heard Annie's cries from her cell. Not knowing what had happened, Sister hastened to Annie's side, knelt down beside her and embraced her. A student from another dorm heard the commotion and looked to see what was going on. Spotting her, Sister shouted for her to get Sister Margaret.

"Annie, you have to tell me what's the matter." Sister Eunice said. "Are you sick? Are you hurt? Please, Annie, tell me what in the world is making you act like this?"

Unable to speak, Annie pointed to the letter that had dropped from her hand and lay spread out on the floor.

"Oh, I see it," Sister said as she reached to pick up the letter. "Let's get you up on the bed so you can calm down a little while I read it."

It didn't take long before Sister had the answer to her question. "Oh, dear," Sister murmured. "I'm so sorry, Annie. This is dreadful news. I understand you've lost your privileges, but I'll ask Sister Margaret to intercede on your behalf. At least to find out how Michael is doing. Now why don't you just rest for a little bit and I'll see what I can do."

"Thank you," Annie sobbed.

The next morning Annie awoke from her troubled sleep by the sound of the cowbell clanging. Seeing herself still fully dressed, she remembered the letter, and the horrifying memory of the previous evening burned through her mind. She wondered why Sister Eunice didn't wake her. Wasn't Sister able to convince anyone to help her?

"Hey!" shouted Lucie. "You OK? You look terrible. We heard there was a problem, but the nuns wouldn't tell us anything. And they said we should leave you alone. So what's going on? It must be pretty bad if you went to bed with your clothes on."

Several girls gathered around Annie's bed when they heard Lucie.

"Oh, you guys," Annie cried. "It's Michael. He's had brain surgery for some kind of a tumor." Spotting the letter in the partially opened nightstand, Annie pulled it out and handed it to Lucie. "Sister Eunice said she would try to help me find out how things went, but I guess she wasn't able to. Looks like I must have cried myself to sleep. That's all I remember."

"Holy cow! This is terrible," Susan said as she sat down next to Annie.

"Sister will do something. I know she will," Jeannie said. "She probably hasn't gotten a hold of anyone yet. You know, if he had surgery yesterday, it's more than likely that his parents don't know anything either."

"Boy, can you imagine somebody cutting open your head and scrambling around with your brains?" Lucie added.

"That'll be enough, Lucille," Sister Eunice said as she came out of her cell. "How are you doing this morning, Annie?"

"I'm doing better than last night, but my stomach is pretty upset."

"I'm sure you'll feel better after you've had something to eat," Sister said. "I'm sorry I don't have much news for you. Apparently they didn't start operating until yesterday afternoon. The doctor told your folks he wouldn't know anything until later today, if then. I imagine they'll have to wait until Michael is fully conscious before they can assess his condition.

"Why don't you get yourself cleaned up so you don't miss your place in line? I'll check again right after school to see if they know anything more. I know this is very difficult, Annie, but worrying won't make it better. Try to remember that if you can."

As Annie went through her daily routine she tried to follow Sister Eunice's advice, but Lucie's words kept sticking in her head. The horror of Michael's surgery prompted old memories of when she had cut her arms as a child. A cold operating table had been her introduction to terror. Her arms and legs were belted in leather straps. A man in white smiled as he walked slowly toward her with a black mask. "Breathe deep," he said as he pressed the mask into her face. Annie felt sure she was going to suffocate as she gasped for air and gagged on fumes from the ether. Struggling violently to free herself, the room began to spin, stars blinked in and out of the blackness that took her into nothingness. Now this whole horrible scene was happening again, only this time to someone she loved. Images of the cold sterile room, with brilliant lights staring at the top of Michael's head, plagued her mind. As he lay on the surgical table defenseless, the stark white of the sheet that covered his stiff unconscious body mirrored the paleness of his face. Annie's heart hammered in her chest as she imagined the ghoulish act. The doctor shaved Michael's head, reached for his scalpel and began to cut. The bony pale skull opened like the lid of a can, allowing the gray mass to empty onto the table. Pushing aside the good tissue, he'd look for the invasive foreign matter.

"Feeling better," Lucie shouted as she slapped Annie on the back. "You should be hearing something pretty soon I would think."

Shocked by the unexpected interruption of her thoughts, Annie stood staring wide-eyed at Lucie.

"Hey! Did you hear me? You look so strange."

"Yes. I heard you," Annie said.

"Didn't Sister say she'd check again after school? Well, it's almost four o'clock. So it's after school, thank heavens. I had the worst day. Sister Mary Joseph socked us with a chemistry exam. I'm sure I flunked it. My folks will be so upset."

As they walked toward the dorms, Lucie continued to ramble on and on. Annie stayed silent. The bizarre thoughts that had ravaged her mind still had her in their grip. Her head ached so bad she felt sure she had the same thing Michael did. After all, she had the same symptoms; she had kissed him and his head had been right next to hers.

Days passed and still no news. Annie began avoiding her friends so she wouldn't have to answer endless questions or be burdened with hideous statements about Michael's surgery. In an attempt to stop her persistent worrying, she devoted most of her free time to practicing the piano. One evening, as she reminisced, she chose to play and hum the melody of the "Merry Widow Waltz" to defer the burden of her thoughts. In the middle of the composition someone knocked on her door. Startled, she banged her hands on the keyboard. Trying to regain her composure she reached for the doorknob of the clouded plate glass door.

"Annie, can I interrupt you for a moment?" Sister Eunice said.

"Sure. Sure. Come in, Sister. You must have heard something, didn't you?"

"Yes, as a matter of fact, I have. I'm sorry to say that it's not the best news."

Sister stood quiet for a moment, trying to choose her words. "All I know is that Michael is not doing as well as expected. It seems he is having problems recognizing people, even his parents. He also has some paralysis on his left side. I'm very sorry, Annie. All we can do now is keep him and his family in our prayers."

After a moment of silence, Annie said, "How can this be happening? He's such a gentle person. It's not fair. It's just not fair."

"Sometimes it's hard for us to understand why things happen the way they do, Annie."

"I'm sorry, Sister," Annie said as she began to cry. "Right now I'm so confused. I feel like I'm coming apart, and I don't know what to do."

"You just have to place your faith in God and ask Him to keep Michael in His loving care. Why don't we go to the sisters' chapel and light some candles for him and his family."

"Will he ever know who I am? Dear God, don't let him be a vegetable for the rest of his life."

Sister Eunice put her arm around Annie and said, "Come Annie, let's go to the chapel and say some prayers for him. Sometimes these things take time. You must hold fast to your faith. God will see you through this. I know He will. Come now, let's go to the chapel."

As Sister Eunice and Annie walked through the hallways that were now blackened by the night, the sound of their footsteps pierced the emptiness with a hollow echo. The cool air struck them harshly as they stepped out of the back door and onto the blacktop that led to the sisters' chapel. Sister Eunice threw her shawl over her back and put her arm around Annie's shoulders to keep her warm.

In an effort to lighten the heaviness of Annie's situation, Sister pulled Annie closer, and said, "That night air is a bit nippy, isn't it?"

"Yes, Sister," Annie replied as she gathered her jacket collar tight around her neck.

They walked in silence through winding paths that were lined with well-trimmed bushes. In the distance Annie could hear women singing—a sweet angelic sound. Then she remembered what Sister Florentine said about the sisters' choir and how their gentle voices could move the soul.

"That singing you hear, Annie, is the sisters practicing for Mass. Isn't it beautiful? I've always admired anyone who could sing. It is such a gift, isn't it?"

Annie stopped and began to cry again. Sister held her in her arms. The sound of rosary beads swishing in the distance could be heard as another nun approached.

"Is there anything I can do?" Sister Margaret asked.

"No. But thank you anyway, Sister. Annie has gotten some disturbing news about her friend, Michael. We were just on our way to the chapel to light a candle and say some prayers for him. We'll be on our way as soon as Annie is able to compose herself."

"Will you pray for him, too? Please, Sister." Annie pleaded.

"I'll be certain to do that, Annie." Sister Margaret said. And I'll tell the other sisters and Father McBride to do the same. Goodnight now."

The flickering candles that were sitting on the altar dimly lit the chapel. In the darkness, Annie could see the outline of a nun as she lit a candle. In silence, Sister Eunice motioned for Annie to wait a moment. As they stood watching the nun, Annie listened to the angelic sound of the sisters singing and found some peace in the gentle melodies. The nun brushed past Annie as she left, lifted her head and smiled. Sister Eunice took Annie's arm and led her to a small altar that was filled with candles in tall, frosted glasses. Some were lit, and some stood half-empty with their black stems telling the story of numerous burnings. A harsh clank sounded against the chapel's silence as Sister Eunice dropped a couple of coins into a little silver box on the altar. Lighting two candles, they knelt in front of the altar for a silent prayer. Numb and glassy-eyed, Annie stared into the flickering lights, praying that God would protect Michael and give him the faith to believe that he would get better. As she did, she felt a tingling sensation sweep over her, and then calm. She allowed herself to melt into the feeling, slipping further and further into a dream-like state of peace, wanting never again to have to face the painful experience that brought her to the chapel that evening.

Chapter Eight

It was two weeks before Christmas when Annie received a letter from Patsy, asking her if she would like to go to the Sadie Hawkins dance at the high school. The thought of going home again sent a sudden surge of excitement through Annie. The feeling faded as she realized she'd have to see Michael and deal with his condition.

> "I know several fellows who would jump at the chance to go with you, especially since they consider you a hero for punching Shirley in the nose. Besides, you have to start dating other guys, Annie. At least until Michael gets better. It's been five weeks since his surgery, and there's still no good news. Think about it and let me know as soon as you can. I'd be glad to make all the arrangements.
> Love,
> Patsy"

As much as Annie didn't want to admit it, she knew she had to listen to Patsy. She'd been stuck at school for almost five weeks, and she did need some excitement. As she held the letter, she remembered how much she had wanted to go to high school in her hometown last fall. Now, she didn't even want to go to the dances. Outside of Patsy, she never had much to do with the other students. And after the episode with Shirley, the handwriting on the wall rang clear. No matter what Annie did now, she'd never be a part of the in-group at that school. They proved that when they had stuck by Shirley, knowing she had started the whole fiasco in the first place.

I should steal all their boyfriends as a payback, Annie chuckled. *It would serve them right for backing Shirley the way they did.*

Annie selected a couple of names from the list that Patsy sent, scribbled a short note and went back to the office to mail it. Thoughts of betraying Michael ran through her mind as she handed Sister Rejeta the letter. Yet she had to get out and do something to shake off the misery of the last six weeks.

As Annie waited for her dad to pick her up for Christmas vacation, she decided she would keep her mouth shut on the way home. This would be her best strategy for avoiding an argument. He would definitely ask the question that would set her off anyway. Sure enough, about a half an hour from home, he opened a Pandora's Box.

"Well, what did you learn from your six week punishment?" her dad asked.

"Not to get caught," Annie blurted.

"Still pretty frisky, aren't you, little lady?" her dad snapped.

"What do you expect me to say? That what happened was OK? And I loved every minute that I had to stay in that dreadful place, week after week? You'll never convince me that I was treated fairly. How would you like to have someone you care about go through a terrible surgery like Michael did, and not be able to be there for him? Or worse yet, not know what was happening to him? Well?" she hammered.

"I'm not going to get in an argument with you, Annie. Mind you, the only reason I'm overlooking your attitude is because I know how upset you are about Michael. It's unfortunate that he had to have surgery at the same time you were being punished. That doesn't change the fact that your behavior was less than ladylike.

We'll talk about this after we get home," her dad said. "Right now I'm going to pay attention to the road."

"Fine," Annie said, raising her chin and pulling herself erect.

By the time her dad pulled into their driveway, the lateness of the hour didn't allow much time to get ready for the dance. A light dusting of snow covered the ground, outlining the sidewalk. As Annie hurried into the house, the crunch of fresh snow under her feet and the cool night air made her shiver. She greeted her mother, ignored her father, and ran upstairs to her room to call Patsy. Curiosity was eating her alive. She had to find out who Patsy had picked for her date.

"Jerry? Oh no, not him," Annie groaned. "Why did you pick him?"

"Because you put his name first on the list, so I thought that's who you wanted to go with."

"I guess I never even thought about the names when I wrote them down," Annie whined. "I'm sorry I barked at you. I know you were trying to help. It's just that he's so short and skinny. He greases his hair with that VO5 gunk, and then his hair starts to kink. After I socked Shirley everybody will think he's the best I can do. I can't wear my high heels with him either. I know he'll have his hands all over me. He's not a gentleman like Michael."

"Slow down! You don't have to worry about your heels. You'll be wearing saddle shoes and some jeans for this dance," Patsy said.

"I don't have any jeans. My mother doesn't allow me to own any. I have to wear what all the other prissity ladies wear."

"Understand. Wear whatever you have to, but keep it casual. My dad agreed to pick you up, so we'll be there around eight o'clock. That way you won't have to walk in by yourself. We don't need a repeat performance like you had at the last dance. I've told Jerry that we'd meet him there."

"I'll be ready for it this time."

"Better change that attitude or you'll end up back in the hoosegow. And you're going to have to stop comparing every guy to Michael. Try to take it as it comes. It's just for one night, for Pete's sake. It'll help you loosen up a little."

Annie didn't mention anything about the dance until just before Mr. Oberly showed up with Patsy. Being caught off guard, and not wanting to make a scene in front of Patsy, her dad reluctantly allowed Annie to go. However, he did remind her that she needed to be home no later than midnight.

"Yeah! I know the rules. That's all I live by these days," Annie said.

Feeling uncomfortable, Patsy started to walk toward the front door.

"Annie!" her mother said in astonishment. "Don't you speak to your father like that! What's come over you? Such a rough mouth you have on you."

That did it. Annie had pushed too far this time. When her mother stepped into the war zone, big trouble lurched in the foreground. Annie decided the smart thing to do was to back off and save her hide.

"I'm sorry," Annie managed to say. "I guess being stuck in a school with a lot of rejects has rubbed off on me."

"Rejects! I hardly think so. You'd better just un-rub yourself, I'd say," her mother said, as she turned to finish clearing the table.

A grimace crossed her dad's face. "Don't worry, Mary. Annie and I will be having our little talk tomorrow. I'm sure that will straighten out a few of her manners."

As Patsy walked out of the door she said to Annie, “You sure know how to borrow trouble, don’t you? After that crack, I really thought you’d be staying home.”

As they approached the school, students were piling out of cars and walking toward the gym. The shaded two-story windows were unable to hide the soft light that shone out into the parking lot. Annie saw Jerry leaning next to the back door, dressed in a jacket and white shirt. As always, his hair had been slicked down, and his pants bagged as though they were two sizes too big for him.

“Hi, Annie,” Jerry called out as Patsy and Annie walked toward him. “Thanks for asking me to the dance. I’ll see to it that you have a better time than you did at the last one.”

“I had a very good time with Michael. We couldn’t help that some little snip asked to have her face smashed in.”

“Oh brother,” Patsy sighed under her breath. “Well, what do you say we go inside and have some fun and forget about the rest.” Pulling Annie close to her, Patsy whispered, “Drop it, Annie. Otherwise, I might sock you. We’re here to have fun, remember?”

“OK! OK!” Annie said as she yanked her arm away from Patsy’s grip. Then she straightened up and walked toward the gym door, pausing long enough for Jerry to open the door.

Annie felt full of vim and vigor by the time she returned to school. She had managed to soften her dad’s foul mood by turning on her sweetest charm. After Christmas, the January blues, accented by the dirty gray snow and overcast skies, had drained the humor out of the adults in the household. Annie decided they could all be as crabby as they wanted. She’d do her best to ignore them and not let them get under her skin. Having to contend with Michael's situation and not knowing how that would turn out would give her enough to handle.

By the end of Christmas vacation, Michael's condition still hadn't changed. His parents wouldn't allow her to see him, saying he wasn't up to receiving visitors. No matter what she asked, they always gave the same answer. Unable to resolve the dilemma, Annie convinced Patsy to go skating with her at the City Park; some interaction with her friend might help with the frustration she felt.

During the winter months, the bathhouse at the City Park was converted to a clubhouse to accommodate a variety of winter sports. Lines of chairs replaced the heavy wooden structure that held the swimming baskets in the summer. Hockey sticks were stacked three deep against the wall, challenging the skaters to some friendly competition. A fire blazed in the fireplace for the frozen toe candidates, sitting with a cup of hot chocolate. The pond had been plowed for ice skating with music piped in. A toboggan slide had been built with blocks of ice stacked two feet deep, directing a course that ended within twenty feet of the ice skating pond. Gleeful riders piled out of the toboggans after their catapulting ride, laughing wildly. Tears streamed down their half-frozen faces from the cold wind as they made their way back up the hill.

Annie didn't care for tobogganing. She much preferred skating, thanks to Sonja Henie. She only went down once and that did it for her. The toboggan had hit the bottom so hard, a snap sounded. She wondered if her tail-bone had cracked. Then the sled veered off at a forty-five degree angle. Aware of an uncomfortable pain in her butt, she got up sure her tailbone had cracked. Besides, she hated the feeling of being totally out of control when on it. To make matter worse, the guys constantly teased her, calling her a chicken. They could do that until the cows came home; she'd just put her nose in the air, flash her new skates, and say she had better things to do.

* * *

The afternoon shadows had already crossed the sky by the time they arrived in the school courtyard. The snow had long since lost its glow, and the blackness of the night was cut only by one dimly lit lamppost next to the front door. As usual, Sister Mary Joseph opened the door. Annie, armed with bags of apples, oranges and a few bananas, greeted the nun as she mounted the foyer steps.

Her dad slid Annie's suitcases onto the first landing, saying, "It's late and I've got a splitting headache, so I think I'll be on my way. They're predicting a bad storm, and I don't want to get caught in the middle of it."

"It's OK, Dad. I can manage from here. I wondered if you were getting a headache the way you were squinting. Maybe you'd better have your eyes checked. You know Michael's trouble started with a headache."

"Oh . . . I'm OK," he said as he bent over and kissed Annie on the cheek. "I'll grab a cup of coffee on my way home and that'll help. I'll call and let you know when I can pick you up again as soon as I know."

"Dad," Annie asked. "If you hear anything about Michael, will you let me know?"

"Sure will, Stinker."

The lateness of the hour concerned Annie. She didn't want to be campused. She quickly signed in and then went to empty her treasures into her locker. She could hear the students marching down from the dorms for dinner. She waited, anxious to meet her friends and find out how their vacations went. The students passed in accordance with protocol, first the seniors, then the juniors. Seeing Annie, Lucie and Helen began jumping up and down, waving their arms for all they were worth.

Unable to contain herself, Annie jumped in line next to them. "How are you guys?" she whispered.

"Super," murmured Lucie. "I'll tell you all about it at the table. Sister Margaret is sort of crabby and I don't want to get into trouble."

"Gotcha!" Annie said.

The students assembled according to their assigned seating arrangements. The usual routine followed with the seniors sitting down first and then the rest of the students. Bustling conversation spread throughout the room with everyone talking at once. Dishes of food were passed to the left without much attention to what was being served.

Massive confusion ruled until Sister Margaret tapped her spoon on a glass on the front table. "Ladies! Ladies! Have you forgotten your manners in such a short time? How can you possibly know what the other person is saying if you are all talking at once? Please be considerate of one another."

"What's with her?" Annie whispered to Lucie.

"I don't know. She was like that when I got here yesterday. I think she's sick or something."

"Sure hope not. We don't need a different nun running the place in the middle of the year, especially now that I've learned her habits," laughed Annie. "You've been here since yesterday?"

"Ha! Habits! That was pretty clever," Lucie sniggered.

"How's Michael?" Helen interrupted.

"I wasn't able to find out anything. I called almost every day, but his parents kept telling me he couldn't have visitors. I finally just told them to call me if he wanted to see me. My dad said he would let me know if he heard anything more."

"That's terrible," Helen responded. "That means he's not much better, for sure."

"Yeah," said Lucie as she looked around the table and shrugged her shoulders. "What do you expect when somebody scrambles with your brains? Say, how did the Hawkins dance go?"

"Actually it turned out better then I thought it would."

"Really? Is this going to get juicy?" Jeannie asked.

"Jeannie! I can't believe that came from you and not Lucie. See what an effect you're having on this poor sweet girl?"

"It's about time I have an effect on something around here. So go on with the story already."

"Anyway, when I got home I found out Patsy had matched me up with this weird guy that I never had much use for. He's short and skinny and greases down his hair."

"Yuck!" Lucie grimaced. "How did that happen? Didn't you tell her who to ask?"

"I did, but like a dummy, I put his name at the top of the list. I was so ticked at my parents for sticking me here for six weeks, I guess I wasn't thinking straight. Like I said, he wasn't as much of a drag as I thought he'd be. I had a pretty good time at the dance. I found out later when I was skating at the park that he's a pretty good hockey player. He can really move that puck around."

"Whoa, way to go," Lucie giggled.

"Lucie, I'm talking about a hockey puck, OK?" Annie said. "I almost started to like him when he stole the knit hat my mother made for me—right off my head. The dumbest move he ever made. Then he wouldn't give it back and all the guys started playing "keep away" with it. That ticked me off. They thought they were pretty cute until they found out I could skate faster than they could. You can bet your booties that it didn't take long before I had my hat back. Nothing like a fast mad female to scare the hell out of some stupid guys. What about you guys? Did you do anything neat over the holidays?"

"Mostly helped my dad milk the cows and my mom with decorations and stuff," Helen said. "I did get to go sledding a couple of times. We have this huge hill behind our barn and it . . . "

"That's OK, but I got some real news," Lucie interrupted. "I got to make some cash clearing tables at the Bunny club. Boy, are those gals stacked. And the guys! They had their hands all over them. As much as I'd like some action, that's not for me. I'll take them one at a time, thank you." Lucie chuckled. "There's nothing like learning what you don't like and getting paid for it."

"You mean the men were touching the girls . . . everywhere?" Jeannie asked. "Isn't that against the law in those places."

"It is," Lucie said. "But these guys get away with murder. A lot of money goes a long, long way."

"What do you mean by that?" Jeannie asked.

"Gee, Jeannie, what haystack have you been living in? Money buys what they want, see? And with enough money, they can get whatever they want."

"Well, you don't have to be so smug about it. Not all of us are as worldly as you, you know. My folks live in a small town and we don't have Bunny Clubs," Jeannie scowled.

Figuring her timing would avoid a war between the two girls, Susan whispered her tidbit. "My cousin and I went to downtown Milwaukee one night and picked up some sailors."

Lucie turned toward Susan, wondering if she had heard her right. “What did you say?”

Beginning to blush, Susan repeated, “My cousin and I went downtown Milwaukee and picked up some sailors.”

“You picked up sailors and got away with it—as strict as your parents are?” Lucie asked.

“We told my mom we needed to do some Christmas shopping, and she never suspected a thing. There are all kinds of sailors on Wisconsin Avenue on the weekends, and they love walking around with you. And they’ll buy you anything you want,” Susan said as sucked her cheeks in and the corners of her mouth turned up into a grin.

“I can’t believe it,” Annie said. “Susan! You, of all people. Isn’t that rather dangerous?”

“I don’t think so, but my mom would say otherwise. They’re just lonely being on those ships so long.”

“I think you’re asking for it,” Lucie said. “Sure they’re lonely. And what do you think they’re lonely for, Susan?”

“Oh Lucie. You have to make something dirty out of everything. They just want to talk.”

“Sure. Sure. Talk first and grope later. I’m telling you, you’re asking for it.”

Seeing Susan and Lucie glaring at each other, Annie said, “Cut that conversation before you two kill each other. Besides I’ve got an idea to run by you. I realized on my way back here that we didn’t have much fun around last semester. It’s hard to believe that the last thing we did was powder good old Jeannie.”

“Not funny, Annie. But you got yours didn’t you?” Jeannie laughed.

"How right you are," Annie said, punching Jeannie in the shoulder. "Here's my idea. What say we have a party in the dorm?"

"You're kidding, of course. Aren't you?" Helen asked as she looked around the table at the stunned faces.

"Listen, you guys. You can be a part of this or not. I'm not pushing anybody into anything. If you don't want in, just say so." Annie sat quietly, watching Sarah squirm in her chair. They all began looking from one to the other, asking each other if they were going to be in on it. Then they turned and nodded to Annie.

"I guess that means we're all game," Jeannie said and looked back and forth between the girls.

"All right! Here's the plan," Annie whispered. "Betsy, the day student I have lunch with every day, has invited me to her house this next weekend. While I'm there, I can get a bunch of supplies like cheese and crackers, the regular stuff, and we can have a party in the dorm the following week. That will give us enough time to hoard some stuff from the cafeteria and plan the whole thing. We can hide the cold stuff in the bushes in the back. I know just the spot. Nobody will ever suspect it. We won't need pop because we can get it out of the machines downstairs. It's a good thing we aren't in the same dorm or we'd have a heck of a time getting permission to retire early. How about meeting right after I get back from Betsy's place, and match our ideas with some action. What do you say? I think it'll be a blast."

"Sounds like a go to me," Lucie said as the others nodded their heads.

Chapter Nine

The cold winter wind held the snow on the streets and sidewalks in its frigid grip. The road was drenched with sand and slush from a previous melt which added to the despair of winter.

As the girls walked along Lake Michigan, Betsy said, “We’ll be catching the streetcar on that corner over there, Annie. It should be here any minute because it has to meet its four o’clock schedule. It’ll take us to the bus line we need to get to my place.”

“This is great, Betsy. I appreciate your folks having me over. My dad said I might have to take the train home once in awhile. This will give me a chance to learn the town a little and find out how to get to the train station.”

“We don’t go that way, Annie, but don’t worry about it. It’s pretty simple. Only two transfers and the streetcar drops you off right in front of the station. The conductors are very friendly so you don’t need to be concerned about asking questions. Betsy laughed."Not that I can imagine you having a problem doing that."

“I guess I’m not exactly bashful, am I? I get that from my grandma. She’s a real character. You wouldn’t believe the stories she tells me, stuff like walking down the street and having poop land on her head after it got thrown out of an upstairs window. That’s why she made Grandpa walk on the outside of the sidewalk.”

“That’s funny,” Betsy said. “I’d sure like to meet her sometime. She sounds like a very colorful person.”

“She’s the greatest. I’ll try to have you over when my grandparents are visiting. They’re my second parents. After I was born I spent a lot of time with them because my mom got pretty sick, I guess. I like them a lot. My grandma loves dragging me all over Chicago.

She doesn't like to drive with Grandpa because she says he's a maniac behind the wheel. I'm here to tell you that Grandpa doesn't have anything on that lady. She can really move, even as old as she is. Sometimes I'm amazed she's still alive. She runs across the street in the middle of the block with streetcars coming from both directions. Then she skips over the tracks and arrives in record time on the other side. And she calls Grandpa a maniac. The funniest part is that Mom hollers at me for running across the street, but she never says anything to her mother. Mom says I'm going to fall someday, and a car is going to go right over me."

"There's the streetcar," Betsy yelled. "Let's hurry so we can get a seat together. By the way, we have a special engagement tonight. I didn't want to tell you at lunch because I didn't know if the party was still on, but it is."

"Party? I like the sound of that. I always love a party, especially if there are lots of new people, like guys to meet," Annie said as she laughed and raised her eyebrows up and down.

"Well there will be plenty of them at this one and probably some fairly rich ones. It's at the Park residence. They're the ones that own all those filling stations."

Astonished, Annie smiled and said, "No kidding!"

"No kidding. They live in a gigantic house a couple of miles from our place. It almost looks like a motel, it's so big. I've never been inside so I'm anxious to see what it's like. It should be fun and, with any luck, we might meet some interesting people. Then on Saturday we'll go skating, Sunday to church, and maybe skating again if there is time before you have to be back at school."

As they traveled to the small town of Elm Grove, the girls chatted enthusiastically about what they were going to wear and who would be at the party. An hour and a half had passed by the time they heard the bus driver holler, "End of the line." Annie looked out of the window and saw that they were stopped in front of a small red brick church that sat on a triangular piece of land.

Betsy got up saying, "I live about a half a mile from here. My dad likes to see me walk home when the weather is good. Of course, I don't call any part of winter good," Betsy laughed. "He says the exercise will keep me from getting too chubby."

"No problem. I walk a lot at home."

The girls entered the home through the back door, greeting Mr. and Mrs. Hogan. They were sitting in the kitchen.

"Well . . . hello there, sweetheart." Mr. Hogan said as he got up to give Betsy a bear hug that matched his physique. "And who do we have here?"

Annie blushed. Smiling, she held out her hand and said, "Annie O'Brien, sir. I'm pleased to make your acquaintance."

"Good afternoon, Miss Annie O'Brien. I'm pleased to make your acquaintance as well," Mr. Hogan said.

"And good afternoon to you, Mrs. Hogan," Annie said. "Thank you for allowing Betsy to have me over for the weekend."

Mrs. Hogan got up from the chair as though it took all of her strength to lift her small frail frame. "You're very welcome. Why don't you take Annie to your room, Betsy, and show her where to put her things. Dinner will be ready in about a half an hour. After that Dad will take you over to the Parks' home."

At seven thirty Mr. Hogan dropped the girls off at the Parks' residence for the evening. Betsy had chosen a soft-yellow chiffon with a scooped neckline for her outfit. Pearls were her choice for her accessories. Annie selected a lime-green silk dress that flared softly from the waist down, accenting her slender waistline. A matched set of pearl earrings and necklace added the finishing touches to her ensemble as well.

Standing in front of the double oak doors that were inlaid with stained glass down the center, they waited for someone to answer the door.

"Good evening, ladies," the butler said as Betsy handed him their invitation.

"Please follow me to the game room."

"Wow!" Annie whispered. "A real live butler!"

"Shh! He'll hear you."

Mahogany graced the walls and doors of the game room which lent itself to a masculine décor. Guests lounged on leather sofas and settees in front of the west windows or stood with drinks in hand next to the fireplace.

Upon seeing Betsy, a tall slender young man with dark circles under his eyes walked over to welcome them. "Betsy, darling! I'm so glad you could make it. Please make yourself at home and feel free to browse if you care to," he chuckled. "And who is this very attractive young woman, may I ask?"

"Gary, I'd like to introduce Miss Annie O'Brien to you. She goes to the same academy that I do."

"My pleasure, I'm sure. I've heard a lot about the academy. It has a fine reputation. You must be very pleased to have the opportunity to attend such a prestigious school."

Annie stood with her mouth open, not believing the syrupy speech she was hearing. However, a poke in the ribs from Betsy closed her mouth and brought a silky response from her. "Why yes, I can see why one might think so. And may I ask what school you attend?"

"Why of course. I am a freshman at Marquette University. Do you know where that is?" Gary asked as he chuckled.

"As a matter of fact, I do. A couple of my older siblings graduated with honors from Marquette. They loved the Jesuits. They are such fine teachers. Don't you agree?"

"Possibly," Gary said as he began walking away. "Why don't you ladies help yourselves to some refreshments? Perhaps we'll have a chance to chat later."

Puzzled, Betsy asked, "Gee Annie, what were you trying to do? I know he can be a pain, but he is our host."

"I'm sorry. I just met him on his own terms. I can be just as uppity as he can. In fact, he was making me nauseous."

"Perhaps some good old American food will help straighten that out."

The girls maneuvered their way through the guests toward the refreshment table. They had just finished a couple of finger sandwiches when the butler entered the room and announced that Mr. Park had graciously suggested he conduct a tour of the mansion for whomever was interested. The majority of the guests paused for a moment, then turned back to continue their conversations.

Annie, surprised by the lack of interest and trying not to look too anxious, said to Betsy, "Here's the opportunity you've been waiting for. We can peek in all the rooms and see how the other half lives."

"I suppose. I wanted to at first, but now I feel a little funny about it. Like we're being nosey or invading their privacy."

"I don't think so, but if that's true, at least we've been invited to snoop. Some rich people like to flaunt their possessions, especially the ones who had to climb up the ladder on somebody else's shoulders. The real rich ones are pretty nice folks and not at all stuffy."

"Well, let's get it over with," Betsy said.

A group of ten followed the butler from room to room. The large portraits of family members emphasized the high ceilings and crown molding throughout the home. Where appropriate, the butler pointed out famous paintings and announced special memorabilia, telling the guests where the articles came from.

"This is a boring house, you know," Annie whispered to Betsy.

"Yes, it's almost like a motel, isn't it? Long wings off of the center house with bedrooms on both sides of the hallway. If you had a room at the end of the hallway, I bet it could take you fifteen minutes to get to the main house. That's not for me."

"Me neither. And whoever did the decorating sure could use a lesson or two in color combinations. And my mom thinks I'm color blind."

By the time the group had gotten back to the game room, the furniture had been moved against the wall and the rugs had been rolled back, displaying the highly polished oak floors. "Now is the Hour" was playing on the phonograph, inviting the guests to pair off and dance. Gazing across the great room, Annie saw a tall well-built young man with blonde hair and bright blue eyes walking toward her. Her heart skipped a beat.

"Good evening, miss. My name is Gene Henderson. May I have the pleasure of this dance?"

"Yes, thank you," Annie said.

"And may I ask your name?"

"Of course. My name is Annie O'Brien." She turned toward Betsy to excuse herself, noticing another young man had asked Betsy to dance.

"You're not from around here, are you?" Gene inquired in a soft smooth voice.

"In a way I am. I go to a private academy in Milwaukee, and I grew up in a small town just north of Milwaukee. Betsy and I go to the same school together. We have lunch every day and have become good friends. And what about you? I don't want to be the one doing all the talking."

Gene laughed. "Of course not. I need to hold up my end of the bargain. I live in Elm Grove, not far from Betsy. In fact we went to the same grade school, but I was two grades ahead of her. Now I'm a junior at Don Bosco. That's a high school for guys not too far from your academy. I do believe your school and mine get together to hold dances once in awhile."

"That is refreshing news," Annie said, thinking she might have an ally. "I didn't think they ever held dances at St. Anthony's. Not unless there was a nun to stand between every couple, that is."

"I don't think it is all that bad, but I must admit you're close," Gene laughed. "The rules at Don Bosco are pretty strict, and we also have a dress code. I know you have to wear uniforms, don't you?"

"I wouldn't even pay them the courtesy of calling them uniforms. Sacks would be closer to the truth."

After a few moments of jovial conversation the music stopped. The couple found themselves standing in the middle of the dance floor, looking into each other's eyes. Annie felt a flush of excitement from Gene's gaze and then a twinge of embarrassment. It felt like everyone in the room was watching them.

Gene asked as he looked down into her eyes. "Would you like to try another?"

"Why yes. That would be nice."

The evening whirled with excitement for Annie as one young man after another asked her to dance. Being spun again and again by her dancing partners, the neatly stacked bookshelves and perfectly placed furniture seemed to disappear into a blur. Gene attempted to occupy most of her time in spite of other requests. It wasn't until the butler clapped his hands and announced that the hour was late that Annie realized the time. Seeing Betsy walking toward them, Gene asked Annie if they could keep in touch. The idea excited her, so she told him about the censoring policy. Laughing, she said they'd have to develop a code.

"Looks like you hooked a winner, Annie." Betsy said as they walked out of the door. "He's a pretty nice guy, and he comes from a good family."

"He sure seems nice. We plan to keep in touch. Do you think he will?"

"It's possible. I do know his parents keep a pretty tight rein on him. I guess time will tell. I'm glad you had a good time."

"I had a terrific time, Betsy. A terrific time!"

"By the way, Annie, you two looked divine together."

The party in the dorm the following week didn't go as the girls planned. Everyone was able to retire early, but things went haywire right after they realized they didn't have an opener for the pop. Remembering that the lock on the tub room door was shaped somewhat like a bottle opener, Annie set out to solve the problem. She strapped four bottles of coke to her body with a couple of nylons and wrapped herself in her heavy wool bathrobe. There wasn't a nun in sight as she sneaked down the hallway. Entering the tub room, a dim light showed overhead from the adjoining room. Thinking it was a night light, she ignored it, unstrapped one of the bottles and began prying the cap loose on the tub room lock. All of a sudden the cap flew off, sending the pop toward the ceiling like a geyser. Annie gasped as she watched the pop splatter off the ceiling and down into the adjoining room. A mini-second later she heard a scream.

Realizing she probably just gave a nun a shower, Annie grabbed the coke bottles and ran for it. She had to find refuge fast. Any second that nun would come flying out of the anteroom, looking for the culprit. Annie darted into the sink room, peeking around the corner to see which way the nun would go. Sister Mary Claudia came out dressed in a wet nightshirt that was clinging to her obese body and a cotton cap that fit tight around her enraged face. Hoping to catch the troublemaker red-handed, Sister looked up and down the hallway, then headed straight for the tub room.

I had to pick the meanest nun in the place to spray, didn't I? I better get a move on and warn the others that she's on the warpath.

Everybody panicked after Annie ran into her dorm, saying the party was off. "Sorry!" Annie whispered. "I accidentally sprayed Sister Claudia with the coke when I was trying to get the cap off. She's really pissed."

"Darn!" Jeannie mumbled. "And we just got started."

Before they ran out of the dorm, each girl grabbed a portion of the food, making sure there wasn't any evidence left behind. Annie shoved the pop bottles along the side of her body as she jumped into bed. There she lay, flushed and out of breath, waiting for Sister Claudia to pounce on her.

It didn't take long before Annie heard a commotion in the hallway. It sounded like a group of nuns had joined forces and were about to disperse into the various dorms. The light lit in her dorm. She listened with her eyes closed, but she couldn't hear a sound. Feeling like someone was standing over her, she thought her skin would crawl right off of her body. Nevertheless, she didn't move a muscle. Within seconds, the swishing of rosary beads and the sound of leather heels hitting the floor announced a nun's departure. The sound of nuns patrolling the hallways continued until the rest of the students came in to retire. Not knowing what had happened in the other dorms, Annie was unable to sleep. It was going to be a long night.

Oddly enough, no one got caught. That didn't stop Sister Margaret from cross-examining Annie for the next two weeks, trying to trick her into a confession. Annie never broke. For the rest of the group the scare was enough to make honest citizens out of them for the remainder of the semester. Annie wasn't about to give up that easily, especially since she got it in her head that if she caused enough trouble she might get expelled. Then her parents would have to send her to a different school. She didn't know where. She just knew she didn't want to be at St. Anthony's. By the end of her freshman year, Annie realized the nuns weren't talking about her escapades to anyone. They were wise to what she was trying to pull and they weren't about to give Annie any ammunition to use with her parents. Nor were they going to allow her actions to go unpunished. So the only things she managed to accomplish with her antics were sore hands and knees from spending hours scrubbing Sister Eunice's classroom floor.

The love-light that glowed so brightly between Gene and Annie went out just as fast. He wrote a couple of short notes and came to one of the dances at St. Anthony's, but Annie didn't show up.

"What's the matter with you, Annie?" Betsy inquired during lunch hour. "You were so wild about Gene when you first met him, all starry eyed and with the goosebumps to go with it. So what's with you?"

"I don't know. I've been so busy trying to get the nuns to expel me that I don't have enough energy to practice the piano. He's an OK guy. I just have other things on my mind right now. Besides, I'm still hoping Michael will get better soon."

"I think you're kidding yourself. He's been out of circulation for too long. It's about time you start getting back on track."

It was an early spring. The tulips were beginning to blossom in her mother's meticulous garden, and her dad had begun to turn the soil for their victory garden. There were a couple of long rows of raspberry bushes along the west side of the home. Annie's job, since they moved there, included picking the fruit during the summer months, along with her other tasks. She hated the job because of the silver dollar size spiders that she often found herself eye to eye with.

The highlight of the summer would be a trip to Chicago to spend some time with her grandparents. To Luke's dismay, he would have to pick the berries and deal with the spiders while Annie was gone.

A week before the school term ended, Annie went to the corner grocery to pick up a couple of things for her trip. Hearing Michael's voice at the front of the store, she needed to double check to be sure. Shocked by his appearance, Annie backed into a corner and began to tremble. His tall frame had sagged under the burden of his illness. Dark shadows hung in the pockets of his gaunt face. The gentleness of his eyes had been replaced with a hard dark stare. Since his surgery she had longed to see him, talk to him, hold him.

This can't be my Michael--the Michael that I loved so much. It just can't be.

She couldn't bear seeing him like this. Suddenly she found herself on the sidewalk, running for home as fast as she could, with tears streaming down her face. Perhaps someday she wouldn't be afraid to face him, but not today.

As Annie readied herself for her trip to Chicago, Michael's condition continued to bother her. She had handled the situation at the store poorly. She felt like she let him down, even though Betsy told her she had done everything she could. There wasn't any sense in both of them being miserable. Perhaps this trip to her grandparents would relieve some of the heaviness she felt in her heart.

Chapter Ten

The windy city was living up to its reputation when Annie's train arrived in Chicago that early June day. As she stepped off the train, she struggled to hold the skirt of her light-blue, silk dress from being tossed above her waist by repeated gusts of wind.

Spotting Annie as she walked down the gangplank, her grandpa smiled and hollered, "There's my best girl."

It embarrassed Annie when he'd call her that in front of her grandma. Grandma didn't seem to mind. She just chuckled and hugged Annie as hard as ever.

"Do we have a surprise for you!" Grandma said. "We just found out your father's nephew has moved over on Armitage Avenue, and they have a daughter about your age. I think she plays the flute and she's supposed to be quite a character. They've lived there for over a year now. Best of all—they own a shoe store! And you know how I love shoes," she grinned.

Grandpa rolled his eyes skyward and moaned softly.

"Oh Henry! That's enough out of you."

Turning back to Annie, she said, "So I thought we could all go over after lunch and see the store. That would give you an opportunity to meet Grace. At least you two would have your music in common, if nothing else. What do you think?"

"Sounds like a plan, Grandma."

By the time Annie had unpacked and was ready to go to the Schaefers, the sun had begun to set. On the way her grandpa remained very intent on his driving. Annie suspected his irritation might be due to having to go to another shoe store or it could be that his usual city driving demeanor had once again crept out of his Irish disposition. He sped through the city, gripping the top of the steering wheel with both hands. The kelly-green Hudson swayed back and forth over the streetcar tracks as he passed one car after another. At irregular intervals he would shout at the other drivers, saying they should learn to drive or get off the road. Annie was amazed at how this otherwise mild mannered man could turn into such a monster every time he got behind the wheel of a car. She hoped it couldn't be hereditary.

Annie always sat in the passenger's seat next to him, a place her grandma never occupied. Grandma insisted on sitting in the back seat where she could concentrate on praying her rosary, so she wouldn't have to see how fast the houses were flying by.

Upon arriving at the Schaefers' home everything fell into place without a problem. Grandma got to try on lots of shoes, Grandpa and Bill Schaefer went outside to have a cigar, and the girls headed for the bedroom where they could tell stories about their boyfriends. Grace's parents, Caroline and Bill Schaefer, were pleasant enough, but yet an odd looking couple. Caroline spent hours sorting sweepstake entries in their upstairs flat as her chubby body swelled over the sides of her armed chair. Bill was the tallest and thinnest man Annie had ever seen. Everyone had such a good time that the Schaefers invited Annie to spend the night. That gave the girls an opportunity to hop a streetcar that evening to a park in downtown Chicago across from Lake Michigan to meet some of Grace's friends.

Just before they left Grace pulled Annie into her room and said, "There's these twin guys that'll be there tonight and they are so cute." Grace was a bright-eyed brunette with silky hair that accented her milky-white complexion, definitely the Snow White type.

"They both have their sights set on going into the priesthood," Grace said, shaking her head and throwing her hands in the air. "Ever since I've found that out I've been on a crusade to change Danny's mind. He's the one I'm partial to. So your job will be to work on Tony. Between the two of us we should be able to convince them not to do such a stupid thing."

Annie asked, "Both of them are going to be priests?"

Grace swooned. "Yeah! And when you see them you won't believe it. They are so incredibly handsome."

"This isn't one of those family deals again, is it?"

"Are you talking about when parents keep track of how many of their kids they can put in the religious orders?"

"Yes. By us it has spread through the community like the chicken pox. If you get my drift."

"Sure do. No, in this case it's definitely their choice."

"Why are they so bent on being priests?" Annie asked. "Frankly, I think it's like going to jail for the rest of your life. And I know what that's like."

"Not a clue. Honestly, I don't think they know what they're doing. I think it's sort of like how a soldier feels when he puts on a uniform. You know, it makes them feel so important and all that crap. That all goes out the window when you're looking down the barrel of a gun. All I know is we have a mission. We have to give them a taste of the good life and change their minds."

"Whoa! What does that mean—a taste of the good life?"

Grace smiled, "Just a little kissing and teasing will stir up those male hormones and unleash the animal within. Don't you think?"

"I don't know. Besides, I haven't seen them yet. Nobody can be that good-looking."

"Just wait. You're going to eat those words."

"Gladly," Annie laughed. "I don't know how good I am at changing anybody's mind on anything. I still haven't convinced my parents not to send me to St. Anthony's."

"I assure you that all it will take is one look and you'll be on your way to seduction," Grace said with a twinkle in her eye. "We'll be doing them a favor by saving them from themselves. I can't imagine either one of them up on the altar saying Mass like some little holy Joe. Now let me ask you. How in the world could you possibly go to Communion with the thoughts you'd have running through your head? And if you didn't go to Communion the nuns would send you to confession to one of them and that would be disastrous."

"This should be very interesting."

"Don't you ever wonder if the nuns think about this stuff?"

"Don't you know—nuns are neuter gender. They're so confused that they can't think about sex," Annie laughed.

"That's funny. I bet they do though."

"I hope there will be other guys there in case I fall flat on my face with this Tony guy."

"Sure. There will be. But you won't care who else is around once you see these guys, believe me."

In the middle of the park's meridian stood a huge ball-shaped sculptured fountain, catapulting pastel-colored water skyward from its center. The water elegantly fell to the basin that surrounded the fountain, ripping outward to the concrete benches that enclosed it. A colorful array of petunias bordered the benches and numerous blacktopped pathways that interrupted the well-groomed lawns.

"There they are. Over there," Grace said as she pointed to the side of the fountain.

"Where? There are a lot of kids standing over there."

"The two guys standing together on the left side. I can feel my skin tingling already. Every time I'm around those two I can hardly control myself. I want to run up and kiss them all over."

"You better restrain yourself. At least until you've introduced me. Then you can start your kissing," Annie smiled and she winked at Grace.

"Hi, you guys," Grace yelled. "This is my cousin Annie from Wisconsin. I don't normally take to blood relatives, but she is A-OK." Grace smiled at Annie and shoved her toward Tony.

"How do you do," Tony said. "And this is my twin brother Danny. The blonde is Carol, next to her is Janet and then Katie, Russell and Ken is on the end."

"Hi, everybody. Thanks for letting me join the gang while I'm here. Turning toward Tony she said, "Tony, huh. Isn't that short for Anthony?"

Tony's black eyes set in his handsome tanned face, flashed. "Sure is," he said. His thick neck and muscular arms gave the impression he spent a good deal of time working out at a gym or at a job where he did a lot of heavy lifting.

"Thought so," Annie said, feeling herself flush as she stared at him. Grace was right about the effect this guy would have on her. He had a charisma about him that made him irresistible. Annie tried to attribute it to the warm balmy breeze that came off the lake, but as she stood next to him she felt an overwhelming desire to stay near him. Her heart began to beat wildly, sending her blood rushing through her veins.

Attempting to steady her emotions, Annie said, "I go to a convent school in Milwaukee named St. Anthony's. It's connected to St. Joseph's Seminary. That's why I was wondering. You sure have one heck of a tan, don't you? I could sit in the sun every day, all summer long, and I'd never get that dark."

"I wish I could take credit for it, but my parents have more to do with it than I do. They're Italian so I come by it naturally."

Before Annie could respond, Danny hollered, "Tony, let's get started with some games. It'll be dark soon and you know we have to be home by nine-thirty tonight."

"You're right! We better get started," Tony yelled to his brother. "Nice talking to you, Annie. Maybe we'll get to talk later. I'd like to know more about your school."

"Great!" Annie said, backing up to position herself for tag football.

The game proceeded with teenagers dashing and turning in rapid succession to avoid being tagged. In the midst of the confusion Annie jumped back when she saw that Tony was about to tag her. She stumbled and tripped over an exposed tree root. As she fell her head scraped against the bark of the tree.

"Oh! I'm sorry," Tony said with a tremor to his voice as he rushed to her side. "Are you OK?"

"I think so," she said, trying to sit up.

Putting her hand to her head, she asked, "I'm not bleeding, am I?"

"No. But then I can't see very well in this light. Let's go over by the fountain for a couple of minutes so I can take a good look and you can catch your breath," as he helped her up. "I could use a break anyway. It's been a long day. My dad is landscaping the backyard and I got to haul all the dirt for him today. I couldn't believe my eyes when this big truck drove up and dumped a ton of it on our driveway. And what did my dad do? He just grinned. I didn't mind so much because my parents have been very good to me. I wasn't always such a perfect little angel. They keep telling me I owe them big time because I used to be such a little hellion. Now let me take a look at that. Looks like you got a nasty scrape, but the skin is not cut."

"Thanks. I'll be OK."

"You sure? I can have Grace call her dad. He'll come and get you."

"There's no way that I'm going to spoil everyone's fun over a little bump. That's interesting," Annie said.

"What?"

"You being a hellion. I'm sure my parents could come up with a funkier name than that for me. Come to think of it, my dad has. I have the worst nickname in the whole world. Don't look at me like that. I'm not telling."

"Come on now. It can't be that bad," Tony chuckled.

Laughing, Annie said, "A herd of turtles couldn't drag it out of me. Of course, my father thinks it fits me just fine." Looking into Tony's warm smiling eyes she stuck her face right up to his and said, "You can plead all you want, but I'll never divulge my secret until the day I die. It's too embarrassing."

"Hey, you two. Who gave you permission to sit around and loaf? Come on—get with it!" Danny hollered.

"Don't get excited. Annie fell and hit her head. She's OK, but she just needs to rest a bit," Tony retorted.

"Hey Grace! Do you know what Annie's nickname is?"

"Sorry. Don't know."

"So neither of you are talking, huh," Tony said.

"This one's on you because she honestly doesn't know."

"Ok, I'll believe you this time. As long as we're sitting here, why don't you tell me about St. Anthony's?"

"Not much to tell as far as I'm concerned. It's a prison. It's a place for parents to send their kids to be tortured. I will say the grounds are beautiful, especially over by St. Joseph's. But that doesn't make up for the rest of it, like the ugly sack uniforms we have to wear, not to mention the bars on all the windows."

"Bars! Are you serious?"

"You bet I am."

"Do you think they are trying to protect you from outside hoodlums and such?"

"Not a chance. My friends and me have it pretty well figured out. It's us that they are trying to keep in. They have guard nuns all over the place. We have to walk single file through the hallways to class and the word for the day is silence. I should say for every day."

"That's pretty rough," Tony said. "I don't know if Grace told you or not, but ever since I've been a little kid, I've wanted to be a priest. I wanted to go into the seminary right after grade school. My parents said I needed to be sure and that high school would help me make the decision. So here I am playing games with my classmates. How long will you be here, Annie?"

"Anywhere from two weeks to a month. I can stay with my grandparents as long as I want." Annie laughed. "They happen to be very partial toward me."

"Then maybe you can come again tomorrow and tell me more about your school and maybe something about St. Joseph's."

The next day Annie spent most of her time thinking about going down to the park with Grace. *This is crazy. This guy wants to be a priest and I'm falling big time for him. Looking for another broken heart to mend, huh? I sure am a glutton for punishment. I should probably just stay home and not see him again, but I want to so bad. He must feel something for me. It seems like he's always chasing me during the games and then somehow he shows up right next to me. Is this my imagination? I'll have to talk with Grace. I don't know what to do. I sure can't just walk up to him and ask him what he thinks about me. I wonder what kind of a sin it would be if you lured a guy away from the priesthood. That's a can of worms I don't care to open. If there's going to be a pass made, he'll have to be the one to make it.*

The O'Reillys kept Annie busy during the day playing board games, going to movies and with a couple of trips to Riverview Amusement Park. After supper her grandpa would take her over to Grace's; the girls would take the streetcar downtown and Mr. Schaefer would bring Annie home. The weeks passed too fast and the time had come for Annie to head home.

During her last night at the park with the gang, Annie decided she would rather sit on the sidelines than participate in the games. She couldn't bear chasing Tony any longer. He was a guy whom she could never catch. After watching for about a half an hour, she began to walk towards the lake. It was a beautiful evening. The sun had just begun to display an array of colors as it slowly sank below the horizon. Several yachts were coming into the harbor under full sail while other sailors were lowering their sails and anchoring their ships in rhythm with the lapping motion of the sea. She breathed in deeply and sighed. The smell of algae and fresh water filled Annie's lungs.

"Where are you going?" Tony shouted after her. "Don't you want to play kick-the-can? We'll be starting as soon as the sun goes down."

"No, I think I'll go for a walk. It's a beautiful night and I'd like to be down by the water where it's still."

"Would you like some company? It sounds like a capital idea to me. That's if you don't mind?"

Containing her desire to be with him, she asked. "Won't the others miss you?"

"Nah. They'll think I hid so well that they couldn't find me. It'll keep them busy for awhile."

"Now I see why your parents think you're a hellion," Annie laughed. "Ok then. It would be nice to have some company. I love the water. Listening to it lap against the shoreline makes me feel wonderful inside. It's almost like a love song."

"Oh, so you're a romantic are you."

"Afraid so,"

Walking north, the shoreline melted into a seawall that disappeared in the distance as it bordered the lake. Wooden benches lined the walkway that was lit by the pale-yellow streetlights. Young lovers sat snuggled in each other's arms, never noticing the passing onlookers. Annie walked along in silence, listening to Tony talk about his dream.

"This St. Joseph's you were telling me about sounds like it might be a possibility for me. I think I'll check into it and see what the criteria is for getting accepted there. It would be sort of funny if we'd end up neighbors, wouldn't it?"

"I suppose," she said. "But I doubt if we'd ever see each other. They keep those guys locked up far away from us. Our principal, Sister Florentine, did say that once in a while the seminarians come over to do a Christmas concert for us. That's as close as we'd ever come to seeing one another. You'll have to let me know what you find out."

They had walked for some distance before Annie saw an open bench and decided to sit down.

"I'd like to rest for a moment," she said. "We've come a lot further then I realized."

"I've come a lot further then I ever thought I would, Annie," he said as he sat down next to her. "I've never met anyone like you. You can slide into home plate, tackle a guy, and the next minute, you're the most delicate creature in the whole world."

Surprised by his words, Annie turned toward him in amazement. Not sure what to say, she kept silent. Tony gently reached down and took her hand. She felt the tenderness of his fingers caressing hers. They fit so comfortably in his like they belonged there forever. He looked up into her eyes, moving her hand close to his heart.

"You know, you are quite a beautiful young woman, Annie. And I've been having a hard time getting you out of my mind. I didn't know that God was going to send me a left curve in the name of an Annie to test my desire for the priesthood. But I guess He did, because here you are."

His words swept through her in joyous waves, leaving behind a feeling of ecstasy. Trembling from his touch, Annie didn't know how much more she could listen to without throwing herself into his arms. Realizing this, she had to leave before she made a fool of herself.

Standing up quickly, she said, "I'm sorry, Tony. Have I done something to distract you from your dream? I didn't mean to."

"No, Annie," Tony whispered as he shook his head. "You haven't done anything wrong. Please stay with me," he begged. "I have to talk to you. I have to let you know what is in my heart."

Not wanting to resist his plea, she sat down and avoided looking into his eyes, knowing that hers would reveal the desire that burned inside of her.

"You're trembling," he said as he took his sweater and put it around her shoulders. "Let me hold you for a moment until you get warm."

Annie allowed Tony's arms to caress her, relishing every moment of his warmth and tenderness. They sat in silence, watching the lighthouse flash its warning upon the sea.

Overhead the northern lights displayed a spectacular blend of lavender as they swayed gently back and forth with the movement of the wind.

"Do you mind if I kiss you?" he asked. "I'd hate to think I didn't give life a fair shake before I made a decision."

Stuttering, Annie whispered, "Yes! I mean no. It's all right. That's if you want to, I mean."

Tony leaned forward and touched his lips softly against Annie's for just a moment. She sat motionless with her eyes closed, allowing him to kiss her again and again. Her deep yearnings mingled with his closeness made her aware of a wanting she had never known before. An hour had passed while they sat together, imitating the other lovers.

Taking a deep breath and sighing, Tony said, "Your touch has filled me with things I don't understand. I have always been so sure of myself. And now there's this uncertainty floating around inside my head like a dense fog. You've given me more to think about than I ever thought possible. I don't want you to go home, Annie."

If only he would have offered a clue to what was going on with him so we could've spent more time together.

Gradually, Tony began to stand up. As he did he took Annie's hand in his, saying, "Even though I never want this moment to end, we'd better be getting back. We've been gone so long even Danny will know something is wrong, and I surely don't want anyone to think you shanghaied me."

"Yes . . . of course," Annie whispered. "It is getting late. We'd better get back."

They strolled back toward the fountain, passing the same lovers as before. Waves lapped against the concrete seawall, at times overflowing onto the walkway. Annie slipped her shoes off so she could feel the coolness of the water. She hoped it would soothe her passion and slow her pounding heart.

Tony continued to hold her hand as he watched her splash in the cool fresh water, saying, "Oh Annie, Annie. What am I going to do about you? You've waltzed into my life and filled it with joy and excitement. Now you are going to disappear and I may never see you again. My heart aches from the thought of it."

"I know, Tony. I've felt the same since the first night I met you. I didn't want to do anything to interfere with your dream. I just couldn't. Now I feel like there is a hole in my heart that's so big that it can never be filled. I'm sorry. I shouldn't be talking like this. It's wrong for me to even hope things could be different."

"No it's not, Annie. I feel the same way. I just don't know what to do about it. I'm so confused."

"Maybe you'll go to St. Joseph's and we can be neighbors, like you said."

"Maybe," Tony said, looking down at her hand .

"Besides, there's always next summer. You know I'll be back then and maybe even over the holidays. I'll be in contact with Grace. She'll be glad to send a message to me about what is happening with you. Of course, a letter from you would be much better."

"The priest that is helping me get ready for the priesthood frowns on any contact with the opposite sex. I can't imagine what he would say if he knew that I kissed you tonight."

"Nobody ever has to know, Tony. It will be our secret—forever."

"I have no doubt that you will keep that promise, Annie." Standing back from her and holding both of her hands, Tony looked into her eyes and said, "Annie . . . I want you to know. No matter what I decide, I'll always remember the beautiful young woman I kissed and held tight as we sat by the waterfront one warm summer night."

Chapter Eleven

"All aboard," the conductor hollered as he looked up and down the platform.

Annie and her grandparents walked toward the train. A gnawing feeling filled Annie's stomach as she forced herself to be pleasant. Turning toward them to say goodbye, she shaded her eyes from the glare of the sun with her hand, and asked, "Will you be up for Thanksgiving and Christmas again this year?"

"I'm not sure, honey. Maybe your folks can come down here," Grandpa said.

A ray of hope flickered through Annie. Perhaps she would get to see Tony at Christmas time. She'd have to let Grace know.

"It's getting more and more difficult for us to travel the distance," Grandma said. "So we'll just have to see. I'm sure we'll see you one way or the other. We're sure going to miss you."

"We sure are going to miss you, sweetheart," Grandpa said as he kissed her on the cheek. Grandma hugged Annie, as she smiled through the tears that ran down her cheeks, "Now get yourself up on that train so you get a good seat. You don't need to be standing all the way to Milwaukee on that shaky old thing."

Not wanting to, Annie walked away from them. As she began boarding the train, she waved, hollering over the roar of the steam engine.

"Goodbye! I love you both."

Standing in front of her bedroom mirror brushing her hair, Annie ventured into her own dream-land and stopped listening to her mother chant a list of messages she had received while she was in Chicago. Every stroke of the brush melted the strands of her long, sun-bleached hair into a flowing river of brilliance. As she looked at her reflection, she realized she had grown at least an inch over the last month. Her breasts were swelling out of her bra, and her buttocks didn't seem quite so round. Luke would be sure to tell her if she was wrong.

Annie never thought of herself as beautiful, except for her hands, of course. During Mass she'd place them on the back of the pew in front of her and admire the creamy smoothness of the skin and their delicate shape. The nuns would heartlessly jab anyone who didn't have her eyes on the priest at all times. So she'd steal glimpses of them without moving her head. Tony thought she was beautiful, all of her. Goose bumps tingled down her body, causing the hair on her legs and arms to stand up. As she reminisced about what he had said, a smile began to cross her face.

"Annie!" her mother said, raising her voice. "Are you listening to me?"

"Yes, Mother," she answered, annoyed that her thoughts had been interrupted.

"You'd better be. I've got more to do than to be your messenger."

"Of course," Annie replied.

"Jerry kept calling and calling this last week to see if you had gotten home yet. I'm beginning to think he is nothing more than a simpleton. He can't seem to understand an uncomplicated statement. Really, Annie, I wish you'd find someone else to go with."

Pulling her hair back into a ponytail, Annie glanced at her mother's reflection in the mirror, contemplating her reply. "It's not that easy, Mom. The girls at the high school already have their claws into all the guys. I'm lucky that Jerry still wants to hang around with me. It's the middle of July so you won't have to put up with him much longer because I'll be gone soon."

"Did you ever stop to consider that if you weren't hanging around with Jerry one of the other nice young men might step up?"

"Guys want girls they can be with, not someone who's gone all the time. Jerry's not my first choice, but he's all I have around here. At times he can be a lot of fun, except when he keeps combing his hair into a greasy ducktail and bragging about his body. That can get pretty sickening."

Luke called upstairs, "Do I have to pick the berries again, Mom? It's Annie's job and I've got other things to do."

"Oh! For crying out loud, Luke!" Annie snapped. "I'll pick the damn berries."

"Annie! Watch your mouth!" her mother chided. "I see being away hasn't done a thing for your vulgar language, now has it?"

"Guess not."

"Oh!" Her mother huffed as she stomped out of the room. "If this is how you're going to act when you come home, I assure you there won't be any more trips to Chicago. We'll see what your father has to say about this."

During the remaining month and a half of the summer Annie made it a point to steer clear of her mother, hoping she'd cool off from their heated encounter.

The summer seemed warmer than usual. To compensate, Annie got up early and rode her bike to the City Park so she could play some tennis before the heat of the day.

After she had avoided the spiders in the berry patch, she headed to the park with her racquet in hopes of finding a worthy opponent. The courts were full when she arrived, so she went to a practice court to warm up.

Hitting the ball with all her might seemed to help relieve the pining she had for Tony.

"You've got quite a swing there," a male voice said from behind her.

Startled, Annie jumped.

"I'm sorry if I scared you. I didn't mean to."

"Guess I was thinking about something else and I didn't hear you come up behind me."

"My name is Paul . . . Paul Mason," he said as he extended his hand to greet Annie. A slender six-foot eighteen-year old with broad shoulders stood before her. Sandy curls fell down on his damp forehead as he looked at her through his horn-rimmed glasses.

"I'm always looking for someone to play in the morning, and you look like you might be a challenge."

"You're on!" Annie commented as she returned his handshake with a firm grip.

Evenly matched, they agreed to meet every morning and squeeze in as many sets as they could before Paul had to leave for work. Paul never mentioned anything other than tennis. She only wanted a staunch competitor, and it appeared that arrangement accommodated Paul as well.

Jerry, on the other hand, had taken a powder as soon as Annie started to play tennis. Tennis had few benefits for him when he could use the time trying to impress the girls.

Not knowing Annie's relationship with Paul was strictly platonic, her mother couldn't contain her delight. Jerry had dropped out of the picture and she hoped he'd stay out. However, she wasn't too happy about Annie being involved with an older man.

The summer days passed quickly. Labor Day weekend arrived. Paul went back to college, and Annie's sophomore year had begun. There hadn't been any news from Grace even though Annie had written a couple of letters.

Annie threw her uniform into her suitcase and slammed it shut, muttering under her breath. “Guess that puts an end to any fun for awhile. At least I got some tennis in before I got sent back to jail.”

On the way back to St. Anthony’s that September afternoon, her mood saddened like the vast gray clouds that swept across the southern sky, threatening a much-needed rain. The heat of the summer had left the grassy areas brown and scraggly, like the head of an old, balding man.

Soon the march would be on for another year: down the hallway to the school, up the stairs in single file, down for lunch in silence, back and forth until classes ended. Silence, silence, silence! Without Lucie’s sense of humor, the everyday drudgery would drain the energy out of Annie.

As hard as Jeannie and Susan tried, they couldn’t shake Annie out of her mood. The only ray of hope Annie had would be her daily trip to the mailroom. A letter from Grace might snap her out of it.

Patiently, she’d wait for the mail-nun to sort the mail. Without looking at Annie the nun would shake her head no. Time after time Annie would stomp out of the mailroom.

“Control yourself, young lady,” Sister Rejeta said one afternoon and continued with her chore. “It’s not anybody else’s fault that you’re not getting any mail. Maybe if you had a better disposition, your luck would change.”

The smell of winter hung in the air as the maintenance man raked the last remnants of leaves that were scattered across the courtyard. Already the middle of November, the thought of winter coming too early ran a chill through Annie's bones.

Annie had given up on ever hearing from Grace. Donning her warmest jacket, hat and mittens, she walked along the black wrought iron fence that divided St. Anthony's from St. Joseph's. Abandoned leaves lay half-frozen in small puddles of ice and twigs snapped easily under foot. Perhaps a seminarian would pass by and she could ask about Tony. Sometimes she'd stand peering at the distant buildings with her hands grasping the cold metal bars until they were numb. But no one could ever be seen anywhere on the premises, not a soul. They were all locked up. Forever.

Returning to her locker, she hung up her things. Out of habit she meandered to the mailroom. Sister Edward was sorting the mail, studying each envelope as though it hid the secret to the atomic bomb.

Without a word, Sister aimed a letter in Annie's direction. "Here! This one's for you."

Surprised, Annie stood motionless with her mouth open.

"Do you want it or not?" Sister Edward chided.

"Yes, Sister. Of course."

Annie glanced at the return address to see whom the letter was from. Grace Schaefer was in bold print in the corner of the perfume laden envelope. Annie ran toward the dorm, ripping open the envelope on her way.

> "Dear Annie,
>
> Sorry I haven't written for a while. The days just seemed to fly by. After you left I did everything I could to get Danny's attention, short of jumping on him, but it didn't work. I got pretty sick of that scene so I set my sights on another guy. He isn't as cute as Danny, but at

least he knows I'm alive. His name is Pete and he has the cutest smile. I haven't heard from either of the twins for some time. I don't think there's much hope of snagging one of them now that they are both under the dictatorship of the Catholic Church. Unfortunately, I think we are both history. I guess we should've known better, but I'd do it again if I had the chance.

I was excited to hear that you might be coming down for Christmas. "South Pacific" is going to be in town around that time with some big Broadway stars. I think Mitzy Gaynor and Rosanno Brazzi are the two lead's names. The tickets will more than likely be very expensive, but maybe I can have my mom see if she can get us in as ushers. Interested?

Your Friend Forever,
Grace"

Astounded by this news, Annie tossed the letter into her nightstand, sat down and covered her face with her hands.

Just remember! You brought this on yourself. You never should've gone back to that park. Someday maybe you'll learn to follow your gut feelings. Out of sight—out of mind, that's what Grandma always says. You must be forgettable as well. And there's nothing you can do about this whole mess. Unless Tony calls Grace there's no way to contact him.

Shattered and feeling she had no one to turn to, she picked up her pen and began to write a letter to Jerry.

Annie's mother had a hard time accepting Jerry back in the picture. Once again the phone rang and rang; she found herself making explanations and trying to be polite to the same young man she had hoped she'd never see again. She continued to beg Annie to stop going with a fellow who was from the "other side of the tracks." The more she insisted, the more she drove Annie toward the relationship, if for no other reason than to spite her mother.

Christmas in Chicago had been scheduled, giving Annie the opportunity to usher with Grace for "South Pacific" on the Sunday after Christmas. The old theater smelled of stale soda pop and dirty mop water. There were three tiered balconies filled with antiquated seats wrapped across the back of the theater. The stage donned a curtain that displayed knights on great white stallions, fighting dragons that immersed them in fiery red and yellow flames. On either side of the room, chrome railings etched the front of the box seats with red velvet curtains pulled into swags as backdrops. In these stood four matching red-velvet tufted chairs that waited for their patrons arrival.

As soon as the doors opened, people began to flood the theater. The ladies adorned in long gowns with sable furs around their shoulders; gentlemen in tuxedos accompanied them. It was difficult for Annie to keep up with the demand, as she walked people to their seats and quickly went back to accommodate others. Looking into the crowd, her chest tightened and she felt a lump in her throat. She thought she saw Tony. She began to wave to get his attention. The man turned and looked at her. Realizing it wasn't Tony, she turned to avoid further embarrassment. Grace had warned her, she needed to forget about Tony. He'd never show up in this type of environment anyway.

As the play went forward, Annie became engrossed in the music and the romance of it. Brazzi's mellow voice captivated the audience with the melodious sounds of "Some Enchanted Evening."

Fantasizing, Annie saw herself on stage. Tony had been searching for her. She called to him. His warm dark eyes engaged hers. Suddenly she fell into his arms and he kissed her soft with passion. The crowd cheered as their hearts met.

Awakened from her blissful state, her mood changed to despair when she realized the audience was giving the performers a standing ovation. Tears poured down her cheeks. She picked up her flashlight and walked toward the back of the theater. Mr. Schaefer would be there soon to pick them up. She'd have to get her coat.

Annie dated Jerry off and on over the next months even though he relished telling her tales about all the girls from other towns that he had dated. Sometimes he'd tell tales about a bunch of guys going to Port Washington to pick up girls. They'd get drunk and sneak into the drive-in theater with four or five kids packed into the trunk. Or they'd go on a farmer's dirt road that ran through the woods like a roller coaster at sixty miles an hour. He'd brag about how they'd pack as many bodies as they could into some beat up old Chevy, even though they thought that one good bump would finish it. Everyone would bounce up and down against each other, screaming and trying not to fly out of an open window. Annie could only assume he told these tales to make her jealous, or if he could be just plain crazy. Whichever it was, the tales were much more intriguing than his far-fetched tales about his love life.

Chapter Twelve

Labor Day weekend, September of 1950, announced the beginning of Annie's junior year, to her dismay. Nothing had changed. The nun-guards paced the hallways day and night, enforcing the rules. The creaking gates still sounded like "Inner Sanctum" when they swung open, and the old building looked just as foreboding.

Annie had never stopped hounding her parents, trying to get them to put her in a different school. It not only didn't work—it backfired. They told her if she didn't drop the subject she would find herself in a school in Minnesota, and she'd only be coming home for the holidays.

Facing the same boring routine as previous years, Annie stood with her friends, waiting for Sister Margaret to make her usual appearance as the moderator for the year.

"The only good thing about this is that we are closer to the front of the line," Jeannie said. "Do you ever wonder how much you might be changing just by being here? You know, are we starting to be like them?"

"Not me," Annie said. "They're never going to be able to claim they "finished" me. Somehow I'll get out of here. I don't know how, but I will."

"You're not going to run away, are you?" Susan asked.

"If you are, let me know and I'll go with you," Jeannie said. "I'm so tired of this routine."

"I don't know yet."

The sound of heavy footsteps coming from behind the hallway door drew everyone's attention. They knew it couldn't be Sister Mary Margaret. Their attention captured, they watched the door. The knob turned; the door flung open.

A shocked moan spread through the group as Sister Mary Claudia's obese body waddled down the hallway. Her angry bulldog face protruded from her habit as she began to speak.

"I can tell by the noise that all of you made, you are more than a little disappointed it's not Sister Mary Margaret who came through that door," she said. "Well, get over it. You've had it pretty easy the last two years. You got away with murder as far as I'm concerned. I can assure you, it won't be so easy from here on in. Now start marching and keep your lines straight and your mouths still."

The only sound heard as the young women began parading down the stairs two by two was the shuffle of their feet. Sister Claudia's reputation rung clear by her consistent nasty attitude in the classroom. She wouldn't think twice about knocking a student out of her seat if she gave a wrong answer or if she hadn't completed her assignment to her satisfaction. Everybody knew that staying out of this nun's way would be the smart thing to do. Annie had been lucky enough not to have her as a teacher. Now it appeared her luck had run out.

The trees had already lost their leaves by November and stood stark against the impending winter evening. Annie had gone out on the fourth floor balcony to see if there were enough empty clotheslines for her to air her bedding. The balcony ran the length of the dorm side of the old building, some fifty feet or so, with a rusty iron fire escape at the far end. There were eight clotheslines hooked to the paint-chipped iron crossbars at either end of it: three for the students' use and five for the nuns. It had taken Annie three days to get permission to go out to air her bedding, so she felt justified in taking her time with her chore. Leaning over the foot thick concrete banister, she imagined an escape. She could barely see the bottom of the fire escape. It looked like it ended about ten feet above the ground. Between the descending stairs there was a flat iron platform attached to the sides of the two balconies below. As she stood huddled next to the edge, a clicking sound came from behind her. Annie turned toward the door and saw the shadow of a nun through the thick plate glass, walking away. Annie ran to the door.

She had been locked out.

She began pounding on the door and yelling in hopes that someone would hear her. But no one answered.

The sun had begun to set and a cool breeze filled the air. She clasped her arms around her midriff as she shivered, trying to decide what to do. Annie hadn't worn a sweater or a jacket as she had only planned to be outside long enough to see how many lines were available.

With no help around, the logical solution was to go down the fire escape. As she stepped onto the rusty metal, a wave of fear sent a hot flash through her body. She felt sifted through the iron bars all the way to the ground. Everything began to spin. She retreated to the safety of the balcony, lightheaded and panic-stricken.

She ran back to the door and pounded as hard as she could. Some students heard her cries and called out that they would go for help.

A half an hour passed before Annie heard Sister Margaret's voice on the other side of the locked door.

"Annie!" Sister shouted. "We haven't been able to find Sister Mary Claudia, and she's the only one who has a key to the door. Everyone is looking for her. I'm sure we will find her soon. Whatever you do, Annie, don't try to go down the fire escape. It's old and it can't be trusted. Try to wrap yourself in whatever you can find to keep warm."

"There's nothing out here, Sister. What about the dorm windows? Don't they open?"

"They've been painted shut for fifty years to keep intruders out. And we can't break one either because they have steel mesh in them. You've got to keep warm, Annie, while we look for Sister Claudia."

"I've been trying, Sister. I've been jumping up and down and running back and forth. I don't know how long I can keep this up. Why did Sister Claudia lock me out? She knew I was out here. I had just gotten permission from her."

"She probably forgot, Annie. I'm sure we'll find her soon. Try to stay out of the wind. Sit down in a corner and pull your uniform around you as a shield if you can. I'll stay right here until we find her. I won't leave you alone, Annie."

The only available corner was directly in line with the freezing temperatures coming off the lake. The opening by the fire escape provided a perfect funnel for the wind to swirl cold blasts against the balcony walls. Annie chose a corner close to the fire escape as it blocked some of the harshness, even though it was the furthest from Sister Margaret.

Sister Claudia is sure an ornery cuss. She must be one of those nuns who were shanghaied into joining the convent. I wish she'd find someone else to pick on. I'm sick of her. How could someone who has supposedly given her life to God lock me out on this balcony in freezing weather? Sister Margaret can talk until the cows come home about how Sister Claudia forgot, but I know better. She's hounded me ever since she was sprayed with the pop. She wants war? Well, war I'll give her. I wonder how my parents will feel if I die out here. It would serve them right if they had to live with that.

Even though Annie forced herself to keep moving, it became more difficult for her to stay awake with each passing moment. As temperatures dropped every bit of warmth seeped out of her body.

About the time she didn't think she could last another second, she heard a click from the door. Looking up, she saw Sister Margaret running toward her, holding a blanket that was billowing like a cape. Susan and Jeannie were right behind her.

"Annie! We're coming. Hang in there," Jeannie shouted.

Sister threw the blanket over Annie as she tried to help her to her feet, "Come on, Annie. You have to stand up so we can get you inside."

Stiffness wrenched at Annie's muscles, refusing to relinquish its frozen grip.

"Don't give up on me now," Jeannie begged. "You've got to get up."

"Let's huddle around her for a moment to try and get her warm enough so we can move her," Sister Margaret said to the two girls.

"I found her, Annie," Jeannie grumbled as she put her arms around Annie. "She wouldn't even come up to see how you are. And she threw the key at me and said you had no business being out on the balcony that long. She's such a piece of work, you know."

"That's enough, Jeannie. You don't know what happened so let's not be too hasty with our judgments. Anyone can make a mistake," Sister Margaret said.

"Sorry, Sister. You don't make this kind of a mistake except on purpose. Believe me, this was no mistake," Jeannie snarled.

"Yeah! You're not kidding," Susan grumbled.

"I said that's enough, you two," Sister said. "OK, Annie. Let's get you inside where it's warm."

Sister Margaret and Jeannie supported Annie as they walked toward the door. Susan ran ahead to open it. When the students heard the commotion they gathered around Annie's open cell to see how she was.

"Wow! You must be frozen to death," Cecilia said wide-eyed. "How long did she have you locked out there?"

"I'll tell you about it later," Jeannie said. "Right now we have to thaw her out."

Sister Margaret had had Susan and Helen place several hot water bottles in Annie's bed so it would be warm. Removing the bottles, Sister helped Annie lie down, covering her with several blankets. As her skin touched the sheets, a surge of shivers ran over Annie's body like waves on top of the sea. She grasped the heavy wool blanket, trying to hold it snug against herself.

"You two stay with Annie while I get some hot soup," Sister Margaret said as she rushed off.

"Don't worry, Sister," Jeannie shouted. "We aren't going anywhere. How are you doing, Annie?"

Annie chattered through her teeth, "I'm damn mad! That's how I'm doing. That nun locked me out on purpose."

"You better believe it," Susan snarled. "That nun is going to fry in hell someday. I don't know what we can do about it. You know these nuns stick together like glue. Maybe we can go to Sister Mary Florentine and tell her what happened."

"I don't think that would help," Helen said. "Everybody seems to have blinders on when it comes to Claudia—no matter what she does."

"It's because they're all scared of her," Cecilia said. "Who wouldn't be with the stuff she pulls."

"I've caused a lot of trouble around here. So who do you think Sister Florentine will believe, me or Sister Claudia?" Annie whispered.

"Guess you're right, but that's not a reason to kill a person. We can't let her get away with it either." Jeanne hit the mattress hard with her fist.

"Don't worry, Jeanne, we'll think of something, something that'll scare the skin right off of her."

Susan looked into the solemn faces of the crowd around Annie's bed, saying, "Sounds good to me."

The group nodded in agreement.

It was Thursday afternoon two weeks after Annie had been locked out on the balcony. Still burning with fever and coughing incessantly, she was cared for by Sister Margaret and Sister Eunice in a cell at the back of the dorm. When Annie didn't get better, Sister Margaret told her she had to call her father and tell him she shouldn't go home for the Thanksgiving weekend because she was too ill.

"Please don't do that, Sister. I'll be OK, I promise. I've just got to get up and move around. That's what the problem is. I've been lying around too much. Just give me a chance. I really want to go home."

"Just listen to yourself. You can't even talk without coughing. Nobody in her right mind would try to get out of that bed. This time you will listen to me, Annie O'Brien. I'm not going to have you go and die on me."

At the beginning of the week, pale and weak, Annie decided to go back to class. She didn't want to be stuck at school over the holiday weekend. Her dad was scheduled to pick her up on Wednesday afternoon around four o'clock. With everyone at home, it was the perfect time for Annie to act out her distressing tale. She was bound to get some sympathy from someone, especially when they found out that she almost died.

Still pretty shaky, Annie decided to remain as calm as possible on the way home to reserve her strength. The temperature had climbed overnight, causing the last snowfall to melt and run rampantly into the storm sewers. Slush separated and slapped against the bottom of the car as her dad drove toward home.

"You look a little green around the gills," her dad said after they got into the car. "Are you OK?"

"I'm fine now that I'm going home."

A half an hour had passed before her dad spoke again. "You're awfully quiet and that's not like you. Are you sure you are OK?"

"I just don't feel like talking. Besides, I don't think anyone in the family cares what I have to say anyway."

"That's not fair, Annie. Your mother and I have made a lot of sacrifices to send you to St. Anthony's and all you do is gripe about it."

"Maybe I have plenty of reasons to gripe. Did you ever think of that?"

"You don't know how lucky you are, young lady. Maybe someday with the grace of God, you will."

Rain spattered against the dining room windows. A whistling sound synchronized with it as high winds forced their way around the storm windows. The soft orange flame on the tall slender candles flickered from the draft and the bustle of the Thanksgiving celebration. The family was in a jovial mood as Annie's mother served the dessert. Annie's parents were seated at opposite ends of the large linen covered walnut table adorned with Grandma O'Reilly's golden-edged, bone china, lead crystal, and ornate sterling silver. Chuck, Annie's oldest brother, sat next to his grandparents, across from Annie. Jane sat on his right side while Mark, Luke and John sat opposite them. Annie's place on holidays was at the end of the table, next to her mother, and close to the kitchen doorway.

It's time to lay the facts on the table. Here goes everything.

She felt adrenaline rush through her body as she began speaking with an air of sarcasm.

"Would anyone like to know why I haven't been home for awhile?"

Chuck pushed his coal black hair to the side and laughed. "We all thought you loved that place so much you didn't want to leave."

"It's just that kind of an attitude that almost got me killed!"

"Oh come on now," Chuck laughed, looking around the table at his siblings' grins.

Annie yelled louder over his put-down. "I'm sick and tired of moldy bread! Rotten liver! Rancid butter! And sour milk! None of your other precious children have to eat what I'm expected to eat. You think just because you're spending a lot of money, everything they do is right. I've talked and talked about the conditions at that school, and you haven't even bothered to check them out. So you don't care about what I have to say as long as I keep my mouth shut and do as I'm told. The rest doesn't matter, does it? You don't even care if I live or die."

Annie moved away from the table, spilling her milk and shoving her chair so hard it tumbled backwards, barely missing the walnut buffet. Running through the kitchen toward the upstairs, she dodged her father as he attempted to grab her.

Reaching the bottom of the stairs, Annie turned to see her Mother start to clear the table, her hands shaking so badly, she could hardly hold on to the dishes. Seeing that no one followed her, Annie stood with her back against the hallway wall to catch her breath and to eavesdrop on their conversation.

"Jane," her mother said. "Please take these things to the kitchen. I'll be right there."

"Yes, ma'am. It's too bad Annie has to act like this, especially on Thanksgiving. Sometimes I wonder if she'll ever grow up."

"I know, dear. I don't know what gets into that girl, Charles. We have to do something about these outbursts. It's gotten to be too much."

"Now, Mary, don't start to cry. I'll think of something."

"She's spoiled our whole Thanksgiving dinner," she sobbed.

"Mary," Grandpa O'Reilly said to his daughter, "Annie's in a delicate time of her life right now. And I'm sure she's having a hard time with that. When Mother and I go back to Chicago, we can stop in Milwaukee and have a look around. If you'd like us to, that is. Nuns can be pretty hard on these young girls. And they don't particularly like young women who are as headstrong as Annie is."

"Thank you for offering, Dad, but that shouldn't be necessary," Charles said.

"She's just being a brat. That's all," Chuck emphasized. "She thinks if she throws a big enough fit she'll get her way. You can't give in to her, Dad. Then you'll just have more problems."

Peeking around the doorway after hearing Chuck's comment, Annie saw her dad drop his weight into the solid walnut dining room chair, shaking his head slowly from side to side.

Jane blew out the candles and turned on the crystal chandelier as the rest of the family began to leave the dining room in silence. The sudden glare from the electric lights accented the blackness of the night as the rain continued to pound against the side of the house.

Annie ran upstairs to her room to avoid further confrontation.

Annie hadn't spoken to anyone over the holiday weekend. Wanting to be left alone, she decided she'd rather take the train back to Milwaukee than go back with her father. The trick was getting someone to take her to the station and not having another argument with her parents over it. On her way back from the store on Saturday afternoon she ran into Jerry. He might be able to take her to the depot the next morning. Patsy had gone to her grandparents for the weekend so Annie didn't have many options. Somewhat uneasy about sharing family secrets with Jerry, she decided to say very little until she felt confident he wouldn't blab everything all over town.

"Hi, Annie," came his cheerful greeting. "How was your Thanksgiving?"

"So-so! How about yours?"

"It could have been a lot better. At least nobody got killed."

"That doesn't sound good. Was there a fight or something?"

Looking down, Jerry kicked at the dirt with his hands in his pockets. "You know how families can be. Everybody thinks stuff has to be perfect because it's a holiday. Ha! Then they're surprised it doesn't work that way. One person has a drink to celebrate and the other one starts screaming. Things went to hell pretty fast after that."

"If it's any consolation, my Thanksgiving was the pits."

"What happened? Come on, you can tell me."

"I don't know, Jerry. I have to be very careful about what I say that's family business. If it gets out that I told anybody, I'd be campused for the rest of my life. Besides, you've been involved with so many other girls lately . . ."

"Oh that's nothing. Just having a little fun, but it was nothing serious. You know me, Annie. I'm not going to tell anyone. I've been wild about you since we've been in grade school. I care too much about you to try to get you into trouble. Besides, why would I do a thing like that?"

"I just have to be extra careful because of Jane. She loves to run straight to my mother with everything I say. I think she thrives on getting me in trouble, if you know what I mean."

"That's not going to happen," he said with a grin. "So . . . come on, tell me—what's going on?"

Dramatically acting out the whole sorry tale, Annie could tell by the concerned look on Jerry's face that he was going to be on her side.

"I thought when they found out I almost died that someone, besides my grandparents, would come to my aid. But no! All my parents were interested in was it was Thanksgiving and I should put on my best lady-like behavior. It was like the turkey was more important than I was. And Chuck! He was absolutely the worst. Don't you think?"

"For sure!"

"Can you believe he said I exaggerate everything? I was so upset I had to get out of there."

"I don't blame you," he sighed. "Brother! What a mess. You've got trouble at home and trouble at school. And I thought I had it bad. What are you going to do?"

"Right now, going back to school is the least of my problems. I can stay out of Claudia's way during school hours and stay in the conservatory after that. She's too lazy to come looking for me. She didn't get fat by chasing after people. My biggest problem is how to get back to school. I don't want to go back with my dad, but I don't have a way to get to the depot tomorrow either."

"What time does your train leave?"

"Around eleven, I think."

"That's not a problem. I can take you. I don't start to work at the theater until 1:00 o'clock and that gives me plenty of time."

"Are you sure? I would appreciate it if it's not too trouble."

"For you, Annie, there's no such thing as too much trouble."

After Annie finished packing, she gave her grandparents a hug and said goodbye. At the sound of Jerry's horn she grabbed her things, ran down the stairs, mumbling a goodbye as she went out the front door.

The train pulled into the station as Jerry and Annie stood in the noonday sun on the old wooden platform. Annie kept looking around to see if her father had followed them to the station.

"Are you going to be OK? It's been a horrible weekend for you."

"Yeah, I will."

"Don't ever hesitate to call me when you get in trouble. I would've picked you up or something. Maybe we could've gone to a movie."

"I'll be fine. It seems lately all I do is fight one battle after another."

"You don't have to worry about that with me. I'll always be there for you."

Seizing the moment, Jerry stepped close to Annie, slipped his hand under her coat and pulled her close to him. Before she could object, he kissed her. Caught off guard by the thrill that ran through her body, she didn't move. He kissed her again—longer and more passionately.

Weakness filled her legs as she stumbled backward when he released her. Staring into his hazel eyes, she said. "I'd—better go. The train is going to leave soon."

"Don't forget me now. I'll see you in a couple of weeks. I'll drop you a line. OK?"

"Sure, that's fine." Annie stammered.

Staring out of the dirt-filmed train window that was half covered by a worn tan shade, Annie pondered her reflection. The coach she rode in was sparsely occupied, by men reading their newspapers. Every so often, a passing train sped by going in the opposite direction, blurring its image. The railroad cars jerked back and forth above the rails in sync with her unsteady emotions. The kiss, still fresh on her lips, triggered thoughts of the future and what it would be like to be married. Tony would have made such a wonderful husband, thoughtful, loving and organized. Jerry she wasn't sure about. He was so footloose and fancy free, nonchalant, even irresponsible.

Life used to be much simpler when she was a child. A jumble of memories tumbled through her mind: the evenings playing hide and seek, horseback rides through the house on John's back, listening to Mark tell scary spook stories and playing with Chuck's lead soldiers when he wasn't looking. Soon her older brothers would be out on their own, and then Jane and Luke. It wouldn't be long before it would be Annie's turn. And the only thing she had been taught about being a woman was she'd get the curse once a month, whatever that meant.

My grandparents were the only ones who stuck up for me this weekend. They're probably the reason I didn't get grounded for six months. I must admit that I wouldn't have blamed my parents this time. I acted like such an ignoramus on Thanksgiving. Betsy will have a fit when I tell her what happened. She'd never talk to her parents like that. And I'll never know how I got away with it. I'd like to be sorry for what I did, but I'm not. I'm so angry that it's turning me into a monster.

Sister Mary Louise had entered Annie in numerous piano contests in the spring of her junior year, to position her for a music scholarship. Because of this Annie practiced five to six hours a day, working on proficiency and memorization. No matter how bored she was with scales and exercises, they were a part of her daily routine. Without them her dexterity would soon diminish and that would mean she would be clumsy on the keyboard when she tackled one of Chopin's or Mozart's works. This was the music she loved most, the music that brought her peace in times of trouble, the music that brought joy to her spirit. On occasion she would practice right through the supper hour without realizing it. One such evening she had hurried to the dining hall, only to find that the students were already clearing the tables. Rather than ask for something to eat and call attention to her tardiness, she chose to get some fruit out of her locker and go back to practicing.

It was almost seven thirty in the evening before Annie decided she was too tired to continue. A game of Ping-Pong with Jeannie or Helen would be refreshing. She headed to the recreation hall, arriving just in time to hear Jeannie yell "21," beating Helen at the game. Jeannie's outburst was easily magnified through the large partially empty room with its high ceilings. A group of students had gathered in front of the TV in the one corner, sitting guru style on the floor. Others wiggled around on either the overstuffed chairs or the sofas, causing the furniture to groan as it moved back and forth against the hardwood floor. Two Ping-Pong tables filled the center of the great hall, and a couple of wingback chairs stood next to the entrance in front of the bookcases that were jammed with musty, old books.

"My turn," Annie shouted.

"Well, I'll be darned. If it isn't the music buff gracing us with her presence," Helen said as she handed the paddle to Annie. "I bet you're pretty rusty at this. Are you sure you want to get beaten by this powerhouse?"

"Sure. I'm game for it. My butt is so flat from sitting on that piano bench that it could use a good workout. Ready, Jeannie?"

"Your loss will be my gain."

"We'll see about that," Annie said as she threw the ball to volley for the serve. "OK! Let the games begin."

They had each won a game and were in the middle of the third to determine the winner when Sister Claudia walked into the room. As her reputation preceded her, the students turned to see what she planned to do. Sister grabbed Annie's arm and yanked her to the side of the room, whispering, "Your grandfather just died."

Annie cried out as she stood wide-eyed and gasped, "No! It can't be," she screamed. "No!"

Slowly, Annie stumbled away from the nun after sister had delivered the blow, as though to try to escape the bitterness. Almost tripping over a chair Annie murmured, "He can't die. I love him so much." She choked out, "What will I ever do without him?" Her eyes filled with tears as she looked toward her friends. Helen and Jeannie ran toward Annie, but Sister Claudia stopped them before they reached her, ushering them, as well as the rest of the students, out of the hall.

"Just never mind what's going on here," Sister Claudia said. "You can all go up to the study hall and get busy with your homework. It's about time anyway."

Bent over and trembling, Annie wrapped her arms around her midriff and began to moan and cry out.

Not knowing what to do, her friends watched, torn between love and fear, as Annie stumbled over to an old wingback chair and curled up in it.

"It's about time you learned that life is about more than how much you can get away with," Sister Claudia sneered. "I'm sure the death of your grandfather will teach you that lesson."

Hitting the light switch, Sister walked out of the room, leaving Annie alone in the dark. Too shattered to fight back, she wept long into the night, swearing she'd get Sister Claudia no matter how long it took.

After the funeral, Grandma O'Reilly moved in with the O'Briens, as she didn't have enough funds to manage on her own. The warmer weather had already coaxed the crocuses and tulips and an array of daffodils into full bloom in the back gardens. And the spring rains were turning the lawns into blankets of soft green velvet. A month had passed before the O'Briens had finished sorting, packing, and moving things out of Grandma's apartment. Willing helpers carried box after box into the O'Brien home, tracking mud through the kitchen, the living room and up the stairs. Although Mrs. O'Brien was thankful for the help, she would be glad when the mess of the move was behind her.

With very little to do, Grandma spent most of her time talking about the past or sitting in her bedroom, pondering her memories. Sometimes Annie would find her grandmother in her bedroom, crying and holding something of Grandpa's close to her heart. Sister Claudia's cruelty had taught Annie about the pain of being alone, a pain Annie didn't want anyone to experience, especially her grandmother. So Annie invited her grandmother to share her room. Being together might help them both ease their sadness.

As Annie readied her room for her grandma, reminders of days past hung on the side-post of her dresser: ballet slippers that had long since been outgrown, a tan star-studded holster housing a metal cap gun used for chasing the masked bandits, and a black paper mask that hung by its rubber headband as the cutout eyes stared vacantly into the mirror. On the floor next to the dresser sat a small cradle with a handmade pillow and blanket that Chocolate, her most favorite teddy bear, used to sleep in when he wasn't with Annie. Other teddies and dolls dotted the room on shelves, and some sat stoically in front of her pillows. Annie gathered her possessions, placing them in a box to be taken to the attic. She rearranged her makeup tray, hairbrush and mirror to the side of the dresser. There would still be room for Chocolate on her bed, but the rest of the teddy bears would have to be put to sleep in a box. They comforted her as a child, but that was over. Now Annie needed to take the time to comfort her grandmother.

Since the loss of her grandfather, Annie hid her sorrow by dating as many different fellows as she could. Patsy said that only someone very fickle would do such a thing. Annie didn't care what anybody thought. She didn't listen either when Patsy told her that trouble dangled on the horizon, getting guys all worked up with her teasing and flippant attitude.

Jerry continued to flood Annie with notes and telephone messages, and Mrs. O'Brien became more and more agitated until she finally told him he was a pest.

"Really, Annie! This can't go on. Can't you find someone with a little more class to spend your time with? A young gentleman would know not to be pestering us all the time. I've told Jerry I would tell you he had called and that he should call around four-thirty in the afternoon. Then ten minutes later he calls again! Next time I won't be so nice. Perhaps I'll give him a lesson in manners."

"I'll tell him again tonight when I see him, Mother. He's just being friendly. That's more than I can say about some people I know," Annie mumbled under her breath.

"See to it that you do. I'm at my wit's end with the likes of him."

It was Friday evening, the second week of May, and the high school had readied itself for its final dance of the year. Annie's dad had dropped her off at the dance with the understanding that Jerry would bring her home on time.

"And no shenanigans," he warned. "Not if you both know what's good for you."

The gym gleamed from the highly polished floor and with fresh sawdust being spread by one of the students when Annie walked into the gym. Several guys were laughing and sliding across the floor, spreading the sawdust in all directions. Musicians for the ten-piece band were setting up their music stands on the front stage that had been decorated with balloons and tightly wound crepe paper. Seeing Annie, Jerry pranced toward her. A group of girls interrupted his jaunt to coax him into a non-musical dance.

It's hard to believe that all these girls mean nothing to him in spite of what he says. Looks to me like Jerry has become quite a Casanova. He sure loves the attention. I don't remember him being like this in grade school. He used to be quiet, almost shy. Maybe it's my imagination.

By ten o'clock that evening Annie was pretty bored with the dance and putting on her best airs. So when Jerry suggested leaving to get something to eat, she agreed.

Driving along a moon-lit country road toward Annie's home, Jerry turned onto a narrow winding dirt road.

Looking at him and then ahead at the road, Annie asked, "Where are you going?"

"Oh, I just thought we could take a side road and enjoy the evening for a little while longer."

As the old dark-blue Chevy continued down the road it swayed and moaned its disapproval with squeaks and rattles from the uneven rocky surface. Without a warning, Jerry pulled into a tree-lined field. The tall grass looked trampled and shiny in the moonlight, lying in different directions, like someone had had a gigantic party.

"Isn't this a beautiful spot," Jerry sighed. "Look! The moon is full and you know what they say about a full moon."

"No, I don't," Annie said, glaring at him. "Except that's when the werewolves come out."

"No. No." He chuckled. "A full moon is made for love. If you believe that nonsense you'd better come over here close to me so I can protect you," he said as he scooted across the tattered front seat, putting his arm around Annie's shoulder. Before Annie knew it, he had slid his hand inside her blouse and started to kiss her.

She tried to pull away, but he held her firmly and attempted another kiss.

Dreamily, Jerry said, "Come on, Annie. Don't be so stingy with your kisses. I just want to see what you're made of."

"Jerry! You've always got your hands all over me. Can't you control yourself?" she shouted and struggled to get his hand out of her blouse.

"What's the matter, haven't you ever had a feel before? You don't need to be shy with me. I've got experience. I can teach you what you need to know. Trust me!"

Continuing to push him away, her anger lit. "Control yourself! Please!"

"What's to control with a beautiful girl sitting at my side," he said as he snuggled closer and whispered in her ear. "I'd like to crawl right inside of you where I'd be nice and warm and . . ."

"Stop that kind of talk right now, Jerry! If my parents heard you talking like that you'd be in big trouble. My mother is already upset because you keep calling all the time. So cool it, will you! I want to go home."

"Come on. Just one more kiss. You're going to love it and beg for more."

"No," she shouted. "Aren't you listening to me?"

"Sure," he whispered.

Realizing she wasn't getting through to him, she tried a different approach. Twirling his tie around her finger and with her face close to his, she quietly said, "You know, it's getting late, and you wouldn't want to get me home after hours. If you do—my dad won't let me see you again."

Jerry pulled back and sat up straight. "OK. But before we go how about just a few little nuzzles. I promise that's all I'll do."

"If you promise."

Annie had decided to start packing some of her things a couple of weeks before summer vacation began. The one dorm window she managed to get open a few inches was providing a warm breeze to the stuffy room. As Annie folded her extra uniform, the thought of Jerry's lingering kiss sent a warm glow through her. A smile crossed her lips and her face flushed. She had felt this way with Tony, but never with Michael. Then Michael never kissed her, so she didn't know how she'd feel. Jerry's kiss was soft but firm, demanding yet tender. In a dream-like state she folded things over and over again, unaware of what she was doing.

Imagining what it would be like to have Jerry kiss her again, she slouched down on the narrow cot. *It's a good thing these nuns can't read my mind. I'd be campused forever.*

"Packing already?" Jeannie asked as she walked into the dorm. "Not that you're anxious to get out of here at the bong of the bell. So what's up?"

"Oh, just thinking about what happened after the dance the other night."

"What's that? But before you tell me," Jeannie whispered as she looked around the room and bit into her apple, "Is Sister in her cell?"

Annie shook her head no, "I'd never be talking about this if she was."

"Go on! Go on!"

"Jerry had taken a back road home and decided to park. All of a sudden I had him in my lap, and even though I pushed him away, it felt so good I didn't want him to stop."

"Whoa! Are we talking about the same thing?"

"He was kissing me, that's all," Annie said and turned her face so Jeannie couldn't see her blush.

"Kissing, my eye. What else was he doing? And don't try to detour me either. I've been around the block myself, kid," Jeannie said.

"This is embarrassing."

"Hey! It's me—Jeannie. You can tell me anything."

"Well . . . he slid his hand inside my blouse before I could stop him and brushed my nipple with his finger. It felt so good I wanted to scream. I knew that anything that felt that good had to be wrong, that I'd have to go to confession again on Saturday and do penance for that sin. Oh, how I hate telling a priest about these kinds of things."

Laughing, Jeannie said, "That's baloney. Do the nuns really have you convinced that feeling good with a guy is a sin?"

"Of course, it is. I'm not married and you don't have any business fooling around like that if you're not. Patsy even said so. She said I was going to get into a lot of trouble, getting a guy all worked up like that. Funny thing is, I didn't do anything. In fact I was rather nasty to him."

"For such a smart gal, you sure are stupid when it comes to sex. Guys don't need you to do anything. They get the whole adventure going in their heads and wham-o, the old sergeant stands up."

"Whatever are you talking about?" Annie said with a confused look on her face.

"With all those brothers, are you telling me you've never seen a guy naked?"

"For heaven's sake, Jeannie! My brothers don't walk around naked. So I'm sorry to inform you that I've never seen a guy—that way."

"I can't believe it. I don't have time to give you a sex lesson right now because it's almost suppertime. And the old wicked witch of the west will get her girdle in a bind if we're late. Just keep your pants on and his hands off of you and you'll be OK."

"What are you two doing in here?" demanded Sister Claudia. "Jean Louise! Are you eating in the dorm? You must be crazy to try a stunt like that."

"Oh! I didn't realize I was eating, Sister," she gulped.

"Sell that one to your grandmother. Don't try it on me," Sister Claudia sneered.

"Really. I swear. I had the apple in my pocket for later. I must have taken it out without realizing it," Jeannie said as she walked toward the wastebasket.

"Don't you throw that in there. Do you think we want rodents up here? I'll see you in my office after supper. And be prompt."

"Darn!" Jeannie grumbled after Sister Claudia left the dorm. "I never heard her sneak up on us. Boy, I wonder how much of our conversation she heard? Too much I bet. She'll probably campus me until the end of the school year now."

"So what's new? Everywhere we turn we get it from either the nuns or our parents. They always have our backs in some corner. At least Sister Florentine is still running the place and, with any luck, we'll get a different moderator next year. One more year and they won't be able to do anything to us ever again."

Chapter Thirteen

The City Park officials in West Bend had decided they needed to do some updating on the grounds since the park serviced crowds of young people every summer. The work began in early spring with the purchase of new sporting equipment and the installation of new hoops for the basketball court. The tennis courts and sidewalks were resurfaced and the pond was drained, cleaned and filled with clear cold water from the artesian well. With the work completed and summer vacation starting, the massive green lawns that surrounded the bathhouse were filled with teenagers lying in the sun.

Although Annie kept a watchful eye on the tawny males playing basketball, Jerry managed to stay in the picture.

Things would be different this summer. Jerry had taken a job in Waukegan, Illinois. Annie didn't know how long that would last because Jerry lost more jobs than any guy around. Most of the time he could be a lot of fun to be with. He loved to entertain in public, cracking jokes and telling witty stories. As soon as they were alone, he turned into a groping octopus. Because of that Annie didn't lament for long, as it had become a major chore keeping him in line. The reason for dating him was that her mother disliked his irresponsible ways. But consciously, she stuck with him because he didn't have it so great at home either, with an alcoholic father and a spacey mother. If anyone could understand her situation, Jerry sure could.

The usual Sunday morning ritual began with Annie fighting with her siblings for the bathroom, getting Grandma to move a little faster so they could get to church on time, and her dad forgetting to pay the pew fees as the family entered the back of the church. As it was Father's Day, her mother didn't remind him of his duty, but rather put the quarters in the pew box herself.

After the fire and brimstone service, her dad swung by the corner drugstore and picked up the Sunday paper before heading home. Grandma sat in the back seat without her rosary. Apparently, with her son-in-law driving, there wasn't a need for prayer.

According to family tradition, every Sunday morning after church, the family was treated to bacon and eggs made by Mr. O'Brien singing, "Home, Home on the Range." Swimming in bacon grease, the eggs stuck to the bottom of the skillet, the toast was cold before it got buttered and the eggs were usually hard before they were served. No one seemed to mind as they fought over their mother's homemade muffins and the last strip of bacon.

Jerry had called earlier in the week, saying he would be bringing his roommate home with him. He said Dick just turned twenty-two, Jane's age, and wondered if they could double date. He suggested that if Jane could get the car, they could go swimming or canoeing at the Long Lake. Although Jane had become more sociable toward Annie since she attended Marquette University in Milwaukee, Annie questioned Jane's response to Jerry's suggestion.

Jane winced at the proposal, "What do you know about this guy?"

"Not much," Annie said. "I guess Jerry had been bragging again. This time about all the lakes and the parks we have. It's not like a real date. It's just so Dick has someone to talk to his own age and doesn't feel like a third wheel."

"Well, just this once. But it makes me nervous being with someone I've never met before."

"Jerry said Dick is a nice and pretty good-looking too. Do you suppose Dad will give us the car so we can go to the beach? He seems like he's in a good mood."

"Oh, so that's it. I'm only going for the transportation."

"No. That's not true. It would just be good if we had a decent car to drive around in. Jerry's beater isn't very safe or reliable. Besides, Dick still needs the companionship."

"I'll see what Dad has to say. What time do you want to go?"

"As soon as we can."

Her dad agreed to the arrangement in spite of her mother's disapproval. She felt they should spend the day with their father and not be running around in a car.

"Oh, Mary. They're young and it's a beautiful sunny day to go to the beach. Remember how we loved to go swimming on days like these? You in your funny long, black and white striped swimsuit," he chuckled.

"It wasn't funny," she retorted.

"OK, it wasn't," he said as he handed Jane the keys. "Just be careful. There are a lot of Sunday drivers out on days like this. Keep your eyes peeled."

"Thanks, Dad! We'll be home for supper, Mom, I promise," Jane said and she kissed her mother on the check.

The road to Long Lake was a narrow two-lane blacktop, sitting above the swamp that it forged through with virtually no shoulder. Dick sat in front with Jane and Jane checked the rearview mirror several times to make sure Jerry behaved himself.

"Pull in here," Jerry told Jane as he leaned over the front seat and pointed at the road. "The beach will be about a half a mile down."

"I guess there must be a beach back here someplace with all this sand," Jane said as she drove along the deeply rutted road, struggling to keep the silver Frazier moving so she wouldn't get stuck. "We'll be digging sand out of this poor car forever after this."

"You're doing great, Jane," Jerry replied. "Just keep going."

As the bushes offered the only privacy for changing, everyone had worn their suits under their clothes. Annie and Jerry readied themselves for the swim. Then they hopped and skipped across the hot sand down to the beach, screaming as they jumped into the lake. Dick, a six-foot fair-skinned fellow, didn't waste any time charming the socks off of Jane. Sitting on the sandy slope that sprouted dried grass, they talked and laughed for the next few hours until Jane realized they'd have to leave in time to be home for supper. Sunburned and tired, they packed up their gear. It had been a wonderful afternoon.

All of a sudden Jane handed Jerry the keys. "Why don't you drive, Jerry? You seem to know the road and how to handle all this sand. I don't know how I got in here without getting stuck. You do have a license, don't you?"

"Yeah—sure! I'd be glad to get us out of here."

Shocked by Jane allowing Jerry to drive her dad's brand new car and yet excited by the idea, Annie said nothing. Another surprise came when Jane allowed all four of them to squeeze into the front seat. Again, Annie said nothing.

Cars were jammed bumper to bumper and loaded with the Sunday drivers their father had warned them about. Jerry had made several attempts to pass the long line of traffic he followed but the condition of the road and the on-coming traffic made it difficult.

Annie's left arm rested on the top of the seat above Jerry because of the crowded space. As he made another try at passing, the car to his right began to pull out.

Annie panicked.

Without a thought, her hand came down to strike the right side of the steering wheel, forcing the Frazier into the ditch.

Billboards and signs raced toward them. Jerry turned the wheel a sharp right and stepped on the gas.

The Frazier leapt forward, grabbing the heavily weeded bank as it headed for the road.

Almost hitting an oncoming car, the thrust shot them across the road and into the opposite ditch. Again the car responded to Jerry's demand as it plowed through mud and grass.

Cranking the steering wheel hard to the left the car began to climb the embankment.

The front tires hit the road at an angle and caused the wheels to lock.

A squeal screeched in the early dust of the evening. The maneuver had caused the car to flip back over front, back over front.

Bodies tumbled.

Doors flew open. Glass broke.

Annie heard screams, not knowing if they were hers.

After an eternity, the car landed with a heavy thud. Annie lay upside down on the passenger side with the loosened seats pinning her down. A chill ran through her body when she realized she was alone.

With all her strength, Annie struggled to free herself but the heavy leather seats didn't want to relinquish their grip on her legs. She continued to push and shove as hard as she could, until she managed to crawl free.

Dragging herself out of the car she saw the tires were still spinning. Jerry began to run down the road toward Dick as he yelled to an onlooker to call an ambulance. A man got in his car and sped off. Annie could see Dick lying entwined in barbed wire about fifty yards from her. Jane lay in a wad of wet swamp grass in a fetal position about two feet from where the car had landed. Blood trickled from her matted hair onto the side of her face. People stood gaping at them, relishing the accident.

Time lapsed.

Annie's legs trembled, her thoughts unclear.

She screamed at the crowd, "Is there enough blood for you? Come on! Get closer so you can have a good look. Then I'll have a better chance to beat the crap out of you."

Razor sharp blades of grass scratched and dug into Annie's legs as she knelt down next to her sister. "I'm so sorry," she cried. "It all happened so fast. Do you know where you're hurt?"

"My side. I can't breathe," she whispered.

"I'll stay right here with you," Annie said and placed her hand over Jane's.

Evening shadows cast their murkiness on the gloomy scene. The Frazier lay upside down in the mud, smashed into a convertible that looked like someone had taken a hammer to its sides. The smell of gasoline mixed with swamp water and liquor filled the air.

Annie sat immobilized. She stared at the car and the broken bottles of liqueurs for her dad's clients that were strewn across the road.

Sirens were heard in the distance, announcing their eminent arrival; as they approached, flashing lights began to whine to a halt. Men jumped from their vehicles and ran to the victims.

"Step aside, young lady, so we can get to her," the ambulance driver demanded.

Jerry helped Dick into the ambulance after he had freed him from the barbwire. Unaware of her own pain, Annie paced up and down on the road, watching the paramedics laboring over her sister. She shouted incoherent comments at the crowd to force them back into their automobiles, until she couldn't stand. The men loaded Jane into the ambulance with Dick and rushed them to the hospital, leaving Annie standing in the dusk embraced road.

Her head in a fog, a voice seemed to call to her. She couldn't respond.

When she didn't answer the sheriff realized the young woman in the road was probably in shock. He approached her, took her by the elbow and led her to his squad car.

Turning to Jerry, he said. "I understand you were the driver, son. I'll need to see your license."

Jerry reached for his wallet and handed it to him.

"This is a temporary license."

The officer's face reddened as he looked at the young man standing before him.

"And it's expired. What were you thinking? Never mind. Don't answer that. Fellow—I think you're in big trouble."

Turning his back to Jerry, he said, "We need to get you to the hospital, young lady." He opened the car door to help Annie inside.

She pulled back and stiffened.

"No! Don't make me go in there. I can't. Don't make me. Please!" she begged as she backed away from the squad car.

"Just calm down. I promise I won't drive fast. You can sit up front by me. And if you think I'm going too fast, just tell me. OK?" he said.

After some prodding, the sheriff got Annie into the car and continued to ask if she were okay.

The next thing she knew she was awakened in the hospital by women moaning. Confused, she tried to get up, but her legs were too swollen and bruised. Then the door opened and her father walked in.

"Jane!" Annie shouted. "How is Jane?"

"Thank God, you're all alive," he said as his voice shook and his eyes teared. "She's got some broken ribs and lacerations, but she'll be OK. Jerry's fine. As far as I know he didn't get a scratch. Dick needed some stitches and a tetanus shot, but that's all."

Embracing him, Annie cried, "The car, Dad—I'm really sorry."

He sighed. "The car can be replaced; you can't be!"

A couple of weeks before school began, Jerry started talking about joining the Air Force. He had flunked most of his classes during his junior year and things had gotten worse at home. He told Annie it would be a welcome change from the constant fighting between his mother and father. Annie did her best to convince him not to drop out of school, telling him that without a diploma, getting a job after he got out of the service could be a major problem. However, he agreed to try one more semester.

The mugginess in the dorm swallowed the air from being shut up all summer. After the accident, Annie spent most of her vacation going to the doctor for her legs. There wouldn't be any tennis.

Being the first senior to arrive, Annie had her pick of any cell she wanted. She headed straight for the one in front of the window that had brought her welcome relief in the past. Annie's main focus this year included winning a music scholarship from the college affiliated with St. Anthony's, the excitement of performing in her own recital and, finally, preparing for graduation. Not realizing what it meant to have a full scholarship, Annie tried to convince her dad that spending funds on a college education for her was a waste of money; however, her parents expected everyone in the family to get a college degree, and Annie would not be the exception.

Sister Mary Louise had no idea how Annie felt about St. Anthony's or going to college. Being thankful to have Sister for a teacher the last three years, Annie wasn't about to say anything that would disappoint her. Sister had been diligent with her training and Annie would forever be thankful for the strides she had made with her music. However, spending another four years at a college for women was not something Annie wanted on her agenda.

The following morning Annie and her friends stood at the front of the line, talking about the highlights of their summer. The freshmen looked tired, after their first introduction to the cowbell, as they compared notes on their new routine. Again the students waited for that fateful moment when the moderator for the year would walk through the door at the end of the hallway.

"Did you hear the latest?" Jeannie muttered. "Sister Florentine is no longer Mother Superior. She went and retired on us. Now we're stuck with Sister Mary Edward. Another wicked witch."

"If this is a joke, it isn't funny," Annie said. "You're kidding, right?"

"No joke," Susan said. "Fact!"

As Sister Mary Edward was not known for her loving nature, the news had spread like wildfire.

"How can they replace someone like Sister Mary Florentine with a rigid old bat like Edward? What a way to start our last year. I knew Florentine was getting old, but I was hoping she could last one more year."

"Not much we can do about it, I guess," Helen said. "One thing for sure, whoever we get for moderator can't be any worse than what we had," Jeannie said. "That old bag was the meanest person."

"I'm holding my tongue until I see who it is," Susan said. "They've got a lot of grouchy bags around here."

Right in the middle of the discussion, the hallway door swung open and Sister Claudia came pounding down the corridor. The warm summer had given way to too much relaxation for Sister, as her face bulged out of her headpiece and her habit floated around her like a tent.

"This can't be happening," Helen whispered.

"See, what did I tell you! The biggest bag of all," Susan snarled.

"That'll be enough whispering and showing your disrespect. You'd think you would've learned something from last year, Susan. So I guess you're ready for another go-around. And what about you, Annie—no smart aleck remarks? Or does the cat have your tongue? Huh!"

Annie glared at Sister. It didn't matter what Annie did or didn't do. Sister Claudia would find some way to get after her. Turning, Annie looked into the fear-stricken faces of the under-classmen. At least she had had two years with Sister Mary Margaret. These freshmen had been thrown into the pits of hell with the likes of Claudia. Looking back at Sister Claudia and the smug look on her face, Annie remembered a pledge she had made to herself last Thanksgiving. It was a vow that needed to be fulfilled. It was just a matter of a little planning.

"Someone has to stop her and if we don't, who will?" Annie said to Susan and Helen. "Did you see the look on the faces of those freshmen this morning? They are terrified. And they should be with the likes of Claudia bearing down on them."

"I don't know how you scare a nun who isn't afraid of anything, much less us."

"There's got to be a way to make her skin crawl, or at least make her think twice about why she's a nun."

"Oh brother—that should be a challenge," Helen said, rolling her eyes skyward.

The next night, right after school, Annie headed straight to the dorm and cornered Jeannie. "Come with me," she said as she pulled on Jeannie's sweater sleeve.

"What's up?"

"I'll tell you as soon as we get to the conservatory where nobody can hear us."

The girls ran down two flights of stairs, turned the corner and went into Annie's practice room.

Closing the door, Annie whispered, "Remember a year ago when I got so sick because Claudia locked me out on the balcony?"

"Who could forget."

"We must've, because we swore we would get her somehow and we never did. The time has come for Sister Pain in the Butt to pay her dues," Annie chuckled.

Laughing, Jeannie said, "All right! What have you got in mind?"

"First off I mentioned getting even with Claudia to Susan and Helen, but that's all I said. I want this to be our secret. If we get too many people involved, it ups our chances of getting caught, and that would spoil the whole thing. We want Claudia to waddle in terror for as long as possible."

"Wow! What in the world do you have up your sleeve?"

"Do you promise not to tell anyone?"

"Hey! First I need to know what I'm getting myself into."

"That's fair enough. Just as long as you agree not to tell anyone what I'm planning if you decide not to get involved. I'm too close to graduation to get expelled now."

"Agreed."

"Here's the plan. These nuns act tough, but take a closer look. What are they doing all the time?"

"Got me, what?"

Annie replied slyly, hoping to draw Jeannie into the scheme. "They keep locking everything up as tight as a drum. Their whole routine goes around locking and unlocking."

"So . . . I don't get the point."

"What if we faked a break-in? Claudia is responsible for the safety of the building the dorms are in. If there was a break-in, she'd be looking over her shoulder for a long, long time."

"A break-in. Boy, I don't know about that. That seems sort of extreme," Jeannie said.

"There won't be an actual break-in. We'd just report seeing a couple of men trying to get into the conservatory. After that, all we'd have to do is sit tight and watch the action. It's far enough away from the dorms and the nuns' quarters, and the balcony overhead would act as a cushion for the sound. So it would be a natural place for it to happen. If it works the way I think it will, there will be cops swarming all over this place."

Jeannie pulled back and cocked her head and asked, "And who is going to do the reporting?"

"That's where you come in."

"Oh no!" she put her hands out to stop Annie.

"I can't do it," Annie said. "They'd suspect me right away. You haven't done much of anything to cause a problem. They'd never suspect you. And since you've been assigned to check the locks on the doors on the second floor, it all works out perfectly."

"I don't know. I'll have to think about this one. Pretty scary stuff. I don't need to get expelled either."

"You won't as long as you do what I tell you. Come on. We've waited a long time to get even. Just think of those poor freshmen. They deserve a break and we deserve to get even. All you have to do is to go screaming to one of the nuns and tell them you saw two guys on the balcony—maybe trying to break in. Hey! That acting class you took is about to pay off."

"Funny."

"Besides, you don't have to run to Claudia. I'm sure that as soon as any of the nuns get the news, Claudia will be the first one they'll go after. Remember—she's in charge."

"I can't see how this can help the freshmen, but it would be fantastic to get even a little revenge," Jeannie grinned.

"Great—then you'll do it. Let's plan it for the middle of next week. I want to wait long enough for Susan and Helen to forget what I had said. With just a little luck, we'll scare the you-know-what out of her."

Over the next few days, Jeannie wavered on her decision to go ahead with the plan. After much planning, Annie managed to convince Jeannine that they wouldn't get caught . . . as long as they kept their mouths shut.

The following Wednesday, a vantage point had been selected, and the melodrama would be performed later that afternoon. A window at the end of the second floor hallway offered a view of the entire area behind the building and of the conservatory balcony. The site was far enough from the front office, giving an intruder time to escape after being spotted, yet close enough that Jeannie could be heard screaming for some distance. The back courtyard bordered the infirmary and linked a blacktop sidewalk to the school and a four-story building that housed the aspirants, novices and nuns. The wrought iron fence that ran along the front continued around to the back, ending in gates that were joined by a heavy-duty chain and two large padlocks.

The sun hung in the western sky just above the horizon as Jeannie listened to the tower clock strike four o'clock. It had been a balmy autumn day. Walking down the second floor hallway to complete her task, a surge of stage fright seized her gut with rapid waves of nausea.

In anticipation of the challenge, her hand shook when she reached to check the last door. She stopped and gazed out of the window.

"Here goes," she whispered. "All I have to do is act terrified. And I don't think I'll be acting."

Running down the hallway toward the office as fast as she could, she began a somewhat contained scream. Annie had told her to be careful not to overdo her dramatics because the nuns might get suspicious. By the time she had reached the first floor hallway, students and nuns had begun to come out of various doorways. Spotting Sister Mary Loretta, Jeannie ran to her, breathless.

"I saw—I saw . . . two men on the balcony by the conservatory!"

Everyone looked back and forth at each other in disbelief.

"Oh my! Jeannie, this is serious. Are you sure you saw two men?" Sister Mary Loretta asked.

"Yes, Sister. Yes!" Jeannie shouted. "They were pulling on a window."

"I'll have to find Sister Claudia. She'll have to see to this right away."

Sister Loretta hurried down the hall, calling orders to the others. "In the meantime, Sisters, call the police and the fire department. They'll need ladders to get up on the balcony. I'll tell Sister Claudia what has happened."

It wasn't long before sirens were heard in the distance. Watching the episode unfold, a group of nuns, wrapped in shawls, stood huddled under the overhang by the back kitchen door. Under Sister Claudia's direction, two nuns worked on the chain and the padlocks that hung on the back gate. Just in time, the nuns opened the gate for the fire trucks and squad cars to enter. A loud squeal echoed in the early evening as it swung open, like somebody scratching a giant chalkboard. One young woman after another gathered at the large windows on the fourth floor, straining to see what was happening.

Annie watched the show from a first floor window. Ladders hit the side of the conservatory. Firemen climbed to the second story balcony, scurrying up and down in an attempt to locate the intruders. The old building was submerged in gray and yellow shadows under the glare of the spotlights that crossed its face. The police continued to scan the building and search the grounds, checking every bush, alcove and doorway. Sister Claudia's obese body waddled back and forth between the men, with her arms outstretched as though she walked a tight rope. Another group of nuns had joined the first group but did not offer Sister Claudia any assistance. Sister Claudia's moment had arrived—the full advantage of the drama was hers.

After a few hours of searching in the darkened skies, the police decided they would come back in the morning for more clues to the attempted break in.

"I'm sure we scared off whoever it was," the fireman said to Sister Claudia.

"Are you sure?" Sister whined.

"We wouldn't leave if we thought the school was in danger, Sister. You'll be OK. You did the right thing by calling us when you did. Goodnight, Sister! We'll see you in the morning."

With the drama ended, the fire trucks and squad cars departed. The lights from the surrounding buildings reflected their glare on Sister Claudia as she stood motionless in the center of the empty courtyard. The gate had been secured.

Anticipation floated on the cool breeze to fill the air with dread and insecurity. The time had arrived to guard the school and keep it safe, nothing more, nothing less.

Delighted with their successful venture, Annie smiled and she whispered, "Gotcha!"

Chapter Fourteen

All through the first semester Jerry continued to complain about his teachers, blaming them for his failing grades. Annie tried to convince him that he needed to try harder. That didn't work, and he ended up enlisting right after Christmas.

The Korean conflict was raging in the Far East, so the Air Force didn't waste any time getting the company ready for duty. The girls at his high school thought Jerry looked so cute in his uniform, and the guys were in awe of Jerry's adventure. Annie felt like her heart had been ripped out of her chest. She didn't know if she would ever see him alive again; and if she did, would he come back in one piece or be eternally wounded like Michael?

It was a clear, cold evening the Wednesday after New Year's Day. The train had already pulled into the station by the time Jerry and Annie arrived. The old, wooden platform was covered with freshly fallen snow that crunched under their every step. As the steam bellowed from beneath the engine, the cool winter air turned the steam into thick waves that climbed the side of the train, almost hiding it.

"I don't know why you had to go and do this, Jerry," Annie cried.

"Just come here and give me a kiss before I have to get on that creaky old train," he said softly. "You've been so worried about me not getting an education. Well, don't—OK! The recruiting officer told me the Air Force would provide all the training I need, so stop your worrying. I'll be all right. Maybe after your graduation we can think about tying the knot. Huh! Then we'll have at least one person in the family with an education. What do you say?"

"I don't know. We're both so young and graduation seems so far away. All I can think of is being here by myself with no one to talk to. I don't have the faintest idea when you'll be coming home or if I'll ever see you again."

"Oh, that reminds me," Jerry said. "The recruiting officer said we'll be in Milwaukee for a couple of days before they ship us to California for basic training. That takes about three months, I guess. Right after that I think I might have a few days leave. If I do, I'm planning to make it back home. Then I'll be shipped to some place in Georgia until they decide what to do with me. Don't look so sad. Three months isn't that long, is it? I'll call you as soon as I get to the holding tank in Milwaukee, OK?"

The steam engine blew its whistle, announcing its departure. As it began to pull its weight, a large cloud of warm steam puffed from under the massive wheels and surrounded them in a soft mist.

"This is awful!" Annie cried over the hissing of the engine. "I'll miss you."

"I've got to go, Annie. I'll call you tomorrow or the next day, and I promise that I'll write every day. You'll be OK."

"Don't forget," she shouted as he disappeared into the haze.

Annie stood on the old platform for a long time that night, looking at the empty tracks. Her aloneness flooded her nerves with nauseating hot tingles. She had no one now, not Michael, not Tony and not Jerry.

Seeing Annie, the stationmaster called to her as he locked the station door.

"Miss. . . it's getting late. Do you have a ride home or shall I call someone to come and get you?"

"No. I'll walk. I'm used to walking. Besides, I have a lot to think about."

* * *

The O'Briens weren't home a few days later when Jerry called to invite Annie to Milwaukee for the evening. Excited about the possibility, Annie ran to her grandmother.

"Grandma, could you please give me enough money to buy a train ticket so I can go to Milwaukee to say goodbye to Jerry? He'll only be there tonight. Please!"

Feeling alone, Annie felt certain that if she could see him one more time, things would be better.

Knowing how unhappy Annie had been, her grandma decided there wouldn't be any harm in allowing Annie to go. She was in charge, and she knew Annie would be home before her parents returned.

Upon hearing the discussion, Chuck cornered his grandmother. "I don't think it is wise for a young woman to be running around Milwaukee at night."

"Now don't be ridiculous, Chuck. Annie's a good girl and she won't be alone. She'll be with Jerry."

"That's the point. It has nothing to do with being a good girl. Well, maybe it does. You wouldn't send a lamb into a lion's cage, would you?" Chuck insisted. "There are too many things that can happen."

"You just don't want to see me have any fun, do you?" Annie challenged.

"Oh, for Pete's sake!" Chuck growled as he turned on Annie. "When are you going to grow up? You don't have the faintest idea what could happen to you. You're so naïve."

"I think you're over-reacting, Chuck," Grandma O'Reilly said as she handed Annie the money. "Now go and have a good time, sweetheart. If something happens that you can't make the ten o'clock train home, just call and Chuck will pick you up later."

"Chuck will do no such thing," he said as he stormed out of the room. "This is a big mistake, and I don't want to be blamed for having anything to do with it."

"Oh, all right then. Here's some money for a taxi, Annie. Just be careful and don't talk to any strangers. I know you'll be just fine."

Jumping up and down, Annie said, "Thank you, thank you, Grandma. I won't let you down."

As the adjoining railroad cars swayed, the heavy steel banged and screeched at its union. Standing between them, Annie balanced herself as the train pulled into the Milwaukee station. She watched the ground passing by, waiting for a wooden platform to appear. The train had just jerked to a stop when Annie jumped off and looked around for Jerry. Upon seeing him, she ran toward him and leapt into his arms. Grabbing her, he swung her around in a circle.

"Boy, am I glad to see you," he said after he put her down. "It's going to be a great evening. A bunch of us were put in a room over the fourth street Movie Theater. We can grab something to eat and take it to the room. Maybe we can even see a movie, if we have time. They told us that the movies are free to the servicemen."

"That sounds great, Jerry!"

There were ten soldiers jammed into the small room. Army cots were stacked like bunk beds against the wall, allowing vacant space in front of the heavily soiled, rectangular windows. Multi-colored neon signs mounted over the stores across the street filled the dimly lighted room with interrupted flashes of light. The multi-colored shag carpet spoke of its era and lack of care. A double bed covered with a red chenille bedspread sat in the middle of the room.

Right after Jerry and Annie arrived; the other soldiers began to leave."

"Have a good time," a soldier shouted.

Realizing she would be alone with Jerry, Annie felt uncomfortable.

"I've never had Chinese food." Annie said. "We'd better eat before it gets cold."

"Now don't go worrying about a little food. We've got all night for that," Jerry said as he patted a spot on the bed next to him. "Just come here and show me how much you've missed me."

"I think we should eat first. I'm really hungry."

"Maybe you need to relax a little, especially after that long train ride."

"It wasn't that long."

He cradled her in his arms and brought her close. Slowly, he began to kiss her softly on her neck.

A thrill sent warmth through Annie.

She pushed him away.

"Relax Annie and just enjoy how you feel."

"Can't we just have something to eat and leave it at that? Your soldier friends could come in at any time."

"We're alone. Nobody's going to come back."

"I thought you wanted to have some fun downtown or go to a movie."

The warmth of his breath weakened her resistance.

With mixed emotions, her thoughts scrambled.

His breathe drew heavy with passion. "You're so beautiful, Annie, so beautiful. . ."

A prolonged kiss pulled Annie into his fantasy.

Suddenly, pain shot inward through her lower abdomen and thighs.

"You're hurting me," she cried.

Realizing she had allowed her virginity to be compromised, she turned away, and sobbed, "I never should've come."

She pushed him aside.

"I'm bleeding. Oh, dear God! I'm pregnant?"

"You're not pregnant," he said. "We both have to come at the same time."

"That's not what I heard at school. You don't have to do much more than hold hands."

"See, that's what I mean. Talk's cheap. We've held hands lots of times, and you didn't get pregnant. Now did you?"

I don't know what to believe, especially right now. I don't feel good about this. I think I better go home."

She began to gather her belongings.

"Come on now, don't be that way. I didn't mean to hurt you. I guess I lost control."

Annie grabbed her purse and jacket. "I don't feel good. I'm going home"

Jerry took both of her hands in his, looked into her eyes, and said, "We didn't do anything wrong, Annie. People do this all the time."

"Come on, what say we try some of that Chinese food?" he chuckled and pulled out a cigarette. "I'm starving."

"I said I'm going home!"

Running down the stairs, Annie took the first bus to the train station.

It would be an hour before she could board her train. It was time she didn't want to spend alone, but she didn't want Jerry or anyone else around, either.

She tried to stop crying, blew her nose and ran to the ladies' room. Her stomach tightened into a knot when she looked into the mirror. Maybe some cold water would calm the thoughts that were ripping her apart.

I have to get myself together. I can't get on the train looking like this. Not a shred of common sense did I use. I shouldn't have come.

The movement of the train speeding through the black night jerked Annie back and forth, as she leaned against the window. She had trusted Jerry to a fault. Now her stupidity had lead to the loss of her virginity. Chuck was right, but that didn't help. The cards dealt lacked the good judgment she usually had. Chuck's insight will rub her naiveté in her face.

I'm no better than that poor girl at his high school that got herself pregnant. Everybody thought it was funny. I don't see anything funny about it. How could I be so stupid? I guess I've watched too many movies with knights in shining armor, because I've swallowed that crap, hook, line and sinker.

Her reflection flicker in the train's window, as they came to a stop. She looked away.

Chuck stood waiting at the station as Annie arrived, and asked, "Well, did you have a good time?"

She attempted a smile but was unable to hold his gaze. "Yeah, I guess so. You know how it is. Time flies when you're having fun."

The Christmas holidays were over, and Annie was back at St. Anthony's for her final semester. There wasn't much Annie felt like doing with the cloud of a pregnancy hanging over her head. The only thing that brought her close to a smile was her grandmother watching wrestling on television. Sitting on the edge of a living room chair, her grandma didn't miss a trick. She acted out a variety of wrestling holds, like a full-nelson, and booed along with the crowd at the wrestler who had beaten the other guy to a pulp.

Thinking her period had finally started, Annie would rush to the bathroom only to find another false alarm. As the days passed and the pressure mounted, her studies began to fail. Sister Mary Louise commented that Annie was falling behind in her preparations for her recital. Sister asked if something was bothering her.

Annie shook her head in response.

Distressed about not answering Sister's question, Annie later made the excuse that it was an early case of spring fever and that she'd try harder.

The feeling of desperation soared with each passing day. She began to scratch her arms and legs until they bled. Annie had to confide in one of her friends. The thought of telling anyone what had happened seemed inconceivable and repulsive. Susan and Jeannie would remind her of how stupid she had been to go into a hotel room with a guy in the first place. Annie didn't need them to punish her; that she managed quite well on her own.

A month and a half after her encounter with Jerry, Annie began to feel ill during Mass. She had to leave chapel and run to the bathroom. Kneeling on the cold marble floor, she sweated profusely and vomited until she thought her insides were going to come out. Jeannie was beginning to get suspicious of Annie's morning trips. Trying to ward off her questions, Annie told her she must have picked up a bug.

Jeannie wasn't at all convinced and commented, "Sure—and horses can fly. Maybe you and me better sit down and have a heart to heart talk about this."

"I'll be fine in a couple of days, I'm sure."

Annie didn't get better, and the trips to the bathroom became a daily ritual. After two missed periods Annie decided to confide in Betsy. At least she knew Betsy wouldn't rub her nose in the dirt. And she might know a doctor in Milwaukee that Annie could go to without anyone knowing about it.

March was coming in like a lion. The radio announcer reported that there were gusts of wind up to twenty-five miles an hour, plunging the temperatures to a minus ten below. Heating the classrooms had become a problem, so the students were told to wear whatever they needed to keep warm. Clothed in her jacket, hat and mittens, Annie slipped a note to Betsy as they passed in the hallway after lunch hour.

"Dear Betsy,

Please meet me in the boarding students' locker room at 4:00 o'clock this afternoon. There's something I have to talk to you about before I lose my nerve. You're the only one on the outside that I can trust. Don't tell anybody about this.

I hope this doesn't make you late for your bus.
Thanks,
Annie"

Annie sat through one class after another that afternoon in a stupor. English class, being the last hour, dragged on as the teacher made students repeat their readings from Shakespeare's "Midsummer Night's Dream" with the proper emphasis. Annie's heart skipped beats as she contemplated her meeting with Betsy.

Darkness began to close in on the windowless room as Annie sat trembling on a cold metal chair in the corner of the locker room. At exactly 4:00 o'clock Betsy entered the room, carrying a stack of books she dumped onto the table in front of Annie.

"What in the world is this all about?" Betsy asked. "I've been worried about you all day."

Looking up at Betsy, Annie's voice wavered as she said, "There's no good way to tell you what has happened to me. I know I was stupid for getting myself in this situation in the first place, but I can't change that now. I need a friend, Betsy. I need a friend badly. And I also need a doctor."

"A doctor! What is it, Annie? What could you possibly need a doctor for?" Betsy said.

"I haven't had a period for almost three months, and I've always been as regular as clockwork. I'm terrified, Betsy. I'm afraid I might be pregnant." Annie bowed her head and cradled her face in her hands as she began to cry. "It happened the night Jerry left for basic training."

"Oh no! You can't be. This is terrible news!" Betsy said and sat down next to Annie. "Don't worry—I won't tell anyone. All we can do is hope you'll get your period soon. In the meantime, I'll get the name of the doctor I know in downtown Milwaukee over the weekend. Try not to worry. You know how bad the food is around here. It could be that you got some bad stuff like you did last year. Remember how sick you got on that liver? And I know for a fact that getting sick can throw your period off schedule."

It took a month before Annie could get in to see Dr. Bristol. Waiting in the cold room, Annie shivered as she sat in a faded light-blue hospital gown at the end of the examining table. Her naked arms folded tightly around her midriff were witness to the repeated scratching they had endured over the last months. A single window in the middle of the outside wall brought a stream of light into the dreary second story office. Betsy paced back and forth in front of the radiator, rubbing her hands together in an attempt to stay warm.

Dr. Bristol, a chunky middle-aged man in a white lab coat, walked into the room. "Well, what have we here?" he said as he read the chart he was holding. "I see you are concerned about being pregnant. Is that correct?"

Looking down, Annie answered, "Yes, Doctor."

"You're not married I take it, are you?" he asked.

"No. . . I'm not," she whispered, wiping the tears from the corners of her eyes.

"I'm sure that if you've missed several periods, and if your nipples have changed, you are pregnant. Let's have a look. OK."

As the doctor unrobed Annie, Betsy turned away and stared out of the window onto the busy intersection below.

Annie sat very still as the doctor exposed her young body to the waist. "I'm sorry to tell you this, young lady, but you are pregnant. It's quite obvious from the change in color of your nipples," he said.

"How can you be sure?" Annie questioned. "You haven't examined me or anything."

"I could do a pelvic exam, but I'd rather not put you through that when it isn't necessary."

"Do it!" Annie cried. "I have to be absolutely sure. My whole life depends on it."

The painful exam caused Annie to grit her teeth and moan in agony as Dr. Bristol examined her. Betsy ran to Annie's side and took her hand.

By the time the doctor had finished, Annie was gasping and trying to catch her breath. "It's OK, Annie. It's over. It's over, isn't it, Doctor?" Betsy demanded.

"Yes, and she's still pregnant. If you want me to refer you to an abortion clinic, I can do that," he said calmly.

"No, that won't be necessary," Betsy said as she helped Annie off the table.

Trembling and glassy-eyed, Annie said, "What am I going to do, Betsy? What am I going to do?"

"Let's get you dressed and out of here. Do you feel well enough to ride the bus to my place?" Betsy asked.

"Yes. I suppose so. Thanks for sticking by me. I don't know how I would've gotten through this without you."

"We're not home free yet, but I'll do whatever I can. You know that. We only have a few weeks left before graduation. That's the first thing on the books. We have to keep this quiet so that you can graduate. I know you have your senior recital in a few of weeks. That'll give you something to concentrate on until graduation. You aren't showing yet, and with a little luck, you won't be by then either. That will give us some time to figure out how to tell your parents. Thank heaven, you've already won the scholarship."

"What good is a scholarship to someone who's pregnant?" Annie said with tears running down her checks. The school will probably jerk the scholarship away from me, I know that'll be a huge blow to my family. I should've listened. It doesn't matter," she sobbed, "my parents just ignore me, anyway."

Annie dropped her head in to her hands and began to weep. "I hope I can keep myself together for another month. I'm shaking so bad these days . . .," she cried, "I don't know how I'm going to get through my recital."

"You'll do it, Annie. You have to. And stop scratching yourself. It's not going to change anything and all it does is draw attention. We'll get something at the drugstore tomorrow to help heal those sores. In the meantime wear things with long sleeves so you can't see them."

The following week, Annie decided to write to Jerry, telling him of the pregnancy. The situation was critical, and she had to know what he intended to do. After all, he did talk about marriage before he left. Was he serious or was it another ploy to get her to do what he wanted her to do?

After four years of watching the nuns with their censoring habits, Annie noticed that they didn't censor the outgoing mail. So she wasn't concerned about her letter reaching Jerry, but she was concerned about the incoming mail and Jerry's letter being read. Thinking it would be wise to have Jerry send his mail to Betsy's home, she asked Betsy to intercept his letters.

"No problem," Betsy said. "I'm the one who gets the mail on my way home from school, so nobody will know about it. I'll bring whatever I get back with me the next day."

It was Friday morning, the week before Annie's senior recital, and she still hadn't received a letter from Jerry. Downhearted, she climbed the five flights of stairs to her homeroom, thankful she wouldn't have to do that much longer. It was a warm, sun-squinting day that begged Annie to come out and lie in the sun. With her senior recital just around the corner, she knew there wouldn't be time for fun, and not after graduation either. As Annie walked toward her desk, Sister Allison, her homeroom teacher, took Annie's arm and whispered to her that Sister Mary Edward wanted to see her right away.

"What's it about?" Annie inquired, shaken by the news. "Did something happen at home?"

"I'm sorry, Annie. I was only given the message that you are to go to her office."

"Do I need to come back here after that or can I go right to my next class?"

"There's no reason why you can't go on to your next class."

Annie picked up her books and began to leave when she bumped into Jeannie. "Where are you going?" she asked.

"I have to go to the principal's office for something," Annie mumbled.

"You're kidding. What did you do now? Give a nun some of your favorite Feenamint chewing gum?" Jeannie laughed.

"I don't know," Annie said. "I must admit that I don't have a good feeling about this."

"Gee! Let me know how it goes. Guess they're going to hound us right up until the time we walk out of here."

In the four years that Annie had attended St. Anthony's, she had never been called to the principal's office. As she descended the stairs, she was oblivious to the sun-lit windows that filled the hallway with the warmth of the day. Her thoughts were occupied with the most dreaded of all possibilities. Trying to control her troubled thoughts, she walked down the hallways and through the tunnel that led to the old building, even though she felt weak in the knees. Annie hadn't told anyone except Betsy about the pregnancy, and she knew Betsy would never betray a confidence. What else could it be? Did something happen to her mom or dad? What about one of her brothers, or her sister, are they OK? Then she realized that if something had happened to one of her family members, Sister Allison probably would have told her that.

By the time she reached Sister Edward's outer office, she was flushed and trembling. The secretary, a plump elderly woman with a flat face, told Annie to be seated. Sister would be with her in a moment. The large impersonal room had only two wrought iron lamps and several gray plastic chairs supported by metal legs. The outer wall was lined with barred windows that looked out onto the courtyard and the front gate. Streaks of sunlight were glistening off the steel bars and falling onto the dark-gray carpet, making it the pattern of a prison uniform.

Annie stared at the cloudy glass in the door to Sister's office as she listened to her heartbeat and tried to compose herself.

I need to stay calm and not panic. It might be something to do with my senior recital, like the staging or an extra recital for the college. They may even be going to honor me for one of the music competitions that I won. Sure—I bet it's something like that.

Just about the time Annie began to calm down, she heard Sister Edward page her secretary, telling her to send Annie in.

"Good morning, Sister," Annie said as she walked into the office.

Seated behind a large oak desk, Sister Mary Edward seemed shorter and thinner than Annie remembered, with her brow furrowed and her frail body dressed in a habit much too big for her. A sly smile briefly crossed Sister's face in response to Annie's greeting. She motioned to Annie to sit down.

"Well, Annie. How have you been these days?"

"Fine, Sister—just fine."

"And how are your parents? I haven't seen your father since the day he came to register you at the academy."

"I'm surprised, because he's been here a couple of times for my recitals and for the music competitions that I was in. It's too bad you missed him. I can see why you might not have seen him lately, because he's been busy with one of his inventions. So I've been taking the train home. My mom is doing OK, too. She still loves baking all that sweet stuff I love to eat," Annie chuckled.

"I see that you have your senior recital in a few more days. I know you've worked very hard for that. Tell me, have things been going well for you?"

"Sure. I know my grades have slipped a little, but that's because I've been practicing so much."

"Honestly, Annie, that really isn't an excuse for your schoolwork to suffer, now is it?" Sister said as she began searching for something on her desk.

"No, Sister. It's not."

Looking directly into Annie's eyes, Sister Edward said, "Do you plan to honor your scholarship at the college next fall? I'm sure Sister Mary Louise would be very disappointed if you didn't follow through with that."

"Yes, Sister. Everything is going well. I'm sort of jittery about the recital, but I guess that's normal."

"I'm sure," she scoffed. "What else can you tell me?"

"I don't understand, Sister."

"About what's going on with you and your plans for the future. The college will need to know."

Annie's throat became dry; no sound came out.

Sister raised her voice. "You have nothing to add?"

Annie stood silent.

Her heart beat throbbed in her head.

Annie grasped her hands to control their trembling.

"I've noticed you've been missing some classes lately. Have you been ill?"

"I had a case of the flu there for awhile. Or else I got into some bad food. I don't know which. I just couldn't seem to get over it."

Eyes narrowed and frowning, Sister said, "And that's all, the flu?"

"That's it, Sister. Nothing serious," Annie said.

Sister Edward sprang to her feet and leaned over her desk toward Annie as she waved a letter in her hand and shouted, "I gave you a chance to vindicate yourself, but all you've done is bury yourself in one lie after another. You are despicable! Did you really think you could get away with this?"

"What—what is it?" Annie stuttered.

"It's the letter you wrote to the man you allowed to violate you. It's the letter that set you up to be expelled from this academy. What did you think the sisters were doing while you were running out of chapel to vomit your insides out every morning? There'll be no recital! There'll be no scholarship! And certainly, not a graduation!" she snarled.

"You can't mean that," Annie choked. "It's not fair. Please! Please, don't do this to me."

"You have broken every rule of this academy over the years, and this is the last straw. I not only can do it, I will. You have until Sunday evening to tell your parents you are pregnant and expelled from this academy. Otherwise, I'll do it for you. Take your choice. You will clear your things out by Monday morning and that's final. Now get out!"

Annie stood frozen and tried to grasp the meaning of Sister's threat.

"Get out, I said."

Picking up her books, Annie walked out of the office. Step by step, she felt her body falter in a daze as she climbed the stairs to the dorm. She made a mistake in trusting Jerry, a mistake that took less than a couple of minutes. Sister Mary Louise would feel betrayed, her family would suffer the social embarrassment and all she had worked for was lost.

Pulling her trunk out of the dorm storage closet, Annie began to finger her belongings. She swallowed hard and stared glassy-eyed at the drawer for a long time. Unable to cry, she began to dump the contents into the trunk and slammed it shut.

She'd have to tell her dad that she decided to start bringing things home early when he picked her up that afternoon. That would give her some time to figure out what she had to do.

Hearing the bang, Sister Eunice called out from behind her.

"Annie! Why aren't you in class?" she paused, and saw the trunk. "What in the world are you doing?"

Annie didn't acknowledge Sister's question. She kept staring at the trunk that held the jumbled mess of clothing.

"Annie. Didn't you hear me?"

"I'm pregnant," she whispered.

Sister gasped, "Oh dear! Oh, Annie, I'm so sorry. I take it Sister Mary Edward knows."

"Yeah, she knows all right. She just threw me out of the school, and now I have to go home and tell my parents. How am I supposed to do that?"

"Here, let me help you. God will give us an answer."

"God!" Annie choked. "He let this happen to me. He isn't going to give me any answers, just problems," she snapped.

"God didn't get you pregnant, Annie. He didn't have anything to do with it. Somehow you didn't use your good sense, and you got yourself in a bad situation. God loves you very much and will see you through this."

"Then why did He sic Sister Edward on me? She didn't have to be so mean. She took everything away from me, my recital and my scholarship. She won't even let me graduate."

"Sister Edward doesn't have a choice, Annie. She is compelled to uphold the standards of the academy. There will be help for you and there will be answers. You'll have to open your heart so you can hear them. You've had some tough times in the past, and you've gotten through them, and you'll get through this. You have such a happy spirit, Annie. Many a time you've brought a smile to my heart with your antics, especially when you sprayed Sister Claudia with the coke. Whoops! You didn't hear me say that," she chuckled. "I know they never proved it, but I knew it was your style."

A little smile crossed Annie's tear-streaked face as she turned toward Sister Eunice, "I don't know how I would've made it through these last four years if it hadn't been for you and a couple of the other sisters."

"Down deep under all that creative curiosity is a very good girl, Annie. And I knew that. There aren't many spunky girls like you around anymore. Most of them are a bunch of sissies, but not you. Always remember, Annie, it's the good girls that get into this kind of trouble because they don't know how to protect themselves. Annie, I will miss you very much. And I know you will weather this storm with the faith you have deep inside of you."

Chapter Fifteen

Mr. O'Brien sat with his face close to the windshield as he drove down the highway through the torrential rain. With little success, the wipers swished back and forth in an attempt to clear the water. The downpour had started right after he picked Annie up from school, ending the need for any conversation. It was almost 8:00 o'clock in the evening by the time they arrived home. Annie went straight to her room, saying that the ride home had upset her stomach.

The small, amber-colored nightlight of her grandmother's cast shadows on the wall in the darkened bedroom. Sitting on the side of her bed, Annie gazed at her silhouette in the mirror above the dresser. Her mother's favorite rule about not sitting on the edge of the bed ran through her head.

What a stupid thing to be thinking about. Here I am almost five months pregnant, and sagging springs are all that's in my head. I wonder if Grandma or Jane ever sit on the sides of their beds. Things have to be so perfect around here. Frankly, I don't care about any of it. I don't care if the springs sag, or how the table is set, or how the silver is washed, or which way the food is passed.

Grandma O'Reilly rapped softly on the bedroom door and entered. She carried a tray with some hot tea and a sandwich. "Your father said you weren't feeling very well so I thought a little tea might settle your tummy." She walked over to the dresser and put the tray down. "You're sitting here all alone in the dark, sweetheart. Is there something you'd like to talk about?"

Annie just shook her head and curled up on her bed, too ashamed to tell her grandmother how badly she had let her down. Silent tears ran down her face in the darkness and onto her pillow.

"Maybe after you've had some tea, you'll feel better." She poured a cup and placed it on the nightstand next to Annie's bed. "I'll be back in a little while to check on you, honey. Try to drink some tea."

The bright light from the hallway streamed in through the partially open door. Annie had just sat up to close it when Jane walked in, followed by her grandmother. Annie turned away from the light so Jane wouldn't see that she'd been crying.

"What's the matter, Annie?" Jane asked. She closed the door and sat down at the head of the bed. "It can't be all that bad—now can it?"

Annie looked at her grandmother, who was standing in front of the two corner windows saying her rosary as the wind beat the rain against the house. How could she utter the shameful words that could break her grandma's heart?

Unable to speak, Annie nodded her head.

"Yes? You mean it's bad?"

Jane waited for Annie to reply, instead Annie began to sob until she gasped for air.

"Are you pregnant, Annie?" Jane's voice faltered at the thought.

Startled by Jane having said the unspeakable, Annie stared into her sister's face. Then she nodded and began to sob.

Jane slid close and put her arms around Annie. "I guess Grandma has been worried about you for some time. She noticed that you weren't having your period these last months when she was doing your laundry. Besides, you've been scratching the living daylights out of your hide. You know you can't put much over on that grandmother of ours," Jane said as she rocked Annie in her arms. "I can't imagine what you've been going through all by yourself. They know at school, don't they?"

Trying to control herself, Annie sat up and blew her nose, “Sister Edward found out. I was sick all the time so I wrote to Jerry to tell him and they read my letter. They never check the outgoing mail, how come all of a sudden?”

“Probably because you were having morning sickness.”

“What’s that?” Annie asked.

“Some women get very sick the first couple of months of their pregnancy. Unfortunately, you 're one of them. You probably wouldn’t have gotten caught if it weren't for that.”

“Just my luck. And to top it off, I really gave Sister Edward plenty of ammunition to shoot me down. I had everything in that letter,” Annie sobbed, blowing her nose again. “I didn’t just tell them about the baby, but on how bad the food was, and how they police us every minute of the day, and how tired I was of having my hide rubbed off from those ugly starched blouses.”

“Well . . . at least you gave her a snoot full. That’s worth something,” Jane chuckled.

“I wish I could’ve given her more than that. She’s so mean. She’s not like Sister Florentine at all. Sister Florentine never would’ve been so mean to me. Sister Edward won’t let me graduate or anything. And I only have until Sunday night to tell Mom and Dad or she said she would.”

“Anything? Does that mean you’ve lost your scholarship, and there’s not going to be a recital?”

“Yes. There’s nothing left,” Annie murmured. “She took everything away from me.”

“Oh, boy!” Jane sighed.

Jane got up from the bed and started pacing back and forth.

“How are we going to tell Mom and Dad? Wow! Who’s going to do that?” she said, overwhelmed as she thought about the task. Then she looked toward her grandmother. Grandma's eyes were full of tears as she shook her head. Jane knew she could never do it.

"Looks like I get the job," she said, taking a deep breath. "How in the world am I going to do this?" The bed bounced as she dropped down next to Annie. "I think I'll go to Dad first. He'll be more rational. I don't know what Mother will do. She's been like a bear in labor these last six months since she's been in the change of life. It sure doesn't take much to set her off. Yeah. I'll go to Dad. That's the best. Annie, you'll get through this. I'm not going to say it'll be easy, but you will. Now have something to eat. That baby needs to eat even if you don't. Then try to get some sleep. I'll talk to Dad tonight."

Annie awakened with a start the next morning by a heated argument. The sound came through the floor register from the kitchen, directly below her bedroom. Even though Annie couldn't understand what was being said, she could tell by the tone of her mother's voice that Jane had kept her promise. Her grandmother's bed didn't look like it had been slept in, either.

Someone rapped on the bedroom door.

Annie jumped to her feet.

She opened the door to find Jane who whispered, "I did the best I could, Annie. Dad took it as well as you can take this sort of news. He got rather pale and said he wished it was me. I'm sure it's because I'm older, and I'm getting married soon."

"I know you did your best, Jane," Annie said, unable to look at her sister. "It's just a horrible situation. Mom has a right to be upset. The whole family has a right to be upset. I'm sorry you had to be the one to tell Dad, but I'm thankful you did. I'll never forget what you did for me."

"Now don't get all mushy on me. I can't handle mushy. Besides, you would've done the same thing for me if the shoe were on the other foot. Did I say that? Egads! Thank heaven, it's not!" she said as she rolled her eyes.

"No kidding! I might as well get dressed and go down and face the music. I'm not hungry anyway, and she can only holler for so long."

"Don't be too sure about that. Frankly, I'd wait a little while and give her some time to get it out of her system. Maybe then she'll be more inclined to deal with it instead of hollering about her social standing. Even Grandma is trying to stay out of her way, and you know she never does that. I'll get you something from the kitchen. Remember what I said. That baby has to eat even if you don't feel like it."

Annie waited until lunchtime before she went downstairs. Dressed in her favorite wine-colored skirt and angora sweater, she stepped into the upstairs hallway. Jane's white satin wedding gown hung on the outside of the hallway closet door. Its elegant lines and purity of color made it a stark reminder of everything that Annie had lost. Behind Jane's wedding dress hung Annie's maid-of-honor gown that would never be used. A soft pink bodice swooped down to a tightly fitted waistline, a waistline Annie wouldn't fit into in two more months. Steadying herself with one hand against the wall, she attempted to get enough courage to proceed. Step by step the bottom landing came closer. Some of the hardwood under the partially carpeted stairs had loosened from years of wear, causing the steps to squeak with the slightest pressure. Many times Annie avoided stepping on the loose boards so she wouldn't get caught coming home late. Today it didn't matter. She had already been caught, and nobody could protect her from what was about to happen, not her grandmother, not Jane and certainly not Jerry.

Her dad sat in his favorite lime-green, wingback chair next to the round leather-top Victorian table laden with African violets. His head was bowed as if he fell asleep when Annie walked into the living room. She began to tiptoe, trying not to disturb him, but he looked up and caught her off balance in the middle of a step.

"Good morning, Annie," he said. "I guess you've been having a pretty rough time these last months—haven't you?"

"I'm sorry, Dad. I never meant for this to happen. I'm so sorry," Annie whimpered.

"I'm sure you are," he said. "We're going to have to do a lot of talking to figure out what to do."

Hearing Annie's voice, her mother stormed into the living room. "Sorry!" she stressed. "A lot of good sorry does at this stage of the game. How could you? How could you do this to your family? I wouldn't have a man who stuck his cock any old place. Have you no shame?"

Charles glanced at Annie. She began to cry and hunched over from the attack.

Charles stiffened and his lower jaw jutted out. "Mary," he scolded. "There's no need to use that kind of language. Besides, you have no way to prove such a thing."

"Oh yes I can. The gossip that flows through this community about him is all the proof I need."

"For crying out loud, our daughter is in trouble. Look at her! She has so much pain inside she can't even stand up straight. This is not our Annie. Can't you see she has beaten herself to death over this?"

"I'll tell you what I see. I see a trollop standing in front of me. A trollop that I've made countless sacrifices for, and my kindness has been repaid by her shaming the whole family. After this, I don't dare show my face in public."

"Good grief," patience turning sour, he said. "Is that all you think about? What people will say? You act as though Annie is the only girl that ever got herself pregnant. What about Alice? Your brother's wife! Yes, Alice was pregnant before they got married and she wasn't seeing anyone else either. That didn't make them bad people. The difference between David and Alice and other couples is that they got caught. The rest of them were lucky enough to get away with it. So come down off your high horse and have some compassion for your daughter."

Mary's faced flushed with anger, "How dare you humiliate me like this? Annie, go to your room!"

Still weeping and not able to comprehend what was happening, Annie continued to sob through her words, "What do you want me to do?" she cried. "Do you want me to go away so you never have to look at me again?"

"Don't threaten me!" her mother retorted. "I'll tell you one thing. If you leave this house, you'll not take one stitch of clothing with you, and you won't get your graduation money either. So let's see how far that gets you."

"This is ridiculous. Annie's not going any place except to the kitchen to get something to eat," Charles said. "She hasn't had anything substantial for some time from the looks of her. I'll fix it myself if I have to."

Mary stomped into the kitchen, opened the refrigerator, and pulled out a variety of foods, throwing them on to the table. "There! Fix it then," she said as she left the room.

Grandma was sitting at the far end of the oak kitchen table dunking her toast in her coffee. Her hand shook as she continued the task. Seeing Annie, she stopped eating and got up and grabbed some dishes out of the cupboard. "Would you like some soup, sweetheart?" she asked with a soft smile on her lips. "I'd be glad to make some for you."

"I don't think I can eat, Grandma," Annie murmured. "My stomach is so upset."

"You have to eat, child. You need your strength to get through this and so does my great-grandchild. Your mother will calm down after awhile. It's just not a good time in her life for this to be happening, especially with the wedding just a couple months away. I know she loves you very much. That's why this is so hard for her."

"After you've had something to eat, Annie, we'll go for a walk and get some fresh air," her dad said. "It's a beautiful day. The sun is shining and it has to be 75 degrees out there."

The Milwaukee River ran along the west bank of the O'Brien home. The lazy weeping willow had embedded its roots deep in the riverbank and dragged its swooping limbs across the water in rhythm with the wind. There wasn't a cloud in the sky to cast a shadow on the silver reflections of the sun. The whitecaps glistened as they danced from one wave to the next. As Annie walked along the riverbank with her father, the roar of the rushing water plunging over the dam downstream silenced any possible conversation. This was all quite different from last winter. Just a few months ago Annie had shoveled enough snow to practice her skating. She had always been careful not to venture out too far for fear she'd be pulled into the freezing current and carried downstream to her death. Today it was spring. And she had ventured out onto the thin ice of life. Now she was drowning in her own tears, even though a new life breathed inside of her.

They were at least a quarter of a mile upstream before her dad spoke. "There's no sense in talking about what happened or whose fault it was. Your grandmother already tried to take the blame by telling us that she gave you money to go to Milwaukee last January. That only made matters worse. On your mother's behalf, I want to say, don't be too hard on her. She had great plans for you and now they're all gone. Just give her time. She'll come around. In the meantime I'll call Sister Mary Edward and make an appointment for Monday morning. You don't have to see her again. Jane told me that she gave you a pretty rough time. I'll talk to her while you are packing the rest of your things. I can understand why Sister can't allow you to stay at St. Anthony's in your condition, but, they can at least give you your diploma. You had more than enough credits to graduate when you were a junior."

"She's really mean, Dad. You'll see. She knew I was pregnant all the while she drilled me, because she had the letter I had written to Jerry. When I didn't tell her anything, she called me a liar and said I was despicable."

"Are you sure you heard her right? You must have been pretty upset at the time."

"I heard her, all right. And I'll never forget it either."

"Anyway, that's behind you now and we can't change it. I'm going to call Jerry's parents to see if we can get him home on an emergency furlough."

"Do you have to call them? His mother doesn't like me as it is. I heard her tell the neighbor lady that I was a snippy little snob."

"Yes, I have to call them," he said. "Jerry is the other half of this situation and I want to know what they intend to do about it. Have you thought about whether or not you want to keep the baby or put it up for adoption?"

"I could never give my baby away, Dad," Annie looked up at him with tearful eyes. "I know what happened wasn't right, but I can't go through life wondering what happened to my baby. I just can't."

"That's OK, Annie," he said. "I'm sorry if I upset you. I just have to know what you want to do. If I can get an emergency leave for Jerry, we can at least get you married by a justice of the peace so you don't have an illegitimate child. We'd better get back now. I have a lot of things to arrange."

Driving along the tree-lined boulevard toward the school, Annie could see Lake Michigan in the distance. The apprehension she felt that first day four years ago was like a pittance from a bag of gold compared to the impending drama that was about to unfold. These last four years, she had tried so hard to get out of the academy. Now she wished with all of her heart to belong. She wished for another chance to make her parents proud of her, another chance to hear the audience applauding after her recital, another chance to be part of graduation and be able to say goodbye to her friends.

After Annie had finished packing, she went downstairs to find her father. Upon entering Sister Edward's office, Annie could hear the muffled sounds of her father arguing with Sister Edward behind her closed door. The receptionist seemed unaffected by the escalating argument as she continued with her tedious tasks.

Suddenly, the door flew open and her dad rushed past Annie, saying, "Let's get out of here."

Annie glanced at Sister Edward as she stood, leaning over her desk. Seeing the look of a victor on her face, the hope for another chance vanished. Indeed, there wouldn't be a recital, a scholarship or a graduation.

In the midst of her despair she felt compelled to say the words that were in her heart.

"I hope you're satisfied," Annie said. "Someday you're going to need someone to show you some compassion. When that time comes, you'll remember what you did to me, and you'll know that you're not entitled to any mercy from anyone. Goodbye, Sister, it was fun while it lasted. Wasn't it? Now I've got more important things to do. I have a life to care for." As Annie walked out of the office, she heard Sister Edward shout.

"Why, you little..."

By the time Annie had gotten to the foyer, there were only two cases left to be taken out. A great sorrow filled her heart as she picked them up. No matter how nasty she had been to Sister Edward, it was nothing compared to what Sister had done to her.

Chapter Sixteen

Searching for some peace of mind, Annie decided to go to the parish priest for absolution. Unfortunately, she left the confessional more humiliated and heavily burdened than when she went in. There would be no absolution for her mortal sin, not until she got married in the Catholic church. In the meantime if she died—she would go straight to hell.

Jerry managed to get a five day emergency leave to come home. That cool May evening Annie paced up and down on the wooden platform and paused occasionally to kick loose a piece of dry rot on one of the old boards. The whistle of the steam engine could be heard in the distance. As the sound of the engine got closer, the tiny pieces of glistening cinders that lay between the tracks began to vibrate from the motion of the approaching train. It wouldn't be long before Jerry would reach his destination, and she would have to face him again. Even though his letters were encouraging, Annie didn't feel at all congenial toward him.

I can't live like this. There has to be an answer. Sister Eunice said there would be. Somehow we have to get married in the church, so I don't have to live in sin.

"Hello there, sweetheart," Jerry shouted as he jumped off the train. "I can't tell you how happy I am about the baby and that we are getting married."

"Really?" Annie glanced up, frowned and let her eyes drop toward the ground.

Laughing, Jerry said, "Why wouldn't I be?" He brought her chin up his finger. "I've landed me the most beautiful girl in the world, and one that has the prettiest smile anywhere. Every guy that sees me with you is going to be so jealous because you'll be all mine."

"This is not the way it should've been, Jerry," Annie said. "You said I couldn't get pregnant. Well, you were wrong, weren't you! This whole thing has been a nightmare. And then the priest told me I was going to go to hell when I went to confession. I haven't been able to sleep for months. I don't know about you, but I can't stand to live with a mortal sin hanging over my head. It's got me scared to death. Besides, I don't know anything about being a mother. We have to talk, Jerry—a lot! I have to know what's going to happen."

"Whoa! Not so fast. We'll do all the talking you want. And there's nothing to be scared about. I'm here now. Come on. Relax. How about a welcome home kiss."

"I don't feel much like kissing you or anybody."

"Well, I know a hug will make you feel better. OK! I bet you haven't had one of those in a long time."

Rather than argue with him, Annie conceded to the embrace. The steam engine geared up to leave the station as they stood in each other's arms. For that brief moment she wavered between feeling safe and wanting to run from him, so she wouldn't get hurt again. The warmth of the embrace began to melt the loneliness she had shouldered the past months. She hadn't had anyone except Betsy to rely on, and there wasn't much she could do. With Jerry home, maybe they could work things out together. They could figure out where they were going to live and what to do about living in sin.

Relaxing a little, she said, "I guess having you here will help some. I don't feel quite so alone."

"That's my gal. Isn't it amazing what a hug can do?"

"That's it," she said, elated that she might have an answer to the quandary. "Once we're married by a justice of the peace my parents won't be able to stop us from getting married in the church. That could be the answer!"

"Could be!" Jerry said, confused by her change of topics. "Could be."

Two days later Annie looked out of the upstairs bedroom window when she saw Jerry's parents, Mr. and Mrs. Hoffa, pull into the driveway to drop him off. The wedding ceremony would take place in Waukegan, Illinois, some 75 miles south of West Bend. The only place her dad could find that didn't require a three day waiting period for a marriage license. Shortly after the car had stopped, Annie saw her mother run out of the front door, yelling something and shaking her fist at the Hoffas. Hearing the commotion, her dad, who had been in the garage getting the car ready, turned and hurried toward the Hoffas' car.

Annie watched her dad take her mother by the arm and lead her back into the house. As they entered the house, Annie overheard, "This won't change things, Mary. Try to get a hold of yourself."

"If they would've taught their son some morals this never would've happened," she yelled. "They're just a couple of low-brows."

"They can say the same thing about us and none of it changes a thing."

Hearing her parents, Annie ran down the stairs, almost falling on the way. By the time she had gotten outside, the Hoffas were gone. Jerry was standing alone in his full dress uniform in the middle of the driveway.

"What did my mother scream at you?" Annie pleaded. "Tell me—please!"

Wide-eyed, Jerry looked at Annie and said, "Never. I'll never tell you. I don't even want to think about what she said, much less repeat it. We just have to get through this day. Then we'll be married and nobody can do anything to us after that."

* * *

The sign in the window of the small white frame house in the middle of Main Street read, "Justice of the Peace." It was the second stop after the couple had their blood drawn. Jerry took the test in stride, but Annie didn't. She hated needles ever since she had that terrible accident as a child.

Seeing that Annie wouldn't cooperate, Jerry said, "Annie relax. You have to do this or we can't get married. Besides, the nurse doesn't have a choice. The laws state that everybody that wants to get married has to be tested for syphilis."

"Does she have to use a bazooka to do it?"

"Afraid so! Here she comes again! So brace yourself."

The elderly justice wore an old black suit that accentuated his snowy-white hair and the glasses that hung precariously on the end of his nose. The ceremony was brief, but not uneventful. A feeling of hysteria had overtaken the couple, causing them to giggle through the entire service. Despite the flutter of interruptions, the justice never stopped his well-rehearsed dialogue. Annie couldn't believe she was laughing at such an inappropriate time and couldn't control it. Even her dad had a smile on his face. After the service her dad handed the justice an envelope, and they were ushered out of the front door.

"Now that we're married, Dad, can I make arrangements to have the marriage blessed?" Annie asked as they got into the car.

"I'm not sure you understand the consequences of that, Annie," he said. "Is this what you've been planning all along?"

"All I know is that we can't go to Communion or receive any of the sacraments until we are married in the church. Father John said that if I died, I'd go straight to hell."

"Well then, I guess you have to do what you have to do."

Jerry picked Annie up early the next morning so they could make arrangements to be married by Father John as soon as possible. The old yellow brick rectory was set back from the street, bordered by the Catholic school and Holy Angel Church on either side. As Father John opened the front door, Annie became aware of the same mustiness she faced at St. Anthony's.

"We don't have much time, Father. Jerry has to get back to his base in Georgia the day after tomorrow."

"Are you sure your father has given you his consent, Annie?" Father John asked. "The last time I spoke with him he did not favor a church ceremony at all."

"I'm sure, Father. Otherwise, I wouldn't be here. I told him yesterday that we couldn't receive the sacraments, and he said I should do what I needed to do."

The couple with Father John arranged everything for a quiet service in the church chapel the next morning.

That evening, Annie and Jerry were sitting on the overstuffed sofa in the O'Briens' living room, talking about some last minute details for the ceremony in the morning.

"It's almost ten o'clock, Annie," Jerry said as he looked at his watch. "I better be getting along home. I have to get my things ready for tomorrow, and I still haven't done my packing to go back to the base."

Just then the telephone rang.

"I wonder who that can be at this hour," Mr. O'Brien said as he walked into the kitchen to pick up the receiver.

"Good evening, Father. What can I do for you? No . . . I'm sorry for the confusion, Father, but I did not give my permission."

Hearing his words, Annie got up and faced her father.

"I'm sorry, Annie," he said after he hung up. "Father John just called, double-checking to see if I had given permission for you two to get married in the morning. As I didn't, the wedding is off."

Shocked by his remark, Annie started to scream at her father, "You did give your permission—you did!"

"No, I didn't, Annie. I said you should do what you had to do."

"If that's not giving your permission, then what is?" Annie snapped. "We're married now so how can you stop us?"

"You're still a minor, Annie, and the church doesn't recognize your marriage."

"A minor," she stammered. "Well, I won't be a minor for long because I'll be eighteen before this baby is due. Then you can't stop me. You can't stop me from doing anything."

"Now don't go getting hysterical," he said as he tried to stay calm. "I did it to protect both of you. I was hoping that Father would marry you without getting my permission. Then if things didn't work out, I could get the marriage annulled. I guess he figured it out."

"How could you do this to me?" Annie moaned. "You've made me look like a liar on top of everything else. "

"I hate you!

I hate you!

I'll never forgive you for this," she shouted as she ran to her bedroom.

"I—I guess I'll be going on home now," Jerry said quietly.

"I'm sorry, Jerry, but I couldn't let you get married in the church. That would've been the biggest mistake of your life."

"No offense, Mr. O'Brien, but it sounds like you had us pegged for failure before we've even begun."

Chapter Seventeen

After Jerry went back to Georgia, the situation in the home intensified. The only conversation between Annie and her mother consisted of her mother walking through the house, slamming doors and directing nasty remarks at Annie.

As the days passed it became obvious that it would be a long time before her mother would forgive her. So Annie decided to take matters into her own hands. She lived in sin whether or not she stayed at home or went with Jerry. One evening before she went to bed, she decided to talk to her grandmother.

"It's been three weeks since Jerry and I got married, Grandma, and Mother is still nasty as can be. I think it would be better for everyone if I left and went to live with Jerry. I can't get absolution, so if I die I'll go to hell no matter where I'm living."

"My dear, Annie, you've always been so protected. You don't have any idea what the world holds for you," her grandma said.

"Maybe not, Grandma, but I know what living in this home is like. I'm surprised that I haven't been asked to hide in the closet so nobody would see me. And I don't even look pregnant yet," Annie explained. "I feel like I'm already in hell the way I'm being treated around here. It can't be much worse out there."

"The world can be a hard taskmaster, Annie. Much harder than your mother can be. You'd be far away from the family, and you'd be having your first child all by yourself. I know what that's like, and I hate to see you go through that."

"I'll be OK. I've lived through the last six months, haven't I? I guess that was a pretty good introduction to life. Jerry said the Air Force would pay for all my care, even the delivery at a hospital in town."

"I know you've given this a lot of thought, sweetheart. I wish I could change your mind though."

"Grandma, I don't want to leave, but I don't want to live like this either. Now stop worrying about me. I'll be OK. By the way, is there any chance I could use that old trunk of yours? I'll take good care of it."

"Oh, sure. I never use it any more. It's down in the basement so help yourself."

"One last favor."

"What's that?"

"Could you find it in your heart to give me my graduation money? That would give me enough money to get to Georgia and a little extra for any emergency."

"Why, of course, I can," she said as she walked over to her dresser and handed Annie the money.

"Promise me you'll write every day and let me know how you are. I'll be beside myself if I don't hear from you. And you'll have to call as soon as the baby is born and let us know if you had a little girl or a little boy."

"I will, Grandma. I promise. I love you."

The sunlight was warm on Annie's shoulders as she knelt on the hardwood floor, packing her things. The large, black trunk sat in the corner on the bedroom floor under the windows. It was the 30th of May, 1952, and the Memorial Day festivities had begun downtown. The parade would be first. Then everybody would march to the City Park. The park would be decorated with red, white and blue flags, the tables would be full of wonderful things to eat. There would be lots of prizes for all those who won the pie eating contest, the frog jumping contest and the one-legged races. Annie wouldn't be going. She had too many things to do before the train left the next morning at nine o'clock.

She didn't have the luxury of maternity clothes, so she'd have to get by with some full blouses Jane had given her to cover her motherhood. Her grandma offered to buy some, but Annie declined. Her grandma had done enough already.

The note Annie wrote, telling her parents about her plans to go to Georgia to live with Jerry, she left unattended on the kitchen table. Annie wanted to avoid as much confrontation with her mother as possible. Listening to more stinging remarks would only drive a bigger wedge between them. Grandma would make sure that her daughter got the message.

Chocolate, Annie's teddy bear, would be packed last. Even though Chocolate's paws showed wear, he could always be relied on for the best hugs. The infamous bear had spent many hours sitting on the chair in Annie's cell, comforting her while listening to her woes. Now Chocolate would be serving the newest member of her family. Finishing her packing, Annie snapped the lid of the trunk closed, locked it and put the key in a zippered pocket in her purse for safekeeping.

The sun was beginning to cast its amber rays in the west when Annie decided to get ready for bed. Standing by the bedroom windows, a breeze gently brushed her face and fluttered the lace curtains on either side of the windows. As she looked at the river, she watched small patches of foam being carried on the turbulent waters as they rushed toward the dam. The simple reality was that it would be a long time before she'd stand there again. These last months' survival had captured every moment. There hadn't been time to consider the life that began to make itself known inside of her.

"Please, dear God," Annie prayed, "Send your angels to guide me and tell them they have to teach me what I need to know to take care of this child. I still can't believe you're sending me a baby. You know I don't know anything about being a mother. I was too busy playing tennis and having a good time to bother with things like that. Now Jane, she knows all about that stuff. She listened to Mother. It's sort of funny. She knows everything, and I'm the one that's pregnant. Anyway, that's the way it is. And remember I need all the help I can get. Amen."

Annie had plenty of time to prepare herself for the new day because her grandmother's snoring awakened her at five that morning. Trying not to awaken her, Annie tiptoed to the corner windows to watch the sunrise. Deep golden and rose hues lined the horizon as Annie inhaled the fresh morning air. After a brief moment she gathered the clothing she had selected the night before and went into the bathroom to get bathed and dressed. After placing her red and white checkered hat that matched her shoes and purse in her overnight case, she fastened the tiny pearl buttons on her wool, navy-blue suit. She had readied everything before she went into the kitchen for her final meal.

She entered the kitchen to find it empty, quiet. For the first time in months, she felt alert and happy, and she wanted it to stay that way. She had just finished her cereal when her dad walked into the kitchen. They exchanged greetings and went on with their tasks. Annie told him she could take a cab if he didn't have time to take her to the station. He said he wanted to make sure she got off safely. All that she had left to do was to say goodbye to her grandmother.

Finishing breakfast, Annie hurried upstairs and gently shook her grandmother.

"Grandma, I'll be leaving in a couple of minutes and I wanted to say goodbye."

"Oh, dear me," her grandmother sighed as she struggled to get her bearings. "I've overslept, haven't I?"

"It's OK, Grandma."

Grandma slipped into her robe as she grabbed her glasses and pushed her feet halfway into her slippers. "You be sure to let us know that you got there alright. I'll worry every minute until I hear from you. Just call collect; I'll pay for it if I have to. I'll expect a letter at least every week. Be sure to go to a doctor as soon as you get there, so you'll know how that baby is doing. You eat plenty of good food now. You have to keep that baby healthy. That poor little soul has had one heck of a ride so far and deserves a break. Come here now and give me a hug."

"I'll be OK, Grandma. Remember what you always told me? No matter what happens—always keep smiling. It's time I pulled myself up by my bootstraps and got on to other things."

"Oh! How I wish I had never given you the money to go to Milwaukee. I should have listened to Chuck. You had been so sad, and I just wanted you to have a good time for a change. I love you so much, sweetheart."

"Grandma, you need to know that I don't blame you for this, the problem came because of poor judgment on my part. So please don't blame yourself for this. I promise I'll write often. I love you too, Grandma."

The ticket master stood behind his barred iron cage as he tapped out a telegraph message. Slightly stooped, his barbershop quartette mustache twitched in sync with the rhythm of the code. After he had finished sending the message, he looked up at Annie.

"A one way ticket to Valdosta, Georgia, please," Annie said.

"You're buying yourself one long trip on that there train, missy. Do you know that?"

Annie smiled and said, "Yes, sir."

He stamped the tickets and handed them to Annie. "It'll take you the better part of a day and a half to get there. Are you going all by yourself? Don't matter. It's none of my business. You're going to have to change trains in Cincinnati. Just ask one of the conductors before you pull into Cincinnati where you have to go to catch the train to Valdosta. Your train will be here in about fifteen minutes. Next," he hollered.

"Thank you, sir." she said, picking up her overnight case.

The last time I stood on this old wooden platform was the night Jerry went back to Georgia. It doesn't look as decrepit as I thought in the bright sunlight.

Standing beside Annie, her dad's hand trembled when he reached to touch her arm, "I wish you wouldn't do this, Annie. You're too young to be by yourself, even if you weren't pregnant."

"I'll be fine. And I won't be by myself. Jerry said he had a nice place for us the first week or so. That'll give us enough time to look for something together. I don't know why you're worried. I've been taking care of myself for the last four years. And if I can't, I guess I'll have to learn the hard way, just like I did with the pregnancy," she said. "You probably don't think I've done a very good job. But one mistake doesn't make everything I've done wrong. Besides, I couldn't be much worse off than if I stayed here. The only person in the family that talks to me is Grandma. Or should I add Mother to that list; that's if you can call her screaming nasty innuendoes at me, talking."

"Your mother will get over it. Like I said, it's a difficult time for her."

"And what do you think it's been for me? A picnic?" she shouted over the clamor from the train. "You act like I have another choice. Well, I don't. Mother saw to it that there was only one choice that I could make. At least Jerry wants me around. That's more then I can say for my family. I don't want to talk about it anymore. I'm not changing my mind." Annie extended her hand to her father, said goodbye and boarded the train.

"Please write and let us know how you are doing," her father yelled over the clamor of the engine. "In spite of what you think, Annie, I love you very much."

Annie paused for a moment as she stood on the metal platform between the railroad cars.

The conductor hollered, "All aboard!"

Turning, Annie looked into her father's tear-filled eyes and said, "I love you too, Daddy."

The train jerked as it started out of the station, throwing Annie off balance. She walked through the crowded smoke-filled cars, grabbing the green metal bar that ran across the top of the straw-covered seats to steady herself. After going through several cars, she became concerned she might have to stand until the first stop at Milwaukee. Then she spotted a seat next to an elderly lady.

"May I sit here?" Annie asked.

Looking up from her knitting through her half glasses and smiling, the lady patted the seat next to her.

"Why certainly, child. I'd love to have some company." A little straw hat covered most of her snow-white hair, and her eyes danced happily as she tilted her head toward Annie.

"Are you making something for someone special?" Annie asked.

"Oh no. Just knitting. Gives me something to do and keeps my mind busy. You know what they say: an idle mind is the devil's workshop," she laughed. "I'm going to Cincinnati to visit my daughter. How about you?"

"I have to meet my husband in Georgia," Annie said.

"You sweet thing. You don't look old enough to be married. Your beau is a very lucky man to have married such a beautiful young lady from such a fine family."

"How do you know about my family?" Annie asked.

"It's the stylish wool suit you have on. Not just any family could afford it."

"Oh," Annie remarked. "I guess you're right. By the way, my name is Annie O'Brien, I mean Annie Hoffa, and I'm pleased to meet you."

"I'm pleased to make your acquaintance, Annie Hoffa," taking Annie's hand and smiling. "You can call me Miss Emma. It's nice to have a young woman as a traveling companion. It hurries the trip along."

Telephone poles flashed past the train window at record speed as they began engaging in small talk. Miss Emma spoke mostly about her daughter and what a minx she was as a little girl. After Annie recognized that she had a captive audience, she told Emma about the pranks she and her friends pulled at the academy. Miss Emma laughed the hardest at the story about how Annie soaked Sister Claudia with the coke. One story led to another until Miss Emma mentioned family skeletons. The suggestion of skeletons in the closet sent a twinge of guilt through Annie. She'd probably be remembered in exactly that same context for generations to come.

"You know, Miss Emma, now that you mention it, I guess I'm the biggest skeleton my family will ever have in their closet," Annie said, looking down.

"You! You're such a delightful young woman. I find that hard to believe."

Annie's face flushed at the thought of divulging the pregnancy. "Believe it, Miss Emma. It wasn't suppose to happen the way it did, but you know all about hindsight I'm sure. The real reason I'm going to Georgia is because I'm pregnant. I humiliated my entire family, and I'm the talk of the town—the kind of talk you don't want to be a part of. All my mother did was scream nasty remarks and call me unspeakable names until I couldn't stand it anymore. I couldn't stay at home and I didn't have any other place to go. So I decided to leave. If I would've used the brains God gave me, I wouldn't be pregnant, and I wouldn't be sitting here next to you. I don't blame my parents for how they feel. They sent me to the finest finishing school in the state and this is how I showed my appreciation. In less than a minute, I lost it all: my music scholarship, my senior recital, my virginity. The academy wouldn't even let me graduate."

Feeling Miss Emma's hand over hers, Annie looked into her face. Miss Emma's eyes were sparkling and lined with what seemed to be hundreds of crow's feet. "It's OK, Annie," she said as she squeezed Annie's hand. "It's OK."

"I don't know why I'm telling you all this. I guess I feel like I've known you for a long time, and I guess I thought you might understand like my grandma does."

"I do, Annie. Let me tell you another little story. A long time ago I remember hearing about a young woman who got herself in a similar situation. The family had turned their backs on her and tried to hide their shame by talking a bushel basket full of gossip. That didn't stop Alice. That was her name—Alice. I hear tell she was one spunky gal, just like you. She held her head up high when she walked down the street. And she was as proud as a peacock once that baby came," Miss Emma said as she smiled broadly and looked up toward heaven. "That baby was a special little gift from God. And Alice told everybody so. Later, after the baby was born, she found herself a right nice young man and they got married. Of course, that was a long time ago, and the baby is probably a little old lady by now." Delighted with her story, Miss Emma chuckled and said, "Yes, Annie. That lady was my mother. The best mother a girl could have. She loved me with all of her heart, and that's what's important. The rest don't matter none. It's only a very small part of a bigger picture. See that bunch of trees over there beyond that field?"

"Yes," Annie said.

"Just look at how beautiful they are in full bloom," Emma chuckled. "Can you see the little sprigs in between the tall trees?"

"No. They're too far away."

"Exactly, Annie. Right now your sprig is sitting right under your nose and you can't see the rest of the trees. That graduation is just like one of those little sprigs in your life. It's only a very small part of a much bigger picture."

With tears in her eyes, Annie said, "I suppose so."

"My dear child, you need to know you have already graduated. No, you didn't walk down the aisle, but you did the important part. You got the education and the musical training and nobody can ever take that away from you. Annie, you'll never be a skeleton in anyone's closet. Skeletons are things that people hide. You don't strike me as the kind that's easy to hide.

You'll be a proud mother just like my Alice was. And you'll love your baby with all of your heart, right until the day that you die. As for your family, as soon as that child is born they'll realize what a blessing you've given them. You'll see."

"Cin-cin-nati!" the porter yelled.

"The time has gotten away from us, Annie. We'll be going our separate ways now. I haven't been fortunate enough to have grandchildren, but if I could take my pick, I'd pick one just like you."

As they gathered their things, Annie said, "I can't believe the time went by so fast. I'll always remember you, Miss Emma. I know I was meant to sit next to you and hear your encouraging words. I will be a good mother, and I will hold my head up proudly, just like Alice."

Standing in the sunlight, the light brown of Annie's hair accented the glow in her eyes. She smiled while she watched Miss Emma hobble down the ramp and disappear into the depot.

Feeling her baby move, Annie put her hand on her tummy. "It's just you and me and Jerry now. We're going to have a new life—a good life. I know we will. Just you wait and see. And that's the important part."

"All aboard for Atlanta and Valdosta, Georgia," the conductor hollered as he bent over to raise the steps of the train.

"Watch your step, young lady. You have a long journey ahead of you."

The End

Chocolate

The Carolee Collectables by Carolee O'Neill

Goodie RudeShoes: Series One, Children 5-10 to 100.
Billy BitterBetter: Series Two, Children 5-10 to 100.
Granny NeatFreak: Children 4-10 to 100.
The Mouse House: Children 4-10 to 100.
That Secret Part of Me: Children 3 to 100.
From Silly to Sinister: Teen, Adult Short Stories.
Book One and Two.
Navigating the Potholes of Life:
Teens and Adults
adventure, comedy, drama.
A Reason to Dream:
Teen and Adult Fiction.
Drama based on a True Story.
The Graduation:
Suspense, survival and humor.
Teens, parents, adults.
May be purchased with or
without a Study Guide.
With God in Mind.
Devotional.
Prose, for Teens and Adults.

Thank you for your interest in my work.

Carolee can be reached at caroleeagain1934@gmail.com

Carolee's books are available as paperbacks and as ebooks.

www.ingramcontent.com/pod-product-compliance
Lightning Source LLC
Chambersburg PA
CBHW071253250626
47159CB00004B/1163
9781947573109